The Duke Who Loved Me

Those Regency Remingtons

Book One

Jennifer Monroe

Those Regency Remingtons

The Duke Who Loved Me

The Baron Time Forgot

The Hero of My heart

Chapter One

Anna Silverstone dreamed of another life. It was not because her fingers were calloused and her body ached. It was not because sweat and dirt stained her dress. It was not because those around her died young due to the terrible conditions of the workhouse.

The truth was, Anna needed to escape because her family had always been poor, and she feared they would always remain so.

The air was stifling and sweat beaded Anna's brow. Dust mixed with tufts of cotton filled Anna's eyes and nose, making her cough.

Once a large stable with the stalls removed, the workhouse was located no more than four miles from Anna's home, which made it a convenient location despite how much she despised the backbreaking work. Heavy wooden beams crossed the low roof, and slits at the tops of the walls allowed in just enough light to see by, making the single open room feel much smaller than it was. It did not help that a dozen large looms in two lines facing one another ran down the center of the room, taking up a majority of the space, a woman at the helm of each.

Wiping her brow, Anna realized that she had another problem. With her flaxen hair, deep-blue eyes, and high cheekbones, her eldest brother, Thomas, was certain that her beauty would attract a wealthy suitor. This, in turn, would fill his coffers and provide him and his siblings a way out of the destitute lives in which they lived.

Many men, married and bachelor alike, offered her congenial smiles while their eyes told a different story.

You're worthy of my bed, but you can never become my wife.

One man, in particular, spent all too much time ogling her, and he repulsed her more than any other. Mr. Albert Harrison, her employer, stood across the workroom, staring at her unabashedly. With nothing more than a few blond wisps of hair upon his otherwise bald pate, he had an appalling habit of licking his lips while he leered at her, which only added to his vile nature and caused her to shiver in disgust.

If he spent his time simply watching her, she might have tolerated his behavior. Yet, one day, three months earlier, he had moved from his usual place beside the wall to stand behind her.

Doing her best to ignore him, she concentrated all her attention on the movement of the loom, praying he would move away. He then leaned in close, his hot, foul breath on her neck as he whispered his desires in her ear. His words had been crude and made her cheeks heat, and she refused him immediately.

Mr. Harrison had not been pleased, which came as no surprise. After all, he was nothing more than an overgrown spoiled child. The workhouse had been a part of his meager inheritance, and he used it to prey on the fears of those who were in his employ. Yet, just like most other men like him, what he did not seem to understand was that Anna feared no one.

He had retreated to his place by the wall, and Anna dismissed the encounter. For she, nor any other woman in his employ, could raise an alarm, lest they lose their position that very moment. Plus, who would come to their rescue if they did? No one.

Beside Anna worked her friend Betty Voss, her dark hair pulled back with a kerchief to keep it from catching in the loom. Seven years Anna's elder, Betty appeared far older. With deep lines around her eyes, her bone-thin fingers worked deftly, making certain that each weft thread lay properly between the taut warp threads.

Back and forth they worked, numbing minds and tiring eyes, to complete the various fabrics sold to linendrapers throughout the country.

"He's been staring at ye for nearly ten minutes now," Betty whispered as she leaned in to make a return pass of the yarn. "He ain't made any of his offers again, has he?"

Anna shook her head as she pulled the thread on her loom tight. "Only the once, and I pray he doesn't do so again."

2

Other women had taken the offer Mr. Harrison had made in exchange for better pay and other favors. Anna held no judgment against them for doing so. But to the man who gave the offer? Indeed, she did. She, however, would never participate in any such barter, no matter how much Thomas schemed for more wealth.

Cutting away the final threads of the fabric, Anna followed Betty to a crude wooden table to place their finished product atop the others. Movement from the corner of her eye made Anna draw in a deep breath as Horace, a young boy of seven, ducked beneath one of the nearby looms.

He really should be more careful, she thought. Indeed, those who did not show the machines their proper respect had the scars— and at times missing fingers— to prove it.

"You've fifteen minutes to eat," Mr. Harrison barked.

Anna and Betty collected their meager meals and followed the others outside where the air was clearer. Nearly three dozen were employed at the workhouse, mostly women and children who worked the looms, while the men deigned to pick oakum or to see to any heavy labor.

The ground was dry this late June. No rain had fallen for nearly two weeks, and an unusually hot breeze whipped dust up around them. Beneath one of the trees, Anna stooped to pluck a blade of grass. Releasing it, she watched it flutter away.

With a heavy sigh, she turned to find Molly Gibbons, a red-haired woman known for a gossiping tongue and loose morals, joining three workers beneath a nearby tree.

"Rumor has it that Mr. Harrison's lookin' to sack people today, or at least until work picks up again. I'll tell ya one thing, it ain't gonna be me. What about you, Anna? Do ya think you'll be here tomorrow?"

Anna fixed her skirts around her, knowing full well why Molly was so full of certainty. "I feel secure in my position," she replied. Unwrapping the food she had packed earlier that morning, she nibbled at a corner of a hunk of bread. "Beyond that, I have no control. I may take many risks in life, but engaging in any form of debauchery with the likes of Mr. Harrison is not one of them. I refuse to stoop to the levels some do."

Betty roared with laughter, and Molly turned away, scowling.

"Did ye ask him for time off to go to London?" Betty asked.

This caught Molly's attention. "London? What business have you in London?"

Anna attempted to quiet her friend with a glare. The last thing she wanted was Molly's opinion on the matter. Yet it was much too late to stop the onslaught now.

"Rumor has it that her father lives there," Betty continued. "She's goin' to London to meet him and see if he's any money for her. Let's hope she uses it to buy this place."

"Not that again," Molly said with a shake of her head. "I'm tellin' ya, you're nothing special. Mum told me the same stories as a child to make me feel better about bein' a bastard. Heya, Susan, weren't your da a soldier but died before marryin' your mum?" she asked one of her companions.

"'Tis true," Susan replied with a smile that revealed several missing teeth. "He done died in France defendin' 'is country." Her burst of laughter said she did not believe a word she said.

"How is it then," Betty argued, "that Anna can perform a perfect curtsy. Or that she can read'n write? Ye've to have smarts to do that, and she got 'em from her father."

Molly snorted. "Fathers are irrelevant if you ask me. And smarts only come from luck. Some have 'em and some don't. It's that simple."

Anna refused to argue either way, for she knew the truth. Whether any of her intelligence came from her father remained to be seen, but it had been her mother who had taught her how to read and write. She had also learned how to set a proper table and even a few words of Latin. The definition of beauty and elegance, Rebecca Silverstone could have been many things, but Anna was certain she had not been a liar.

Anna tore off a bit of mold from a corner of the cheese and tossed it aside as Molly continued her tirade.

"'Tis all right to dream, Anna. We all do. But 'tis time you faced the truth. Your father's not an earl, and your mother only told you lies to protect you from the truth. That might make her a good woman, but she still told a fib."

Anna made a fist but refused to respond. Her mother had revealed on her deathbed how Thomas and Anna were conceived. According to her, she had been in a secret romance with an earl who professed his undying love for her. Sadly, as time progressed, he was given no choice but to enter into a marriage of convenience with a lady from his class. Thus her mother was left brokenhearted and caring for his children alone. Since that revelation, Anna had dreamed of searching out her father.

"Would it not be well worth our troubles if we were to find our father?" Anna had argued when she and her brother had broached the subject. "After all, if we do learn he's an earl, surely he can provide some sort of financial support."

Thomas had refused to discuss it, which only confounded Anna. His goal in life was to save enough money to become a part of the landed gentry, which would take a great deal of work on the part of all the Silverstone children.

In Anna's opinion, proving their bloodline would open a whole new world. Yet, until she had the proof she needed, she kept secret the name of her father.

"I don't care what ye think," Betty snapped, bringing Anna back to the present. "Her father's an earl, and she's gonna leave here and never return, ain't ye, Anna?"

Anna gave a small nod as she watched Mr. Harrison walk over to Geraldine Malley, a widowed mother of three. "Indeed, I'll leave this life behind one day," she replied as she glanced at the other women chatting with one another as they ate. "Not only that, but I'll also marry a handsome man who has a strong will and great courage."

To this, Molly snickered. Anna ignored her, turning her attention once more to Geraldine, who now stood with arms around two of her children, both under the age of eight. The youngest, a boy named Samuel, wore shoes with so many holes, his toes stuck out the tips.

With gaunt cheeks and threadbare clothes, they looked very much like the children of the other women who worked there. Not for the first time, Anna was grateful for what little she had.

Standing, Anna drew closer to the widow and her children, straining to hear what Mr. Harrison said.

"I'm sorry. Your children may continue working, but there's no position for you until September."

With a choked sob, Geraldine pulled her children in closer. "Please, sir, we can barely afford to live as it is. If I lose me wages, I'll not be able to pay the rent, and we'll be tossed outta the house. Please, I beg of ye, be merciful."

Mr. Harrison crossed his arms over his chest and eyed the woman up and down. "Perhaps we can speak privately and come up with a solution that will work well for both of us."

The look of consideration and fear that crossed Geraldine's face made Anna want to strike the taskmaster, and she was not opposed to using violence to put him in his place.

She had done very much the same thing just last year when a well-dressed man had pinched her bottom as she walked past him in the nearby village of Wanesworth. A quick fist had the man doubled over in pain with what was most certainly a broken nose.

Sadly, this was no alleyway, so striking Mr. Harrison was not the best of choices. Instead, Anna joined them, keeping a tight rein on her emotions. "Excuse me, Mr. Harrison, but I meant to ask permission to have a few days away. Geraldine is welcome to take my place in my absence."

Mr. Harrison's lip curled. "You're willing to give up your work till September, are you? And what will your brother have to say to that, eh? Won't he be angry? You've younger ones relying on you, don't you?"

Besides Thomas, Anna had two other brothers— Christian, who was fifteen, and Henry, eight. The younger boys did not have an earl for a father but rather a drunk who had died six years earlier from a knife to the heart during a fight at the local tavern. Since then, Anna had done all she could to care for her siblings.

She had put aside a bit of savings over the past two years to pay for her journey to London, but that would have to wait. Her conscience would not allow Geraldine and her children to suffer.

"I'm sure there will be no issue," she said.

"Then I've no reason to deny your request," Mr. Harrison replied. He raised his voice. "Everyone, back to work."

Several women groaned as they pulled themselves from their seated positions. Geraldine whispered a quick "Thank you" before she and her scrawny children hurried into the building.

With a sigh, Anna explained to Betty what had transpired, and soon, she stood outside alone. The walk home would take her just over an hour, if she maintained a leisurely pace. She was in no rush to give Thomas the news. He would be raving mad when he learned she had given someone else her place, and doubly so when she revealed that she had money hidden away.

Yet, that was her life— hidden farthings, burlap dresses, and dreams that gave her hope. And as she made her way down the road toward home, Anna began to wonder if the dreams she wished for would ever come true.

Chapter Two

Colin, 9th Duke of Greystoke, dreamed of life far different from the one in which he lived. In it, people spoke to him honestly. One would think that a duke could demand it of them, but alas, it was as if it never occurred.

For as long as he could remember, it was as if every person he encountered went out of their way to lie to him. Oh, he had no mad notion that they were plotting any nefarious schemes to rid him of his wealth. Or searching for a way to manipulate his good character in order to receive gifts.

The fact was that he was a duke from perhaps one of the most powerful bloodlines England had ever known. Many could benefit from his position in one way or another, whether it be an invitation to an exclusive party or a whisper of a favor at the Royal Court. It was no different when it came to the women who craved his attention. They did not want him, they wanted the title that with marriage to him.

He had lost count of the number of times he had considered how different his life would have been if he were bred from common stock. Although he loved the many luxuries his title afforded him, he despised the cost with which it came.

He had been drinking tea and reading in the library early this morning, a routine he savored that allowed him time to escape his monotonous life. Whether it was a highwayman planning a robbery or a hunter facing a wild beast in the Savannas of Africa, the enjoyment of not being a duke for a full hour pleased him.

Yet his freedom had come to an abrupt end. With a sigh, he returned the tome to its place on the shelf amongst the others of green or brown leather binding. It was time to face his life once more.

And as if to remind him of this fact, the door opened and Pendleton entered the room.

The butler was older than England itself. Or so Colin had believed as a child. Even today, a full head of silver-white hair and a face so lined it could have mapped every river in every country in the world confirmed the man was ancient. The often cankerous man was a welcome delight who added a much-needed presence to Hemingford Home.

"Your Grace," Pendleton said with his customary bow, which consisted of folding one arm across his stomach as the other remained rigid at his side. "Her Grace requests your presence to escort Lady Katherine Haskett through the rear garden before you leave."

Colin had planned a short holiday to Wilkworth for ten days, where he would stay at an estate belonging to his cousin Markus Remington.

The term cousin was a bit of a stretch, really, for they did not have parents who were siblings. How far back they had to go to find the connection was several generations, but regardless, they all still used the familiar term whenever they saw one another.

Which meant that there were many "cousins" in the Remington family, all of who invested in each other's various schemes. He was acquainted with most of them, or he had met them at least once, but he did not keep in touch with them all.

Nash and Albina Remington, Markus's parents, had always been amongst his favorites, despite the fact they had held no title. Whenever he visited, he was treated like any other Remington, and that was his reason for choosing Redstone Estate for this particular escape from his usual life.

Colin had not been to Wilkworth in nearly six years. Markus and his wife, Tabitha, who were a part of the merchant side of the family, did not keep residence at Redstone Estate. Instead, it was left in the care of Markus's yet-to-be married sisters, Evelyn and Caroline.

A month ago, Colin had sent word of his arrival and had received a prompt response that his visit would be most welcomed. It would be there at Redstone Estate that Colin would be free. At least as free as a duke could be for ten days.

Before he could enjoy himself, however, Colin had to deal with Lady Katherine, the daughter of the Earl of Haskett. Lovely in her own right, she was the woman his mother wished for him to marry. Although the choice of any potential bride was Colin's decision, he had yet to do so, and his mother had grown frustrated with his bachelorhood.

Oh, but if only he could become a butler and thus unencumbered by such expectations!

"Pendleton," Colin said as he leaned a shoulder on the bookcase, "you served my father for many years, did you not?" The old butler nodded. "And now you serve me."

"Yes, Your Grace."

"Tell me, in all those years, did you have any moments when you wished you had lived a different life? Perhaps you could have become a blacksmith? Or a soldier who fought for King and country?"

Pendleton reared his head back as if Colin had slapped him. His thick eyebrows pushed together, forming a single hedge even the expert gardeners in Colin's employ could not have trimmed. "I'm one and seventy, Your Grace, and therefore far too old to begin a new trade. If you mean to dismiss me, then please say as much so I may leave with some semblance of dignity."

Colin barked a laugh as he pushed away from the bookcase. Taking three long strides across the fine Aubusson rug, he stopped in front of the butler. "You're not going anywhere unless you wish to. I'm simply curious as to whether you ever desired a different life."

"No, Your Grace. I'm quite content where I am."

"And if I told you that I wish my life had been undistinguished from the one I live now, how would you advise me?"

"Good heavens," Pendleton gasped as he took a step back. "You must be jesting, Your Grace. I cannot entertain such a thought." He had grown so pale, Colin worried the poor man would faint.

"Indulge me," Colin said. "What advice would you give me?"

The butler glanced around as if hoping someone else would intervene. When he returned his gaze to Colin, he replied in a shaky voice, "You're a duke, Your Grace. Whatever you decide is best."

"But pretend I am not a duke," Colin said, forcing calm into his tone. "Say I was… a servant, perhaps."

Pendleton placed a hand over his heart and closed his eyes. Was the man praying? Colin swore he heard a plea of divine intervention.

This did not stop Colin from continuing with his line of questioning. "Would you advise me to become a tradesman? And if so, what sort? A cobbler, perhaps? Or better yet, a tailor?"

"Wh-whatever you wish to be, Y-Your Grace," Pendleton stammered. "You're a duke, Your Grace, and your wisdom's unparalleled to mine, just a lowly butler. In fact, there's none who can compare to you in wisdom or character in all the land."

As the man went on praising his name, Colin's thoughts drifted. He, Colin, was human, yet his peers, his servants, and even those who had yet to meet him treated him as if he were some sort of deity. Was there not one person in all of England who was willing to be truthful?

"In fact, Your Grace, many should want nothing more than to be in your presence."

Colin had heard enough. "Thank you, Pendleton," he said as he placed a hand on the butler's shoulder. "Your advice has been most helpful."

Color returned to Pendleton's face as he offered up another prayer, this one of thanksgiving. "I'm pleased to have been of help, Your Grace," he said with a diffident bow.

Grateful that the butler had not fainted, Colin exited the library and made his way to the foyer. Massive paintings hung from the walls, some depicting hunting scenes and others ships at sea. Between them hung rich tapestries of purple and gold. The chandelier held dozens of tapered candles. Blue and green porcelain vases filled with freshly cut flowers sat on highly-polished side tables. It certainly was not the home of a tradesman.

The sound of his low-heeled Hessian boots echoed in the room as he walked down the long corridor that led to the back gardens.

He drew in a steadying breath before stepping out onto the veranda where his mother and Lady Katherine sat at a round table enjoying a glass of lemon water. Beside Lady Katherine sat another young lady, likely her companion.

"Ah, my son," his mother cooed, "Lady Katherine rose while the moon still shone in the sky to prepare herself so she could be here to see you off this morning." She waved a hand at Lady Katherine. "Please, stand so he may inspect you."

This treatment by his mother of a potential daughter-in-law was not unusual. She often acted as if she were a merchant considering the purchase of a horse. His future wife, whoever she may be, was nothing more than an object to be measured in every possible way. Was he to count how many hands high she stood? Perhaps he should ask her to open her mouth so he could inspect her teeth!

Two months earlier, he had overheard his mother and two of her friends discussing how many children Lady Katherine would bear for him. Upon hearing them discussing the woman's "childbearing hips", he had decided it was best to leave them to their conversation and hurried away.

Lady Katherine dropped into a curtsy that nearly had her nose touching the veranda floor. She wore a white day dress of fine linen, the stitching likely done by the most skillful hands in London. It fit perfectly with a rather generous neckline that showed what his cousin Evan, Baron of Westlake, would have described as a "bountiful bosom." With red hair in tight curls and eyes greener than any he had ever seen, there was no doubt that even a blind man could see she was attractive.

Yet after four months of sharing tea and conversation, Colin felt nothing for her.

"Is she not beautiful, my son?" his mother whispered in his ear. "She awaits the engagement announcement with bated breath as much as I. Surely there is none more deserving. Go, take her on a stroll and I shall chaperone. If you wish to ask her anything, feel free to do so. I promise to give you some semblance of privacy."

Collin knew exactly what question she hoped he would ask, but he would not do so. Not today.

"Please, rise," he said to the young woman who had remained in the midst of her curtsy. "May I have the honor of escorting you around the gardens?" He offered Lady Katherine his arm, which she took without so much as a word.

They began the tedious journey over the cobbled path. Neatly arranged flowerbeds filled with colorful rows of blue, yellow and red flowers lay on either side.

"Lady Katherine," Collin said, "I have a question that has been on my mind as of late, and it requires an answer only you can give."

"Of course, Your Grace," Lady Katherine replied with a smile. "I am ready to give you such an answer."

Colin cringed. He was not speaking of their possible engagement. "Would you prefer addressing me as Greystoke like my friends and family do?"

"If that is your wish, Your Grace, I shall abide by it."

Sighing heavily, Colin stopped beneath a large tree and took hold of her gloved hands. "No, I'm not asking if you wish to adhere to my request but rather if you would prefer to address me in a less formal manner."

She drew in a quick breath and glanced toward his mother, who had stopped some ten or so paces away.

"You may tell me the truth," he said, offering her a smile to ease her obvious discomfort. "And look at me, not her."

"When we... forgive me. If you have decided that I am worthy to become your wife, I shall address you less formally."

Colin whispered a prayer of thanksgiving, but the words tumbled away as Lady Katherine added, "If that is what you desire, Your Grace."

"What I desire is someone willing to speak to me with honesty," he snapped, doing everything he could to control his frustration. When he did finally marry, he refused to settle with a wife wanting nothing more than to placate him. Seeing Lady Katherine drop her gaze, he sighed. "Ignore what I said—"

"I shall, Your Grace," Lady Katherine replied. "Shall I ignore the entire conversation or simply the last words?"

All Colin could do was shake his head. Could this woman truly ignore and forget everything he had just asked? He doubted it was possible, but her face said she would do all she could to do so until her dying breath.

"It was not an order," he murmured before releasing her hands. "I must go. It was a pleasure to see you again." He searched his mind for a compliment that would please her. "Your dress is lovely." He turned and marched away.

"I am sorry for offending you, Your Grace!" she called after him.

Colin ignored her and stopped before his mother, whose eyes narrowed at him. Although her hair was dark like his, silver had invaded it over the last few years. His mother was considered a great beauty. It was unfortunate that her words never matched her outward loveliness.

"I still don't understand why you must go to your cousin's estate," his mother said with a frown. "And what compounds my worry is that you refuse to take any staff with you. What duke goes anywhere without at least the benefit of his valet?"

Colin smiled. He would never be a blacksmith, but the idea of going without staff for nearly a fortnight intrigued him. "I'm sure that Newbold has plenty to keep him occupied here, Mother. And I'm not an invalid. I'm quite capable of dressing myself."

His mother sniffed. "Just because you can does not mean you should."

He gave her a smile and kissed her cheek. "I must go."

"When you return, it is my hope you make clear your intentions towards Lady Katherine. Once you've done that, we'll begin the preparations for a lavish party to make the announcement. In fact, I see us hosting several parties in the coming months."

Colin understood his mother meant well, but too often she had to be reminded of her place. "It's my hope that you remember that I'm the duke. Whom and when I marry will occur when I decide and not a moment sooner."

The truth was, Colin had no desire to marry Lady Katherine— or any other woman he had met thus far. Yet even he could not escape one simple fact. He was a duke. At four and twenty, his years of bachelorhood were numbered. Many of his peers were already married, and of those, most already had children. Yet he had no illusions that the inevitable marriage would take place. He just did not wish to see it happen today.

As he moved to step past his mother, she grasped hold of his arm. "This girl has been training all her life to marry into a noble family. I've no doubt that she will serve you well."

"I've no doubt she will," Colin said as he glanced at Lady Katherine, who waited beneath the tree, likely awaiting her next order. "Yet she has not been trained to think for herself. Nor to serve Colin Remington, the man behind the title."

His mother let out a small laugh. "You must learn that there is no difference between the two. Lady Katherine is virtuous, beautiful, and will bear you many children. Don't forget what is important in your life. What is expected of you!"

"And what of what I want?" he asked, although he knew her reply long before the question was asked.

"I speak of what is needed to see that the dukedom remains strong. I've no doubt you'll succeed. Especially if you follow my advice and marry the young lady I've brought to you."

"I'll succeed," he said with a smile. "Jut as I have all along. Your worry for me is appreciated but unnecessary. Now, I must go."

His mother sighed. "I suppose I do worry far too much, but is that not what mothers do? I'll speak to you soon."

Once in the waiting carriage, he released a heavy sigh. He would have ten days of leisure away from here, but he was certain of one thing. Whether it be his fiancée or the butler, no one he encountered had been honest with him. Nor sought to know the man behind the title.

As the carriage pulled away, he closed his eyes and considered that it would always be that way.

Chapter Three

The wind gusted as Colin soaked in the home belonging to his cousin, aptly named Redstone Estate. The three-story house was made of a reddish stone that came from the local area. In circular recesses above each of the ground floor windows sat a bust of one of the men who once lived in the house after it was erected several generations earlier.

Tall trees grew on either side, and deep-red flowers mixed with yellow lined the ground floor windows. He recalled a visit here during his childhood when he enjoyed the freedom of horseback riding and exploring.

Indeed it had been a much simpler life. Now, he was a man with far too many responsibilities to enjoy such pastimes.

Although not as large as Hemingford Home, Redstone Estate offered a large ballroom, a vast library, and twenty bedchambers. Even the stable that sat to the right of the house was grand.

The drive circled a grassy area with a large birdbath, where three sparrows splashed in its cool water. A single tree provided a circle of shade. All around him spoke of luxury, a word synonymous with the name of Remington.

That and scandal.

The Remington family possessed a fortune so vast that even distant cousins far removed owned homes as grand as this. He knew of none who did not benefit from the many trade agreements and business contracts their ancestors had made. Indeed, there was much to go around.

Not for the first time, Colin wondered if his family was as unhappy as he. For the more the Remington wealth grew, so did their problems. Infidelity, blackmail, and even bribery were among the list of suspected troubles the society columns of the London papers attributed to them. And although no names had ever been attached to those articles, Colin always recognized a story about a Remington.

As Barclay, his driver, saw to his luggage, Colin made his way to the set of double doors of the house. At once, they opened, and he laughed as Miss Caroline Remington threw her arms around him.

"Oh, Colin!" she exclaimed. "I've been waiting for you all day!" She drew back, her eyes wide. "I'm sorry. I mean Your Grace."

The last time Colin had seen Caroline, she was only eight. Now at fifteen, it was as if he were meeting an entirely different person altogether. Gone was the straw-like, mousy-brown hair, which now fell in a lustrous natural deep chestnut wave down her back.

"We're cousins, Caroline," he replied with a grin. "When it comes to family, we don't necessarily have to adhere to such strict formalities. And look how much you've grown!"

Her cheeks reddened and she sighed. "As have you," she replied. "We all have. Well, at least some of the Remingtons have matured. Father often joked that scandal..."

Her words trailed off, and Colin offered her a sympathetic smile. The loss of her parents had been a great blow, not only to Caroline but to Evelyn, as well.

"Well, that doesn't matter anymore," she said with a wave of her hand. "What does is that you're here. And I'll make certain that your stay here is as perfect as it can be."

"Don't exhaust yourself at my expense," Colin said, grinning. "In fact, I demand that you do not. So, tell me. What has been going on since we last saw one another?"

Caroline bit at her lower lip as if unsure how to respond. "So much has changed, yet much has remained the same. Come inside, and we'll talk more about that and other matters."

Colin followed her into the house, and Caroline motioned to the butler, who appeared older than Pendleton. "Davis will see to any needs you may have during your stay."

The butler gave a bow. "I'll have your bags taken to your room, Your Grace. And if you need my services as your valet—"

"Thank you," Colin replied. "But I'll see to dressing myself. If I need my shoes shined or my coats brushed, however, I'll be sure to ask."

Leaving Davis to his task, Colin looked over the foyer. The marble floor and highly polished oak banister were just a taste of the fantastic decor of Redstone Estate.

"Do you not find the house too large for just you and Evelyn?" Colin asked as he followed Caroline down the corridor. With her parents deceased and Markus living two days' journey away, he would have found the place a bit overbearing if he had to live there alone.

"I prefer the ample space," Caroline replied as she stopped before a closed door. Brushing back a strand of brown hair behind an ear, she sighed. "It allows me to read in peace without worry that Markus will fuss at me."

Colin recalled a younger Caroline with her nose buried in a book, much to her parents' chagrin. In fact, she read so much that her mother had begun forbidding her from reading as a form of punishment for any acts of misbehavior. Colin never understood his aunt and uncle's disapproval of their daughter reading. So much could be learned from such an activity.

"Evelyn is inside waiting," Caroline said, pausing as she gripped the door handle. "I know she's as excited as I to see you again."

She opened the door, and Colin stepped inside. The drawing room had not changed any more than what he had seen of the house thus far. Red tapestries with gold trim hung from the walls, their patterns of gold vines and cherubs matching the fabric on the furniture. Three large windows draped in red looked out over the back gardens.

What caught his attention, however, was the lone figure of his cousin Evelyn, sitting in a window seat. Dressed entirely in black, even down to her gloves, and her dark hair pulled into a severe bun at the nape of her neck, one would have thought she was still in mourning.

When Evelyn gave no indication that she noticed Colin and Caroline approaching, Colin leaned in closer to Caroline. "Is she unwell?"

A look of sadness crossed Caroline's features. "Not long after Father died, she began to withdraw. She can go for several days without speaking any words at all, but then she'll go for an entire week as if all is normal. Nothing I do or say seems to help. I just don't understand how one can be so withdrawn one day only to suddenly become happy the next and then draw back within herself again without any obvious cause."

She walked over and lowered herself to her knees in front of her sister. "Evelyn? Evelyn, look who's arrived. It's our cousin Colin." She spoke as if addressing a child rather than an elder sister.

Evelyn tilted her head, reminding Colin of a dog listening to a strange new sound. Then she rose as one crippled with old age despite her six and twenty years.

"Hello, Evelyn," he said, pushing down the shiver from peering into her cold blue eyes. He did not embrace her as he had Caroline, and he could not have said why. Cursing himself inwardly, he added, "Thank you for having me as your guest."

"You are most welcome," Evelyn replied in formal tones. "Forgive me for not greeting you upon your arrival, but I was deep in thought and had not realized you were here. May I help you settle in? I can have tea sent up if you would like. Or something to eat?"

"Thank you, but no. Perhaps we can speak later at dinner."

Evelyn gave a nod and returned to her seat beside the window, looking exactly as she had upon his arrival.

Caroline signaled to Colin to follow her, and they exited the room. Back in the foyer, she went to a large table and returned with a dark brown bottle.

"What's this?" he asked.

"Honey wine," she replied with a smile. "A gift to welcome your return. It was made locally. I think you'll enjoy it."

"Thank you. I had planned to spend my days in leisure, and this will help." This made them both laugh.

He studied his cousin, and although she was eleven years younger than her sister, she carried herself like a woman far older. "Tell me more about Evelyn. Does Markus know of her condition?"

She crossed her arms over her stomach. "He believes it's a charade in order to gain attention after Father's death."

"And you? What do you believe?"

"It's pure rubbish. She refuses to see anyone, has closed off every friendship, and rejects every offer to receive suitors. And the doctor agrees with me, that she is still grieving."

Colin had heard of a mourning period lasting longer than six months, maybe even longer than a year. But three years? That was an obvious sign of something far sinister at play.

"The doctor has prescribed honey wine, just like what you hold, but you can see that it has done no good." Colin went to return the bottle, but Caroline waved it away. "We have enough bottles to last us twenty years, so please, keep it. As I said before, there are days when Evelyn speaks as we are now, and you would think it's always that way. Yet days like today outnumber those by far."

Collin wished there was a way he could help. He was acquainted with many who were distinguished in the area of modern-day medicine. Perhaps he would make inquiries later. But he needed more information before he would do that.

"And this all began after your father's death?"

Caroline nodded. "Markus hosted a party... well, perhaps party is not the correct term but rather a gathering to celebrate Father's life and to begin the mourning period. Although I believe it was more an excuse for food and wine. The day after the party, Evelyn refused to leave her room or speak with anyone. Several months later, she refused to get out of bed. I suppose the fact we've been able to convince her to dress and come downstairs is an improvement, but this is as far as we've come."

A sense of hopelessness washed over Colin. Here he was worrying over his problems, especially Lady Katherine, but his issues paled in comparison to those of his cousins. The air around him became stifling, causing his breathing to come in short gasps.

"I think I'll go for a stroll and perhaps a bit of this wine." Somehow, he managed to keep his voice even. He stepped out onto the portico and drew in a lungful of fresh air.

"Do you remember the river?" Caroline asked.

"How could I forget?" Colin asked with a laugh, glad to feel normal again. The last time he had gone to the river, Markus still lived at Redstone Estate, and he had joined Colin and the girls for a swim. Evelyn had gotten her shoes stuck in the muddy bank. Colin, in an attempt to rescue her shoes, had slipped and fallen on his backside, muddying his breeches and coat. Everyone, including himself, had shared in riotous laughter.

It suddenly occurred to him that he had not laughed like that since.

Caroline smiled. "Why not take a walk down there? The sound of the current can be very calming."

"I think that's a wonderful idea. Will you join me?"

Caroline glanced at the closed door and shook her head. "Evelyn does not like me going there, even with friends. But you enjoy yourself. Dinner is served at half-past six. Oh, and don't drink too much of that in one sitting. It's quite potent."

Colin bounded down the steps and made his way to the stable. Halfway there, he stopped, uncorked the bottle, and sniffed at the opening. An overwhelming smell of honey and nutmeg filled his nostrils. Although he was curious as to where Caroline had procured such a drink, he summoned his courage and took a sip.

It was quite good.

"Potent?" he mumbled. "It's more fruit and honey than wine." Then again, Caroline was not accustomed to truly strong drink.

As the sun beat upon his head, Colin removed his coat and flung it over his shoulder. The unusually dry air stung his cheeks as he made his way into the small forest beyond the front gardens. Memories flooded his mind of a time when he was but nine years of age, when he and Markus spent an entire afternoon climbing various trees and romping through the underbrush. Yes, this was exactly what he needed— time alone to contemplate his life before returning to the number of hefty responsibilities heaped upon him like manure in a dung heap.

Ten minutes later, the babbling of the river reached him well before he arrived at its bank. He had forgotten how soothing the sound of the rushing water could be. A tree long since fallen joined the flanking banks, connecting his cousin's property to another.

Colin had never met the family— the Silverstones if he recalled correctly— who owned the adjoining property, but he had heard of them. From what Markus had told him, they were a thieving lot who believed that anything they found belonged to them, even if it was discovered on another's property. Apparently, they had stolen quite a number of tools, so many that Markus had been forced to place locks on all the outbuildings to keep them out.

What worried Markus the most, however, were not the objects they pilfered but rather that the Silverstones had claimed the river as theirs when it clearly belonged to the Remingtons.

Regardless of who owned it, Colin found the sights and sounds relaxing, and he took another drink of the honey wine. It really was quite tasty. In a way, it reminded him a bit of sherry only sweeter. He had drunk something else that was very much like it, but he could not bring to mind what it was.

As he watched the water flowing past, his mind drifted of its own accord. His mother was relentless in her insistence that he marry sooner rather than later, and Colin had no valid reason to argue with her.

The problem was the woman he was meant to marry. If only he could find one who had her own opinions, who made up her own mind and did not feel the need to agree with everything he said. An intelligent woman without being obstinate or shrewish. If he could find a woman with those qualifications, he would have the banns read that instant. He could not remain alone forever, nor did he want to.

He desired a bride at his side, but she had to be more than his wife. She also had to be his friend and confidante.

He would not be disappointed if she also had attractive features.

Taking another drink to quench his thirst, Colin walked along the riverbank. Many young ladies had gone to great extremes to catch his eye. What they wanted, however, was not to know him for who he was. No, their interest lay in the fact that if they were to marry, they would then become the duchess. Could he fault them for such aspirations? No. Yet, could he not find one, just one, who wanted to know *him*?

Perhaps that was far too much to ask. After all, did he know himself? He glanced down at his finger. The gold band with its red ruby indicated he was a duke, but surely he was more than that. But what exactly he did not know.

"Colin Remington, blacksmith," he said with a laugh. If only it were true.

The river had done its job, for his bad had a kind of weightlessness to it and the sound of his own laughter delighted him.

"What woman would marry me then? No, they want a duke, not a blacksmith. They're all the same."

And nothing could have been truer. Every young lady he had been forced to meet was exactly like every other young lady, both in appearance and demeanor. All wore the latest fashions, styled their hair in the same coiffures. Not one stood out amongst the others as an individual. Oh, they had different hair and eye color. Some were rail-thin while others were plump. Tall, short, sharp nose, button nose. Yes, they had their own individual qualities. But in too many ways, in the ways that mattered, they were far too much alike.

A bead of sweat trickled down his cheek and his head suddenly felt light. He had clearly spent far too long in the sun. Turning his back to the river, he walked over to the shade of a nearby tree. Indeed, it was far cooler there.

He leaned his back against the trunk, placing his coat on the ground beside him, and took another large swallow to wet his dry throat. Then he placed the half-empty bottle beneath his coat and watched the river rush past. It had been a very long time since he felt this relaxed, and he stretched his legs out in front of him and allowed the smooth bark of the poplar tree to press into his back.

Oh, yes, it felt so nice to relax.

His eyes grew heavy, and promising himself to nap for only a few moments, he allowed sleep to wash over him.

Chapter Four

W as there anything more relaxing than a lovely swim in the river? Anna did not believe so as she balanced herself with her arms extended at her sides, a shoe in each hand. The fallen tree acted as a bridge between the Remington property— which she had just cut through— to her own.

The river had been a source of contention for the two families for generations, although no arguments had ensued for many years. It was quite evident that the body of water had once belonged to the Silverstone family, a fact her mother had shared with her on more than one occasion. And her mother did not lie.

With the roar of the rushing current just beyond the pool below, Anna shimmied the knotted tree trunk, whistling a tune. Not once had she fallen into the river, a feat of which she was quite proud. Few could make such a claim. Even Thomas had lost his footing when he was younger and plunged into the water below.

Once she reached the opposite shore, she allowed her toes to sink into the soft mud of the riverbank as she gazed at the flowing waters. Anna had come to the river often to swim alone, even after dark when the moon was full. Doing so, of course, was not ladylike. But seeing as she was not of the *ton*, nor would she ever be, her confidence allowed her to do as she pleased.

Besides, no one but her family ever came out to swim. Not anymore. Many years ago, she and Miss Caroline Remington had gone swimming together on several occasions— in secret of course— but after the death of Mr. Remington, Miss Caroline never returned.

As it was only midday, Anna thought it wise to take her time returning home. Once she did arrive at the cottage, she would have to inform Thomas why she chose to leave her position for the remainder of the summer. Although the argument could not be avoided, it could be delayed. Thus the reason she now removed her burlap dress. Swimming made for a wonderful way to pass the time.

She despised the course fabric she used to make her dresses. How wonderful it would have been to wear soft muslin or royal embossed satin. But the cost of such fabrics was more than she made in a month, and she would rather put food on the table than purchase fabrics that would only need extra care. Burlap was strong and held up well. Too bad it was so unattractive.

Wearing only her shift was freeing, and she set her shoes on a nearby rock and draped the dress over an arm. The water was cool when she waded into the river, far different from the heat that hung in the air.

She inched forward. The water covered her ankles. Then her calves. Her knees. Deeper and deeper she moved into the pool beneath the log, stopping when she was immersed to her neck.

As she swirled the dress in the water to rid it of the dirt and dust of the workhouse, her mind drifted back to the events of the day. Although she had no regrets for helping Geraldine, the cost of doing so pained her. Her plan to journey to London to search out her father would now have to be delayed, for she would have to hand over her savings to Thomas to make up for what she had done.

It would take at least another year to save as much again. One did not simply leave for London without money to pay for passage as well as the food and lodging while there.

Then a new thought made Anna shiver. What if Mr. Harrison demanded what he deemed "a favor" for her to return in September? She could say as often as she liked that she would never do such a thing, but if there was no work, trouble would ensue at home.

That is, of course, unless she married one of the men Thomas had mentioned over the last few months. Some were her age of eighteen, while others were old enough to be her grandfather. But all had some sort of wealth, whether it be a shop or his own small estate. Each time her brother suggested one, she had rejected him, causing Thomas to scowl and his voice to rise. He simply did not understand what she needed in a husband.

So often, their mother had spoken of the love a couple could share. That was what Anna sought— the mysterious force that few were able to experience. Although her mother had sworn she loved Anna's father, she also admitted that she had not loved Hugh, Christian and Henry's father and Anna's stepfather. Their marriage had been one of convenience for them both, her mother needing security and he wanting someone to warm his bed.

It was not as if Hugh had not been kind to all the children, including Anna and Thomas, for he had. Yet his days of working soon ended after marriage, and his drinking had increased. What little money the family had was soon gone, leaving them with nothing but the property on which sat the tiny cottage in which they lived. And that came from her mother's family, not from Hugh's.

Wanting to clear her mind of those times, Anna drew in a deep breath and ducked her head beneath the water. A moment later, she resurfaced, swiping back the wet hair from her face with a gasp of fresh air.

As Anna wiped water from her eyes, she caught sight of a man propped up against a tree, his head lolling to one side. Was he even breathing?

With a pounding heart, she lowered herself into the water up to her chin and glanced around in search of any signs of an assailant. All was quiet except the fluttering wings of a sparrow and the babbling of the river over the rocks. That did not mean she was alone.

Her concern that a dead man lay on the Remington property equaled that of who could have possibly murdered him. What if a highwayman still lurked about? Would he murder her to make certain he left no witnesses?

Despite her fears, her curiosity grew stronger. Making a decision, Anna swam to the opposite bank and crouched in the mud as water dripped from her body. The sun warmed her skin as she glanced around once more. When she was certain no one was waiting to attack her, she wrung out her dress and spread it over a boulder to dry.

Although her mind screamed that she should turn around and run, Anna could not resist inspecting the body and crept toward it. Perhaps he was still alive and needed aid. Not that she knew much about doctoring.

Once she drew close enough, she was certain of two things. The first was that the slight rise and fall of his chest confirmed that he was not dead, although he might be close to it.

The second was that he was handsome, devilishly so.

"Hello?" she whispered. When there was no response, she said the same again, this time much louder.

With his head at such an awkward angle, Anna wondered if he had climbed the tree and fell.

No, he was far too old to be climbing trees.

Unsure what to do, she straddled his outstretched legs until her knees pressed into the grass on either side of him. "You're very handsome," she whispered, her cheeks burning more than they ever had before.

With his short, dark wavy hair, strong cheekbones, and an equally strong jaw, he was far more dashing than any man she had ever seen before. Her heart pounded so hard against her chest that she was sure it would waken him.

Reaching out, she placed a palm on each of his cheeks and righted his head. A mischievous thought came to mind, and biting at her lower lip, she ran a finger along his jaw. Although they were protected from the sun by the overhanging boughs, a fire erupted inside her.

She glanced around once more to see if anyone was nearby. Seeing no one, she dared to look over the man's strong form. His shirtsleeves clung to his broad chest, and Anna considered how large his arm muscles were. His fine breeches and shiny boots said he came from money. But who was he?

When her gaze fell on the large ring on his finger, her eyes widened. She had never seen such a large red gem in her life! That ring alone could feed her family for at least two years if not three.

But no, she was not a thief.

His coat lay on the ground beside him. She reached for it and laughed when she found a bottle beneath it. "So, you're drunk," she said.

Returning her attention to the coat, she ran a hand across the dark-blue fabric, which was soft and finely woven. She decided to don it.

"There," she said. "Now I'm decent."

Then she picked up the bottle, removed the stopper, and took a drink. "Honey wine? Not a common drink for a man of your wealth."

She studied him for a moment. He drew in a deep breath and snorted, but his eyes remained closed.

"Who are you?" she asked. "Do you know the Remingtons? It's rare to see anyone out here these days."

Of course, the man did not respond.

Taking another drink, she then held the bottle against her chest. She was tempted to kiss him, for even his lips appeared strong. Yet there were certain acts in which even she dared not partake.

But she could touch.

With a trembling hand, Anna placed a finger on his lips, causing a thrill to run through her. What would it be like to have a fine gentleman kiss her? Would his lips be soft and languid or harsh and urgent?

Shaking the thoughts from her head, she took another sip of the wine.

"What a life you must lead," she said with a frown. "You're able to drink all day and discard such a fine coat as if it were nothing. I imagine that you can purchase another just as fine, if not finer, without thought of how much it will cost you."

Glancing down at his open hand, she traced the tip of a finger across it. "Your hands are smooth, unlike mine. Days of labor are foreign to you." She pulled her hair back over her shoulder. "You must understand. I'm not jealous of your life, but I wish you to know what I need in my own. I wish I had the funds to take me to London, to pay for a small room for a few days so I can meet my father."

She took another drink from the bottle and replaced the stopper. "But I imagine you'll never comprehend such wants in life. How fortunate for you. That ring could provide everything I need and more. And you, drunk sir, could do nothing to stop me from taking it. Not in your current state." She let out a hearty laugh. "But today good fortune has befallen you, for I am no thief."

Without warning, the man's eyes opened. Before Anna could speak, he let out a great roar, grasped her by the arms, and threw her onto her back, promptly straddling her just as she had him.

The bottle rolled away as she struggled to escape. Yet, although Anna should have been terrified, she found she was not. In truth, she found having the man's body atop hers exciting.

When his deep blue eyes met hers, the fight inside her receded.

"Who are you?" he demanded, his breath reeking of honey wine.

"I would ask the same of you," Anna retorted. "What man thrusts himself upon a woman who's attempting to aid him? A rogue, I tell you!" Oh, he was a delightful rogue, he was! She tried to withhold the giddiness that filled her, but it was a terrible struggle.

"Aid me?" he said, his scowl turning into the most delectable smile Anna had ever seen. "I awoke to you speaking of my ring and your desire to have it. Tell me, woman, are you a thief?"

"I'm not a thief," she repeated, her words faltering for the first time. Not from fear but rather from the piercing blue eyes. And having him on top of her, which was nearing the obscene.

Even a woman of Anna's station knew she should demand that he remove himself. Her mother had once warned her about handsome men and what they could do to a woman. Yet, as she studied his face, the words of wisdom trickled from her mind like water seeping beneath sand.

"But I am a fool," she continued, "for trying to help a beast such as yourself. Tell me, rogue, do you set upon helpless women often?"

"Rogue? I'm no rogue. I'm a duke."

Anna snickered. "A duke?" She pretended to study him for a moment. "Your eyes tell me you're honest, and I'm a very good judge of character. I would even go so far as to say that your eyes are wonderfully appealing."

Had the honey wine had that great of an effect on her? She was acting like a silly girl of thirteen speaking to a boy she liked from the village.

As Anna considered this, the duke had taken the opportunity to look her over. Although that very action had brought her anger from other men in the past, she found his gaze welcoming.

Then, like a rock striking her head, realization of her situation hit her. A man she did not know was sitting on top of her, and she was wearing his coat, which had come open to reveal the wet— and disconcertingly clingy— shift.

What had come over her? She had to do something to keep herself from succumbing to these feelings before it was too late!

Fearing that all decency was about to leave her, Anna feigned outrage. "You're a brute!" she cried. "Your eyes betray your lust! Get off of me at once!" She pushed against his hard chest and immediately scolded herself for enjoying the feel of his muscles.

It was a relief— and perhaps a twinge of regret— when he rose and offered her his hand.

"Please, allow me to help you," he said, smiling. "It's the least I can do. And I'll have you know that I'm not a brute. I would never harm you in any way."

Eying him with suspicion, Anna reached out and placed her hand in his. Immediately, the warm sensation returned. His hands, though smooth, were strong, and she was soon on her feet standing before him.

He towered over her, and despite his current state of inebriation, she felt safe in his presence.

Glancing down, she saw he remained holding her hand. When he released it, she could not help but give a sigh of regret.

"I'm the Duke of Greystoke," he said with a half-bow. "I thank you for not robbing me of my ring, though I do request that you return my coat."

Anna laughed. Perhaps he was truly a duke, but whether he was mattered little to her. Rather, it was the question of how badly he wanted his coat.

She ran a hand down the lapel. "I imagine this coat cost more than a few shillings," she said, grinning. "And to be honest, I've come to like it very much. It would make a fine addition to my current wardrobe."

"Are you saying you don't mean to return it?" he asked, his face scrunched as if she had thrown a fist into his stomach. Clearly, he had no idea she was teasing, and his bewildered look as he scratched his head said as much.

Anna was laughing so hard that she had to grab hold of his forearm to prevent herself from topping over, which was a mistake, for the heat once more washed over her.

"Tell me, are you truly a duke?" she asked once she was able to catch her breath. He nodded. "Well, I suppose keeping this coat would be a crime against the Crown." She gave a mock frown. "And although removing it would please you greatly, I have no choice but to inform everyone how a duke made me indecent."

When she reached for the lapels once more, he groaned and grabbed her arms. "No, you keep it," the duke mumbled.

For a moment, he held her, and Anna had the strong urge to have him kiss her. To her surprise, he licked his lips as if considering doing just that.

Then, as suddenly as he had grabbed her, he released her.

Pushing aside the sense of regret, Anna smiled. "Come on, then," she said, picking up the bottle from where it had landed. "It will be some time before my dress is dry, and I would like to learn more about you." She walked over to the boulder where her dress hung and leaned against it.

The duke had not moved.

"What?" she demanded. "Is a duke too good to drink with a commoner like me?"

To this, the man laughed, and Anna suspected she had never heard such a wonderful sound.

"Before we drink together," he said as he joined her beside the boulder, "you must tell me your name."

"Anna Silverstone. You may call me Anna."

Taking the bottle from her hand, he took a drink and wiped his mouth in a very unduke-like manner. "You may call me Colin. In fact, I insist on it."

Chapter Five

Colin considered that perhaps he had died and gone to Heaven. The woman who lay beneath him was most certainly an angel. How else could one describe her beauty? Honey-blonde locks fell down her back— or in her current position created a halo around her head. Blue eyes sparkled more than the ruby on his finger. A fire roared inside him at her pouty lips begging to be kissed.

Oh, but how she tempts me!

Perhaps his cousin had been correct in her description of the honey wine. The fact that he had fallen asleep drunk— and his aching head— said as much. But when he heard someone discussing his ring, he had used all his strength to subdue the would-be thief. It was not until he had her back pressed to the ground that he realized she was of the female persuasion.

As they exchanged words, he could not help but consider their positions— both literally and figuratively. After all, any man with his form atop that of a woman should have retreated immediately upon realizing his mistake, but he found he did not have the strength. She wore a mischievous grin that caused a most welcoming sensation to come over him.

His eyes took on a life of their own, and he found himself staring at the damp shift that showed off a very pleasant feminine form.

You are a duke, by God! he chastised himself. He was no rogue, nor was he a man who gazed upon women with lust! Surely, he had damned himself to Hell with his scandalous actions. Yet, whether it was due to inability or unwillingness, he did not look away. No, this woman was to be admired, and was he the only worthy man to do so.

"You're a brute! Your eyes betray your lust! Get off of me at once!"

Could he argue with her words? There she was, pinned beneath him. Although her voice held anger, her eyes displayed something else, something he could not name. Something he found welcoming. Any gentleman worthy of his title would leap to his feet and apologize for such brazen behavior, yet Colin feared that if he allowed the woman to go, he would never see her again. And he found the idea dreadful.

Finally, rational thinking returned, and he stood.

Well, offer her a hand up! his voice of reason snapped.

The woman hesitated before placing her hand in his. It was rough, the fingertips calloused, telling a story of a life of hard work. Although her hair was damp and she was wearing only his coat over her clinging sift, he found her natural fragrance alluring. A strange desire came over him, a craving to touch her face, to taste those pouty lips just begging to be kissed. Standing there above her, a primal need to protect her overtook him. From whom or what was unknown, but he would gladly do it all the same.

The throbbing in his head lessened, and for a moment, he was uncertain how to proceed. Should he be the gentleman he was brought up to be and apologize for his actions?

"I'm the Duke of Greystoke," he said, offering her a small bow. "I thank you for not robbing me, although I do request that you return my coat."

Had he taken on the role of jester in the King's court? It was not the intoxication of the honey wine that made him say such witless words but rather the woman who stood before him. He had never felt so weak in the presence of any other person— even the King himself! Her laughter did not help ease his frustration, either.

Oh, but what a sharp tongue this little vixen had! She wielded it as well as any master swordsman, dueling him in wit and teasing. And she was unwilling to return his coat, or so she claimed. Never had a woman made him feel so alive! Blood pulsed through his veins faster than the water flowed in the river beside them.

She leaned against a large rock, a mischievous twinkle in her eye that awoke a yearning inside him. Twice she had called him handsome, yet he had not yet expressed how beautiful he found her. But he planned to. Although he feared the word was not strong enough to do her justice.

"Colin is a fine name," she said with that playful smile. Then she knitted her brow in thought. "I believe it means strong. Or is it handsome?"

When she tilted her head just so, Colin had to rein in the beast within him. He was a gentleman, not a lion!

"Regardless," she continued, "I'll call you Colin." Then she grinned.

He took a small sip from the bottle without thought that it had gotten him into the strange— and quite alluring— predicament and handed it back. "My cousin may believe you to be a thief, but I do not."

He cringed. What had made him utter such a statement?

"Do you mean Master Markus?" she replied. "He's accused my family of all sorts of atrocities, as did his father. I can assure you, what they've said is all untrue."

Colin took a half-step toward her. "I believe you. At least that you're no thief."

"Your opinion does nothing to change the truth," she said with a laugh. "And why are you out here of all places? Do you not have a hunt in which to partake? Or perhaps a party in London where your attendance is expected?"

That same mischievous grin made him laugh. Already he found this woman quite fascinating. "As a duke, I'm expected to do many things, in that you're correct. But I've come to the home of my cousin to escape. Not from a fox hunt or a party, but from something far worse."

Anna raised a single eyebrow. "Well, I must hear what would be far worse than a hunt."

He walked over and leaned beside her on the rock. "As a duke, one would believe that my life would be mine, to do as I please. But that is not the case. There are responsibilities, customs, expectations, so many requirements with which I would not wish to bore you." He turned toward her. "You don't plan to run off with my coat, do you?" he asked, hoping to change the topic of conversation to something more pleasant.

She gave an exaggerated gasp and placed a hand to her breast. "I've never been so insulted in all my life. And by a duke, no less! Please, insult me again. If you dare to face my wrath."

He wanted nothing more than to take her up on her offer. "For a woman of your advanced years, you are quick with your tongue."

"My advanced years?" she replied with a voice so flat, the cook could have used a rolling pin on it.

"Why yes," he said, pressing as much innocence into his tone as he could muster. "You must be at least thirty. Perhaps even closer to forty."

This time her laugh was accompanied by a playful fist to his arm. How could he know this woman no more than ten minutes yet feel as if he had known her forever? He found her a breath of fresh air, and their oral fencing was a delight. After calling on Lady Katherine for several months, he had yet to feel this close to her. Yes, this was a delightful change, indeed.

As their laughter died down, Colin allowed himself the privilege of soaking in her feminine form. Or what he could see with his coat covering her. Why the girl was not married was a mystery, one he hoped to unravel.

"Are you always this friendly to those you first meet?" she asked.

"Not typically," he replied. "Too often, when I first meet people, it is for matters of business, which does not allow for much friendliness."

Her smile was as warm as the breeze that blew around them, and she walked over to pluck a blade of grass. She held it high above her and released it, and it floated away on the air.

"And you?" he asked. "What are you doing here. Of all places?" He added the last belatedly.

"Oh, I often come here to swim. Or to sit on the log bridge to listen to the flow of the water." She returned to stand in front of him and, to his surprise, placed a hand on his chest. "Now that we've been properly acquainted, and seeing that my dress is now dry, I must go."

An odd sensation of the world closing in on him threatened to take away his breath forever. He had to— no, he needed to— spend time with her again. "When shall I see you next?"

She removed the dress from the rock, folded it and held it against her hip. "Meet me here in two days at midday. Oh, and if you're truly a gentleman, see that you bring a basket of food with you." As she took another step closer, Colin's heart thumped harder when she looked directly at him. "One more thing."

"Yes?" he said, preparing himself for the kiss he knew she would request. One he would be happy to oblige.

"I need something from you."

Colin wet his lips and dipped his head. "And I shall give it to you."

When he placed his hands around her waist, she sighed. He pulled her against him, and he was overcome with desire.

She smiled, not taking her eyes off his as the tips of her fingers trailed down his upper arm with aggravating slowness, making his skin pebble beneath the sleeves of his shirt. They then continued down his forearm, sending heat to his midsection. Her lips parted, and he leaned closer.

Then she winked and pulled the bottle from his hand. "Thank you."

Colin found himself in a state of disbelief when Anna laughed. "You're horrible!"

"I can be at times," she said, poking him in the chest. "You really should be more careful in my company."

"Anna!" came a male voice.

"It's my brother," Anna said, her voice filled with fright. "You'd best run!"

"Anna, what are you…"

A man near Colin's age emerged from the trees on the opposite side of the river, a boy of perhaps seven at his side. His eyes went wide only a moment before rage crossed his features.

"You rogue!" he shouted. "I'll beat you to a pulp!"

Anna pushed Colin toward the woods. "Run!" she hissed. "I'll see you soon!"

Colin nodded. He was in Wilkworth for leisure, not to engage in a bout of fisticuffs. He was no coward, but fighting would only make it more difficult for him to see Anna again. And that, he could not have!

So, he ran into the woods, the cries of her brother following after him. Within a single hour, Colin had fallen asleep in a drunken stupor, been awakened by a beautiful woman straddling him wearing nothing but a thin, wet shift that did more than hint at the shapely form beneath. And now her irate brother wanted to fight him. It was a far cry from anything he had ever experienced before.

And he loved every moment of it!

Chapter Six

Anna was well aware that there was no escaping Thomas's wrath. She hurried across the fallen log where her brothers waited. Henry, the youngest, grinned up at her, a gap where a tooth had once been. His patched trousers and threadbare shirt were a stark contrast to the clean coat and breeches Thomas wore.

Any extra money went to her eldest brother, which he used to purchase clothing to impress the many men to whom he presented his latest propositions. He had to have the "proper attire," or so he termed it, or the best port as an offering during those various meetings. One would believe he was of the landed gentry if they took in his appearance, which was all Thomas ever wanted.

"Who was that man?" Thomas demanded, his fist raised. "Tell me at once so I may go find the coward. I'll challenge him to a duel if I must."

In Anna's opinion, if her brother was as furious as he made himself out to be, he would have given chase. But his words were rarely followed up with meaningful actions.

His tall form cast her in shadow, and he let out a sigh of frustration as he brushed back a wave of brown hair from his brow. Although he and Henry had different fathers, both shared their mother's hair color.

Thomas looked her up and down, his face purple with rage. "I don't wish to ask what took place here, but I've no choice. And why are you wearing that coat?" Anna went to respond, but he lifted a hand to forestall her. "Please tell me my fears haven't been realized."

"Nothing happened in regard to your *fears*," she snapped.

He heaved a dramatic sigh. "Thank goodness."

"What did you fear, Thomas?" Henry asked with the innocence of a boy of six. "Was that man gonna thump her?"

"It's none of your concern," Thomas snapped. "I'm just thankful our dear sister remains honorable. I would hate to think she would ruin her chances of finding a wealthy suitor interested in calling on her."

Anna shook her head in annoyance. Thomas was not concerned for her sake that she had acted properly. Instead, he was relieved she was still worthy of finding a proper gentleman who would ask for her hand in marriage, a transaction of which Thomas reminded her almost daily.

And why would he be concerned about scandal? He acted as if the Silverstone name was on the tip of every tongue of those of high society. The truth was, perhaps he should consider his own actions before berating her for hers.

"Why're you home so early?" Henry asked, and Anna winced. "Did you miss me?"

She ruffled his hair. "I always miss you while I'm working." She sneaked a sideways glance at Thomas and added, "Work's been delayed for a while. That's why I'm home earlier than usual."

"What do you mean 'delayed'?" Thomas demanded as they exited the sparse woods that bordered the small field beside their cottage. "Are you saying that you won't be returning to work tomorrow?"

Anna shook her head.

"Next week, then."

Again she shook her head.

"Henry, run along and prepare for your lesson. I'll be there in a minute."

The boy darted away, running past the pen where their brother Christian was working one of the horses.

Sighing, Anna said, "I'll not be returning until September."

Thomas pinched the bridge of his nose. "Anna. No one suddenly shuts down a workhouse for so long. Tell me the entire story."

Anna sighed. He would learn the truth soon enough. "Remember when I told you about Geraldine Malley and her children?"

The Duke Who Loved Me

Thomas raised a single brow but gave no indication that he had any memory of said family.

"Today I heard a rumor that Mr. Harrison wishes to release some of the workers." For several minutes, she explained what had transpired, including her offer to give her work to Geraldine.

When she finished, Thomas stared at her, his face a thundercloud. "Have you lost your mind? We rely on that money to survive, and you give away your position? For once, will you consider the needs of your own family and let Mrs. Malley worry about hers?"

Anna's jaw tightened. "Geraldine and her children barely have enough to eat as it is, Thomas! Unlike you, I can't walk around in good conscience knowing that others suffer! Not when I can do something to help."

"What's that supposed to mean? Unlike me?" His red face had darkened to puce, and his tone became quiet, a sure sign she had gone too far.

"It doesn't matter. I've enough money set aside that you may have. It's more than enough to carry us through until I return to work."

As she had expected, Thomas went into a rant, demanding to know how she could have kept back any money, when they needed it so much. One would have thought he was her husband rather than her brother.

"After what I've seen today," he said with a disappointed shake to his head, "I don't know who you are anymore. And what was this money you deprived your family of intended for?"

Anna dropped her gaze. "To go to London and search out Father."

Thomas took a firm grip on her arms. "That man doesn't deserve the title of Father. I forbid you to see him or even speak of him again. Do you hear me?"

"But why?" Anna asked. "Why is it that you can have such lofty dreams, but when I wish to meet the man who can open up the world to us, you become angry?"

He released her, and Anna wiped tears from her cheek. He had not hurt her, not physically, but if she were not arguing with Thomas, Christian was. Thomas spent every waking moment consumed with

42

the idea of being accepted by those far above them. It was why every farthing went into the horses Christian trained so they could sell them, which would have been a respectable way to make money. The problem was, what they earned from those sales went to new suits, gifts of expensive wines, and hired carriages, all to impress those who would never accept them.

The only result of that hard work was continued poverty and incessant arguing, and Anna despised it all.

"You're no longer a child, Anna. It's my duty to protect you. Trust me, that man cared nothing for our mother, nor you or me. Erase him from your mind. He's not worth a moment's notice. Now, that man whose coat you wear. Who is he? And how is it that you are still wearing it?"

"A cousin of the Remington's. A duke. And he...gave it to me."

"A duke?" Thomas snorted. "I doubt that. He probably lied to you. I forbid you to see him again. People like him believe that women like you are easy to seduce. Once he gets what he wants from you, he'll cast you aside. Mark my words. That coat is merely the beginning, Anna. I'd rather you return the garment than see you pay for it in ways that cannot be taken back."

Anna's cheeks heated with embarrassment. She had not partaken in any unscrupulous acts today, but she *had* hoped that Colin would kiss her. At one point, it appeared he would. If he had, she was uncertain if she would have stopped him if he asked for more.

Yet a larger problem than receiving a kiss from a handsome duke was at hand. Thomas had forbidden her to see Colin, and she simply could not allow that to happen. Not that she would inform her brother of this fact.

"There's no need to worry, Thomas. He was bragging about returning to his fancy estate first thing tomorrow. I doubt we'll ever see him again."

"Good. Now, get supper started. I'll see to Henry's reading lesson. He was looking forward to a swim today. Until you ruined it."

Anna clenched her fists in her skirts as her brother walked away. Every problem that arose, he blamed on her. Or Christian. Neither made any sense, as it was he, Thomas, who made all the financial decisions in the family. If anyone was to blame, it was he!

Her gaze fell on the cottage. How she wished their mother were still alive! In the long line of grandfathers on her mother's side, one had purchased the property and built the house. Over the years, it was parceled out and sold, most to the Remington family.

Eventually, all that remained was the house and the small patch of land on which it sat, which was left to Thomas. It was not fancy, by any means, but it had enough bedrooms to allow Anna and Thomas a bedroom of their own, leaving the last for the two younger boys to share.

The thatched roof leaked, the window in her bedroom had a crack that resembled a wide grin, and the paint— like the happy memories— had long since faded. Yet Anna found their home charming, and like her dreams, she believed there was still hope for it.

She smiled as she approached the pen. Christian was a handsome boy, so much so that he attracted as many smiles from women as she did from men. Although it was not in fashion, he wore his blond hair long, allowing it to flow around his shoulders as he worked. Christian, like her, dreamed of better days, but he had his feet firmly planted in reality, unlike Thomas.

"Do I dare ask how you came by that coat?" he asked as he closed the door to the stable. "Or that wine bottle?"

"A cousin of the Remingtons— a duke, no less— gave them to me." Christian raised an eyebrow. "Well, that may not be the complete truth. I donned the coat and refused to return it."

"That's my sister," Christian said with a chuckle. "And Thomas? What's upset him this time? That could not have been just about your new coat."

Anna explained the situation about work as she walked alongside her brother to a large tree, leaning against its trunk as she finished her story. "So, it appears our poverty is once again my fault."

Christian frowned. "He's no right to your money. He believes he's so wise with finances, but the truth is, we'd be better off with you doing them." Pulling his hair over a shoulder, he motioned to the bottle. He took a large swallow and wiped his mouth on the sleeve of his dusty coat. "Well, it doesn't matter, none of this does. Our fate's only temporary. We're bound to hit a streak of luck sometime. After all, we are Silverstones, aren't we?"

Anna smiled as she accepted the bottle once more. In the past, their family had indeed enjoyed better days due to wise investments in mining and wool.

But that had been several generations back, and every subsequent generation since had squandered any wealth gained. If Thomas were given the opportunity, he would do the same. Had done the same. And now her tiny nest egg would be gone, too. She would hand it over to Thomas, and like the Silverstones before them, she would be left with nothing.

A moment of fear overtook her, causing her heart to seize and her breath to stop. Would she truly never meet her father? Would the bloodline she so desperately desired allude rather than save her?

As if reading her thoughts, Christian threw an arm over her shoulders and said, "You're my sister and tougher than most men I've met. Don't let our brother, who chooses to grovel at the feet of every lord there is, bring you down. You'll figure this out and get to London one way or another."

"Do you truly believe so?" she asked as they made their way to the cottage. "I'm beginning to have my doubts."

Christian grinned. "That's when we recognize our true dreams. When they're just within our reach."

Anna considered his words. They eased her worries, if only by a bit, and allowed her mind to turn to the man whose coat she wore.

Chapter Seven

After a hot bath and a short nap, Colin made his way downstairs to join his cousins in the drawing room. Thoughts of Anna still occupied his mind. Was her brother very angry with her? He prayed not, for the thought of anyone harming her in any way caused his ire to ignite.

Plus, he hoped the picnic they had planned would not have to be canceled.

Well, he did not have time to think about that now. He would speak to the cook after dinner about preparing a basket of food. For now, he needed to focus on his cousins.

When he entered the drawing room, he smiled upon seeing Caroline, who sat with a book in her hand and a smile on her lips. She had always been one with an insatiable appetite for reading, and he hoped she would always remain so.

Evelyn appeared far different from her earlier mournfulness. Gone was the black, now replaced by white gloves and a fetching dark-blue dress with tiny yellow flowers. A pretty woman with dark hair and blue eyes, she should have been married and raising children, not living as a spinster in waiting. She was family, and guilt tore at him for not inquiring after her and Caroline sooner.

"Colin," Evelyn said as if seeing him for the first time. Her dress swished as she walked over to kiss his cheek. "I'm so pleased you're here. It's good to see you again."

Colin welcomed the embrace, and then she held his arms and gave a small shake of her head.

"The days have passed so quickly since we last saw one another. Has it truly been seven years? Or is it six? My memory does not serve me well these days."

Her odd behavior brought Caroline's earlier words to mind. She had made mention that Evelyn had moments of lucidity, but this only made her actions that much more bizarre. Nonetheless, she was his blood, so he held no judgment against her.

"I'm afraid it has been too long," he replied. "I beg your forgiveness for my lengthy absence."

Evelyn returned to her seat. "There's nothing to apologize for. Please, sit. Davis can pour you a drink."

The drawing room consisted of a couch for two and four wing back chairs, all covered in cream-colored fabrics with blue flowers. Blue drapes had been drawn and held back with cream ropes, and a blue rug with white roses sat beneath a dark-stained table in the middle.

Selecting a chair, Colin indicated to the butler that he preferred a measure of brandy.

"Markus sent word that he'll be arriving early next week," Evelyn said. "You will stay here with us until then, will you not?"

"Oh, yes," Caroline added as she closed her book. "Please say you will. He plans to stay for a few days. Though I hope he'll stay longer."

An image of Anna came to mind, and he nodded. "I'm in no hurry to return home," he said with a wide smile. I may stay longer than I had originally planned. If you'll have me, of course."

Evelyn laughed and waved a hand at him. "We are Remingtons, dear cousin. None of us ask permission for anything we wish to do. But your request will be honored all the same. Although I love my sister, having another family member around will bring about a nice change."

Davis presented Colin his glass on a silver tray, and Colin took it in hand. Taking a sip, the liquid warmed his throat. Thankfully, the effects of the honey wine had worn off. "This is excellent," he said. "Who selected it?"

"Markus did the last time he visited," Caroline replied, rolling her eyes. "Twice a year, he comes for a visit that lasts no more than three days. He schedules everything ahead of time, including ordering whatever drinks he deems necessary. As far as he's concerned, he's the only one who has the ability to do anything correctly. Is that not right, Davis?"

The butler, who now stood in the corner of the room awaiting his next order, bowed his head. "You are correct, Miss Caroline."

"Markus even instructs Davis on how to do his job," Caroline continued. "Can you imagine the absurdity of it? Davis is the finest butler in all of England and, therefore, needs no one's help. I find it offensive if you ask me. Is that not right, Davis?"

Colin had to hide a smile. Poor Davis had the very same look Pendleton gave him when Colin had made his strange inquiries before leaving Hemingford Home.

"Miss Caroline is much too kind in regard to my work. I have reminded her often that I'm only a simple butler who believes it an honor to receive instruction from any member of the Remington family."

"What Davis means to say is that Markus is a fool," Caroline said with a laugh. "He's just too much of a gentleman to admit as much."

The butler's lip twitched, and Colin wondered if the smile would win its place on his lips. But although it appeared to be a worthy battle, the man's face remained solemn.

"Enough with questioning poor Davis," Evelyn said. "Now, Colin, tell me. Have you not yet found a bride? Were the women last Season so poor in appearance?"

"It's their reputations," Caroline interjected. "Ladies' reputations are being scrutinized far more now than ever before. I'm telling you, a time will come when men will have to beg women to look their way."

Evelyn frowned at her sister. "Caroline," she snapped, "enough of that nonsense. And put that book away. We have company." She returned her attention to Colin. "Please, go on."

Colin took a sip of his brandy and crossed one leg over the opposite knee. "I must admit that the beauty of the young ladies I encountered last Season cannot be matched anywhere in the world." An image of Anna appeared in his mind. "Well, nearly." He smiled. "I've been speaking with a Lady Katherine Haskett, but I've no desire to wed her."

He turned the glass in his hand as another image of Anna came to mind. This time the image was of her beneath him as he held her by the arms.

Such thoughts will surely send me to Hell, he thought, and he pushed the memory aside.

"Why is that?" Caroline asked.

"I find her far too dull," Colin replied. "She is so like all the other women who've been paraded before me. They all think the same, act the same. So much so that if you were to speak to one, you've spoken to them all."

Caroline stood. "You're not alone in your assessment. Men are no different. All they speak of is hunting and playing games of chance. A woman does not wish to discuss such topics! It's beneath us."

"And what men do you mean?" Evelyn retorted. "There have been no men here other than our brother. I do hope you've not been speaking to any in the village and therefore have ruined your good name!"

"I speak of what has been written about in the newspapers," Caroline said with a jut to her chin. "This past Season ended in nothing short of disaster. Some are saying it may be the worse Season ever. Men and women kept to their own circles, men speaking of their hunts and women of fashion. It saddens me, for not a single soul spoke of love." She dropped back into her seat. "If there is no love to be found, then why live? This has been an important question asked since the beginning of time and yet ignored for far too long."

Evelyn shook her head. "Forgive my sister. She is prone to dramatics. I've tried time and again to explain that her life is not like the heroines in her romance novels. That is one subject in which I agree with Markus and Father. What she reads corrupts the mind of the youth far more than any words of politics. Do you not agree, Colin?"

Colin set his glass on a nearby table. He knew nothing about love but also despised the politics discussed in London. "I must admit that I've never read a romantic book, nor would I, so I cannot attest to its worth."

"You see?" Evelyn said with a gratified nod. "He has confirmed what I told you. You would do good to listen to Colin. He is a duke, after all. Now, no more foolish talk. You don't want to embarrass our cousin and force him to leave."

Davis left the room, and the conversation changed to matters of the estate. Colin learned that the arrangement under which the sisters lived was extremely generous. Markus paid all their expenses, and each sister received a generous allowance. Once Evelyn married, the estate would be gifted to her husband.

"Markus prefers to spend the Season in London," Caroline explained. "He may not be invited to all the grandest parties, but being a Remington has its benefits. Then he returns to his estate in Barstow once the Season ends. He finds both far more desirable to here." She leaned forward and lowered her voice. "I think he's hiding from the papers."

"The papers?" Colin asked.

"Oh, yes," Caroline said with a wide smile. "Lady Honor, who writes for the Morning Post, keeps her column ripe with gossip. Although I don't necessarily condone such reading, a lady must keep abreast of what is going on with the *ton*. Rumor has it that Cousin Evan has been mentioned in one of her columns as of late."

Colin gave a polite smile. He was not surprised by this news. Although he and Evan had been close as children, their lives had gone in different directions once they were grown. Evan was unscrupulous at best, but Colin still felt a bond whenever they encountered one another.

The conversation changed, and as the three talked, Colin considered Evelyn's situation. The woman was nearing spinsterhood, if she was not already seen as such. If she waited too much longer, she would be deemed undesirable, Remington or not. What of her episodes like the one he had witnessed earlier this morning? Would any man be willing to accept her despite her varying moods and appearances?

Well, that was a riddle on which he did not care to dwell at the moment, but he would seek help for her one way or another.

"Dinner is served," Davis announced, breaking Colin from his thoughts. Rising from his seat, he offered his cousins each an arm and walked them to the dining room.

The long table could seat twelve, and Colin was directed to the position at its head. Footmen hurried to pull out chairs for the women, Evelyn to his left and Caroline to his right. Several candles lit the table, and the large fireplace remained untouched. A large mirror hung on the blue-papered walls, flanked by two paintings of fruit on either side of it.

"You'll find that the soup is wonderful," Caroline said. "Mrs. Montgomery makes the finest dishes. I'd go as far as to say that her cooking is unmatched."

A footman placed a bowl of white soup in front of him. The aroma of chestnut made his stomach growl with anticipation. He dipped his spoon into the liquid and took a sip. "You are so right," he said, unable to keep the awe from his voice. "You must have Mrs. Montgomery give me her recipe before I return home so I may give it to my cook. If she's willing," he added with a light chuckle. He had encountered more than one cook, his included, who held their secrets close to their breast. Oftentimes as close as their purses.

Caroline seemed pleased by his reaction. "I'll see that she does."

When the soup course was done, the meat course was served. Tender venison, roasted potatoes, and vegetables slathered in butter. Colin, not realizing how hungry he was, had to pace his eating lest he choked.

"So, Evelyn," he said to keep from devouring the entire slice of venison in one go, "how goes the hunt for a suitor?"

The room became eerily silent, the only sound the light click of his cousin's utensils as she placed them on the plate with careful deliberation. Caroline gaped at him, her fork halfway to her mouth and her mouth on the verge of opening to accept the bit of potato on the fork's tip.

Evelyn placed the tips of her fingers on the edge of the table. "My responsibility is to prepare Caroline for the day she attends the Season," she replied in a tight voice. She clearly was doing all she could to not shout. "I've no time to engage in the absurd rituals myself, such as attending balls or accepting courtships."

The silence that followed her outburst was deafening. Wanting to return to the lighthearted conversation they were having before he spoke, Colin said, "I believe your decision wise. Now, I would like to learn more about what has been happening here at Redstone Estate since I was last here." He turned his attention to Caroline. "Do you have many friends?"

A look of relief crossed Caroline's face. "I do. Many come during the week for tea."

As they continued the meal, Colin learned about how Caroline spent her days. She had indeed grown in the years since they last saw one another, although reading novels had remained her favorite pastime. Friends called for what she deemed "polite conversation," which he knew meant gossip. By the time they had completed the meal, his head was aching with its attempt to keep up.

"Coffee will be served in the drawing room," Evelyn said as she rose from her chair. "I, however, shall not be joining you. My head aches and I must rest. Please forgive my rudeness."

"Not at all," Colin said, concern filling him. "Rest and we'll speak tomorrow when you're feeling better." Once Evelyn had hurried from the room, he turned back to Caroline. "May I speak to Mrs. Montgomery?"

After the lavish meal, he had nearly forgotten about the food basket. Nearly. It was as if Anna never left his thoughts, but at times, she waited in the recesses of his mind, jumping out at him at some of the strangest times. Like now.

She beamed. "Of course. She'll be so pleased. Follow me."

Collin followed his cousin to a door hidden at the far end of the corridor, down a narrow staircase, and into the kitchen area. "Mrs. Montgomery is very protective of her kitchen. And I should warn you, she's not afraid to speak her mind to anyone she meets."

"Thank you for the warning," he said with a chuckle.

The kitchen was alive with maids and footmen hurrying this way and that. A woman of perhaps fifty with thin arms and a pile of red hair atop her head barked orders. When she saw Caroline and Colin, she hurried over and gave a small curtsy.

"Mrs. Montgomery," Caroline said, "I would like to introduce my cousin, the Duke of Greystoke. His Grace wished to tell you that he believed your soup to be quite tasty."

"Did he now?" the cook said with a wide smile. "Well, I'm pleased to hear it, Your Grace."

Colin had hoped to speak to Mrs. Montgomery alone, but Caroline made no indication that she meant to leave. "I must admit," he said, "I've never enjoyed such a splendid dinner." He glanced at Caroline. He would have to simply make his request while she was there and hope his cousin did not become too inquisitive. "Also, I was hoping to ask a favor. I'll be needing a basket prepared, with food for a picnic, in two days. Can that be done?"

"Of course it can be done," Mrs. Montgomery scoffed. "And it'll be the best you've ever had." The clang of a pot falling to the floor had the woman's jaw tightening. "Excuse me, Your Grace. I've got to attend to a certain clumsy maid. But I'll have your basket ready by ten."

After thanking her, he followed Caroline back to the main corridor.

"A basket of food?" Caroline asked with a grin. "And you were at the river earlier. That can only mean one thing. You've met Anna."

Colin suppressed a grin. "I did meet Miss Silverstone."

"So, it is she!" his cousin said, clasping her hands together and bouncing on her toes. "How romantic!"

"There is nothing romantic about it," he said. "We are meeting as friends and nothing more." Perhaps that was not the complete truth, but how could he explain that he found Anna much more exciting than just a simple friend?

Caroline waved a dismissive hand at him. "Yes, of course it's not romantic. A woman as beautiful as Miss Anna Silverstone attracts many... er... friends." She giggled, but Colin had never been more embarrassed in his life. "Oh, don't give me that look, Colin. Anna makes men look as silly as you do now all the time. I've seen it in the village many times."

"I look silly?" he asked as they entered the drawing room.

"Oh, yes, quite. It's the look of a man smitten. But do be careful, for it can consume you."

Colin smiled. He certainly was not in love, but he could not argue the fact that Anna intrigued him. So much so, he began counting the hours until he would see her again.

Chapter Eight

I t was pure luck for Anna that Thomas had chosen this morning to go into the village. With no one to question her activities for the day, she prepared for her outing. All three of her best dresses— meaning that they were not made of the stiff, drab burlap of her everyday dresses— lay on the bed.

The blue had yellow and pink flowers embroidered on the bodice, the yellow had a white ribbon around the waist, and the pink had tiny white lace roses sewn at the waistline. None would have been considered fashionable, the bottom edges were in dire need of re-hemming, and what little lace they had needed repair. But they were far better than anything else she owned.

Blue had always been her favorite color, so that was the one she chose. Plus, the ribbon on the yellow dress was frayed on the ends, and one of the white roses had fallen off the pink. The blue was simply the best option.

Once she was dressed, she looked at her reflection in the small, jagged mirror. There was a bit of visible discoloration in the fabric, but she could do nothing about that. She had no hats or gloves to don, and the idea of choosing jewelry made her snicker. Jewelry, indeed. What would someone like her do with jewelry? She did own a few hairpins but decided to brush out her hair and allow it to hang freely down her back. This was no ball she was attending.

Her reflection said that she would not impress Colin, but that did not bother her as it would have other women. This was who she was— a girl with nothing more than dreams. She would never allow a threadbare, outdated dress stop her from going on this picnic!

The excitement of meeting Colin washed over her anew. She had never gone on a picnic— or gone on any type of outing, for that matter— with a gentleman. The previous year, a boy her age had asked her to accompany him on a walk. She had considered accepting. Until the heavy scent of honey wine on his breath made her think better of it.

At least Colin would be different. Oh, he had also smelled of honey wine, but he was different from that boy. Not because he was a duke, for nobility could be worse than commoners in their behavior. No, she had a sense about people, and she could tell immediately that he was no rogue.

The opportunity to kiss her had arisen more than once, and Anna wished he had. The first had been when she was lying beneath him. The second soon after. But it no longer mattered. Somehow, she knew he would soon.

I need him to kiss me.

But first she thought about their meeting today.

Her mother had often spoken of the outings she enjoyed during her youth, enjoying food at a picnic as one of them. That was the reason Anna had made that particular request of Colin— to experience what her mother had.

She had been surprised at his acceptance. Dukes did not eat their meals out-of-doors without benefit of a tent and servants, did they? He was a duke. She was a Silverstone. The two did not mix, and yet somehow, *they* did.

She walked over to the vanity table, a crude desk with a missing leg her stepfather had procured from an estate in which he had worked. Like many of the objects in their home, it had nicks and missing pieces, but it did its job holding what few treasures she possessed.

A bottle of perfume her mother had given her rested beside an old brush. For a moment, she considered using what little was left but decided against it. She would save it for a special occasion, if one arose.

After leaving her room, she walked outside to find Christian speaking to a well-dressed gentleman. It was not unusual for members of the gentry to call, for although her brother was young, he was renowned for the fine horse he trained.

The gentleman appeared to be nearing forty with gray specks dotting his otherwise dark hair. His gaze fell on Anna, and a sly smile crossed his lips. This clodpate dared to cast sheep eyes at her while wearing a ring that said he had a wife? Men could be foul sometimes.

All too often, buyers took an interest in her and hoped to be given the opportunity to introduce themselves. But Anna detested feigning interest in conversation. Yet if it helped Christian procure a sale, she did so.

Christian had joked on more than one occasion that he should sell her and retire before his sixteenth birthday. Although they both had laughed, she had warned him not to mention that idea to Thomas in case he took it to heart.

Yet had he not considered it already? She knew a time would come that unless she found a man first, Thomas would do so for her.

With a single nod to her brother, Anna lowered her head and hurried away. Making her way through the woods, she arrived at the river. On the opposite bank, Colin paced back and forth, a blanket folded over one arm and a basket hanging from his other hand. Anna watched him with interest from behind a tree.

She allowed herself a moment to absorb his masculine form. He wore a fine dark-gray coat, and his hair was neatly combed up in the latest fashion. The ruby on his finger glinted, and she could not help but wonder what she was doing here. She was a simple girl and would likely marry a cobbler. If she were lucky. Colin was a duke, wealthy beyond anything she could imagine and could have any woman he wished. Surely even a lasting friendship between them would never be allowed.

"I see you own more than one coat," Anna called out.

Colin came to an abrupt halt and turned.

"Do you own many?" A thrill went down her spine at teasing him, as did the smile it brought him.

"I own more than two dozen," he replied with a laugh. "Though I only brought three to Redstone Estate. You don't plan to take another, do you? If so, you must warn me ahead of time so I may find a tailor to replace it."

She stepped onto the fallen log. "That remains to be decided and depends on your actions. If you fall asleep drunk, I may need to help myself to even more this time." She leapt to the grass on the other side of the makeshift bridge and motioned to the basket he held. "I see you honored my request. Did you pack it yourself?"

"No," Collin replied. "Mrs. Montgomery, the cook at Redstone Estate, prepared it. Does it bother you that I did not see to it myself?"

The innocence in which he asked made her nearly giggle, and she drew in a deep breath to calm the urge. "First, I learn you are a drunk. Now I see that you're a man unable to pack a simple picnic. I fear any honor associated with your title will soon be lost."

When Colin laughed, two deep dimples appeared in his cheeks, and she had to bite down on her lower lip. "Anna, I've never met a woman quite like you. Tell me, have you always spoken your mind so easily?"

"Follow me if you wish to know," she said as she entered the woodsy area on the Remington side of the river. "I've never had to worry about the peerage or nobles judging me because those of us down here don't pay them any mind. We of the working class see one another as the same and don't bother to compare ourselves to the likes of the aristocracy. Oh, we have gossips just as your people do, but few of us care much for what they have to say. The wealthy seem to have some strange notion that being poor should make us more reserved somehow, that people like me should remain in the shadows and have no opinion on anything. But I do have thoughts on all sorts of matters. And although some refuse to listen, I see no reason I should not make the attempt to be heard. I do hope you agree, for if you don't, I may have to leave."

Colin laughed again. "Oh, I agree wholeheartedly. Those people who refuse to listen to you are fools, for I wish to hear your opinions on all sorts of subjects. In fact, I could listen to you all day."

Anna stumbled, although the path was clear of roots or anything that would have caused her to trip. Drat her legs for going weak!

She stopped beneath a tree free of debris and leaned her back against the smooth trunk. How could his simple words make her feel as if she had drunk an entire bottle of honey wine?

"I find you quite intelligent," Colin continued. "You have something about you... a passion that shines in your eyes. I don't lie when I say that I would enjoy your company for hours on end. Perhaps even days."

Anna could not stop the sigh from escaping her lips. Drat uncontrolled sighs! She was no lady who swooned at the slightest kind word from a gentleman!

"I'll set up our lunch," he said, although he stared at the ground as if it were a chained mastiff waiting to pounce on him.

"Is this your first time setting up a picnic?" she asked. "You cannot tell me you've never eaten out-of-doors."

"Oh, I have. Quite often, actually," he said as he straightened out the wrinkles in the blanket. "But this is the first I've ever wanted to attend. And the first that was not set up for me by a servant."

Anna realized she was grinning like a fool and quickly looked away. When she turned back to face Colin, her heart skipped a beat to find him standing in front of her.

"Allow me to help you sit," he said, reaching out a hand to her.

Without hesitation, she placed her hand in his. The grip was firm, protective, and Anna considered never letting go.

Once she was seated, he sat across from her, his legs stretched out in front of him as he reclined on his elbows. Never had she admired a pair of breeches more in her life.

"I do like your dress," he said.

Anna bit at her bottom lip. "Is that so?"

"It fits you well."

She smiled. "It appears the duke can speak his mind. Though I dare not ask what else you're thinking."

This had him laughing, and she could not help but wonder what had come over her.

She glanced down at her hand, which seemed to have a mind of its own as it was midway through smoothing the skirt. She had no conscious memory of asking it to do so.

"Why did you agree to this?" she asked. It was not that she did not trust him, but she had yet to come up with a reasonable explanation for such a decision. "You're a duke, a Remington, and I'm a Silverstone. I'm sure you know our families' history."

"Indeed," he replied. "I learned some of it last evening from Caroline." He opened the basket and pulled out a bottle of wine and two glasses. "But I'm like her in that I don't care for petty family squabbles." He looked up at her, and her mouth went dry. "It's no mystery why I'm here with you, and I'm willing to confess why. I wish to know more about you, Anna."

The way he said her name sent a strange warm sensation from the pit of her stomach to the tips of her toes and fingers.

"So," he said as he handed her one of the glasses, "what brought you to the river the other day? Besides a desire to wash your dress, that is."

She had told this very story twice already and had no reservations in telling it again. If anything, she found she wanted to share everything with Colin.

"A woman at work, Geraldine, had been told that she was no longer needed." Between sips of wine— which was far lovelier than anything she had ever consumed in her life— she told the events that led to finding Colin asleep against the tree. "Drunk, I might add," she said with a laugh. "A drunk duke. Thankfully, you were not dead, which had been my first suspicion."

"I'm afraid I cannot deny my drunkenness," he said, raising his glass of wine. "I've learned that honey wine is far more potent than I would have ever suspected. I just ask— no, I beg of you, please— tell no one what you witnessed. I do have a reputation to uphold."

"I'll consider it before I give you my answer," she replied, drawing a smile from him. Her gaze went to the ring he wore. "Where does that ring come from? Or was it given to you?"

Colin lifted his hand and sighed. "My father gifted it to me before he died. It has been in my family since the first Duke of Greystoke received it four hundred years ago." He tilted his head and was silent for several moments. "It's more than a simple piece of jewelry. It represents my title, my family name, and all I should be in life."

Anna detected no enthusiasm, no sense of pride, in his words. Instead, his tone said that the ring was more a burden than a gift. "You wear the finest clothes, and I'm sure you are able to purchase anything your heart desires. I imagine that people bow to you wherever you go and that you receive invitations to all sorts of gatherings. How many fathers throw their daughters at you in hopes you'll marry them?"

"Too many," Colin said with a chuckle. "And all you've said is true."

"Then why do you speak as if your life is a terrible weight you're forced to carry?"

Twisting the stem of the fine crystal glass in his fingers, Colin said, "I know it appears that I'm just a spoiled duke complaining about his life. And that may be true. But have you never wished people to be honest with you? To treat you as the person you are rather than whom they believe you should be?"

Anna considered this question. Being poor, coupled with her family name, led to others treating her unfairly. "I suppose so. I have dreams I'd like to pursue, dreams of my own. My brother, Thomas, the one who found us here together, he believes my dreams are a waste of time. The women with whom I work think me a silly goose— except Betty. She believes in me. Men see me as an object they wish to own. Thomas wishes to sell me to the highest bidder. And none— except you— have ever taken the time to listen to what I have to say."

That realization made her heart warm. Duke or not, Colin was a considerate listener.

He smiled. "I'm glad to be the first. And I do hope you're able to resolve your problems."

"As I hope you're able to resolve yours," she said. "Although, I've an answer to my problems already. Or so I hope."

"Oh? And what would that be?"

She gave him a small smile. "As I've yet to put my plan into place, I'll explain another time."

"Very well," Colin replied. He offered her a portion of cheese from a cloth, which she accepted along with a selection of cold meats.

"I've never eaten anything so delectable," she said in awe. "The cheese has such a wonderful flavor."

"I'm glad you enjoy it."

Silence fell around them as they ate. Finding the quiet more than she could bear, Anna asked, "When we met, you insisted that I call you Colin, and you seemed overly pleased when I agreed. Why is that?"

"'Your Grace' can be tiresome after a while," he said with a grin. "I wish to take a vacation from being a duke while I'm here." He lifted the wine bottle, and she nodded. "Addressing me informally seems to unnerve you."

"It's not that," she said, feeling the heat rise in her face. "I find your name quite handsome, and it's comforting to say."

She clamped shut her mouth. Now she was acting the drunken buffoon! What had made her say something so outrageous? Speaking her mind had never been a problem, but her mouth had said it without the thought coming to mind. It was one thing to be honest with a man who was in a drunken stupor, but daring to speak so intimately with one who was in complete control of his wits was quite another.

Colin, who was staring out toward where the river sat beyond the edge of the woods, did not appear to have heard. Thank goodness.

"Anna," he said as if sampling her name for the first time. "It's a beautiful name. Quite fitting for a woman unlike any I've ever encountered."

She took a large swallow of wine to ease the sudden dryness in her throat. "What's that supposed to mean?" she demanded in an attempt to cover the uneasiness his words caused her. She was not one who was easily distressed!

Colin threw his head back and laughed. "That's what I like about you, Anna. You're quick with your tongue and will strike anyone!" Then his laughter died. "I was speaking of your uniqueness, which is very much like your beauty. I've met nearly every lady who has set foot in London, and none can compare to you. Not in the slightest."

When he turned to look at her, a blaze lit a fire within her, and she considered leaping into the river to cool herself.

"You're a treasure, Anna."

The river looked even more inviting as Anna attempted to match his gaze. "You're handsome in more ways than one," she said. With a trembling hand, she gave him the empty glass. The tips of his fingers touched hers, causing her heart to race and her mouth to go dry.

My, how things change in such a short time! If only Betty could see her now.

And Molly? She would have a fit!

Now the silence that fell between them was awkward as Colin repacked the basket. Had each said too much? And why had her heartbeat not slowed? Unable to take the silence any longer, she stood. Just as Colin did the same. Facing one another, Anna considered asking him for a kiss but did not. She might speak her mind, but she would not be that forward!

Prying her gaze away, she said, "You mentioned that you came to Wilkworth to escape. Although you may not wish to explain from what you're fleeing, I want you to know that I'm willing to help in any way I can."

"I don't mind telling you," Colin said. "I want to be free of my responsibilities as a duke, to be Colin for ten days. That is why I'm grateful that we met and have become friends."

"If the girls at work knew I've befriended a duke," she whispered with a shake of her head. "Yes, we are friends. And I can see now that you do need to escape being a duke."

He frowned. "And what makes you recognize that exactly?"

She knew what he needed, what he wanted. To be seen as the man inside him, just as she wanted to be seen as a woman with dreams. "I see a man who needs change, and I would be happy to help you do that. We'll begin slowly, so you don't become overwhelmed."

Colin gave her a devilish grin. "And you believe I'll be overwhelmed, do you?"

"Most definitely," she replied with a firm nod. "The next time we meet, leave your coat at home. And be sure to bring honey wine."

"Next time?" he asked as if surprised. "You'd like to meet me again?" She raised a single eyebrow, and he quickly added, "I mean, I would like that."

"Much better." She gave him a wink and then tapped her lips with a finger. "We can't meet at my home. Thomas might challenge you to a duel. But don't worry, we own neither a pistol nor a sword." This had them both laughing.

Then he took her hand in his, and the laughter died on her lips. Her head became light and her legs weak as he brushed a thumb across the backs of her fingers. "When shall we meet again?"

"I promised Henry that I'd spend time with him tomorrow, and I have housework I must see to. The day after, however, I would like you to bring a horse and meet me at the crest of the tall hill just east of here. Precisely at midday. Do you know of which hill I speak?"

"I do," Colin replied. "Am I to teach you how to ride?"

Anna laughed and then raised herself onto the tips of her toes. "It's I who will teach you," she whispered before leaning in and pressing her lips to his cheek. His masculine fragrance overwhelmed her senses. "I'll see you then."

With wobbly legs, she walked over to the fallen log. It was only by a miracle that she did not topple over into the water below as she crossed. It was not until she reached the opposite side that she realized what she had done. She had kissed a man, a duke no less! No one would ever believe it!

Anna turned around to find Colin staring at her. She raised a hand, and he returned the wave. An overwhelming desire washed over her to return to him, but she did the sensible thing and turned to head home instead.

Chapter Nine

Anna peeked from behind a tree at the edge of the woods closest to the river. No one. She darted to another and caught sight of Henry scurrying to the right of a small bush. He lacked the skills to find appropriate hiding places during their games. She was lenient with him, however, taking far longer than was necessary for her search. He would learn to be a better hider as he grew older.

After an early breakfast, they had used sticks to play at fencing, gone hunting for wild beasts, and drawn several masterpieces in the muddy riverbank. But his favorite pastime had always been hide and seek.

Henry had been just a babe out of swaddling when their mother died, and although Anna was young herself, she had slipped into the role with the youngest of her brothers. Whether it be times like this or stories at night, she made certain he always felt loved.

Christian, on the other hand, had been much too old to need a mother, or so he had said. After all, he was only three years younger than she. And Thomas... well, he never needed anyone.

"Now, where has that boy gone?" Anna said in a voice much louder than normal. A snicker from her left made her force back a smile. "Well, I suppose I'll never find him."

In truth, there were few places to hide in this area, and she stifled a chuckle when she caught sight of Henry hiding behind a tree far thinner than himself.

Feigning frustration, she threw her arms in the air and called, "I give up! He must've run away. I do hope to see him again one day." She turned toward the house as if to walk away, but the sound of

Henry's stomping and his shout of "Anna!" made her turn back around.

"I'm right here," he said, his face filled with anxiety. "I'd never run away and leave you!"

Dropping to one knee, she said, "Oh, thank you for saying so, Henry. Because I don't know what I would do without you."

He wrapped his arms around her neck. "Me, too!" he murmured into her shoulder.

"What do you say about having a bite to eat? Then we can read a story together."

"I'd like that," he replied with an adamant nod. "Wanna race me back?"

"I'm afraid you've tired me out far too much for that," she said, smiling. "But you go on. I'll be right behind you."

Dipping his head, he pumped his arms and ran as fast as he could, disappearing into the woods.

Anna turned her attention to the river. She had hoped to find Colin waiting for her, but, of course, he had more important things to do than sit beside a river to see if a workhouse laborer appeared. It did not matter, anyway, for they had an appointment to go riding together. And she was certain they would plan another outing after that.

By all appearances, they were becoming fast friends, but the reality was that it would not last long. The number of ladies from whom he could choose was far too many to count, and if she did happen to gain his admiration, she was not of noble blood. Well, none that she could prove at the moment.

Yet he had called her beautiful. A treasure. The echo of those words still made her body heat. Surely he did not use such honeyed words with just any woman.

As she made her way back to the house, she considered the impossible prospect of Colin courting her. If, by some strange miracle, he did, she would most definitely accept. The fact he was a duke mattered not at all, for he was far too handsome to deny.

Furthermore, he conducted himself as a true gentleman in every sense of the word. He asked her opinions and then listened to her responses. He was the very example of the type of gentleman she had always desired and about whom she spoke endlessly to the other women at work.

Above all, however, it had been the playful teasing that had drawn her to him most of all. He had wanted to kiss her, she was certain of it, for it showed in his eyes. Yet he had refrained from doing so. Although it had been a disappointment, she also took it as a sign that he was no rogue like so many of his station could be.

"You mustn't waste your time on such dreams," she whispered. "Not now. And certainly not with him. He's far beyond the realm of possibility to even consider."

The sound of crunching leaves had her searching for Henry only to have her breath catch upon seeing another man standing before her.

"M-Mr. Harrison?" she stammered. "What are you doing here?"

A light breeze lifted a few strands of his blond hair. His tongue flickered across his lips as he grasped her by an arm. "Forgive me for startling you," he said, although she had no reason to believe he was remorseful. "You seem agitated. Are you all right?"

She could not stop the tremor that ran down her spine. "I'm quite well, thank you." She attempted to pull from his grip. "I really must get home."

"I spoke to Thomas," Mr. Harrison said, ignoring her plea. And not releasing her arm. "He's upset that you've left my employ. I have to admit that I've missed seeing you at the workhouse."

Anna's stomach knotted, and she swallowed back bile. "I'll return in September as we agreed," she said, wrenching her arm from his grip. "If the position is still open. Good day to you, Mr. Harrison."

She hurried past him and made her way through the woods until the cottage came into view. The carriage belonging to Mr. Harrison sat in front, Thomas pacing beside it. When he caught sight of her, he paused and waited for her to draw closer.

"I assume Mr. Harrison found you," Thomas said.

Anna nodded and made a mental note to speak to him about sending men out alone in search of her!

"Did he tell you the good news? You're to return to work tomorrow." He seemed rather pleased with himself.

Tomorrow? She had plans to meet Colin this week. In fact, she planned to spend a great deal of time with him during his time in Wilkworth.

"That's kind of him," Anna said. Mr. Harrison joined them. She turned to him and added, "I appreciate you thinking of me, but I must politely decline."

The man took a step back as if she had slapped him. "You know, I've got others who've requested more time at the looms. I didn't realize the Silverstones were in a position to refuse work." He turned to Thomas. "Your sister really should control her wild ways. I'd counsel that you both consider the requests I've made if you want to remedy your current situation." With that, he turned away.

"Wait, Mr. Harrison!" Thomas said, his hands wringing. "Sir, I'll speak to Anna. You can expect her at work very soon."

Mr. Harrison gave a deep snort of derision and climbed into the carriage. As the vehicle pulled away, Thomas turned on Anna like a wild dog.

"How dare you! The man offers you your job back and you refuse? I've a good mind to accept his offer for your hand in marriage!"

"My... what?" Anna demanded. "Marriage? That man disgusts me. I've told you how he treats the women at the workhouse."

"Are those women being dragged into a corner or behind the building against their will?" Thomas retorted, his voice as loud as Anna's. "I imagine not. They're making the decision freely."

"They aren't being dragged, but they have no choice! You'll never understand, and even if you did, it would no likely change your thinking anyway."

Thomas waved a dismissive hand at her. "They do have a choice. But what does it matter? Every suitor I've selected for you, you turn away. This can't continue on forever, and you know that. The excuses, the delays, they end now. Tomorrow, you're to return to work, and I'll consider Mr. Harrison's offer of marriage further."

Anna pursed her lips. She had had enough! "No," she said flatly.

"What did you say?" he hissed, his cheeks turning a deep crimson.

"I said no. I'm not returning to work tomorrow, nor next week. I'll find other work when I'm ready and not a moment sooner."

Thomas took a threatening step forward. He had never struck her before, but Anna had a sudden suspicion that this might be the first. "You'll return to work tomorrow, and I'll not hear another word about it." He turned to walk away.

Anna clenched her fist as memories of the past years flooded her mind. The cycle of working to bring in just enough money to get by lay over her like a heavy blanket. Her destiny was to spend her life at Mr. Harrison's workhouse— or one similar— and that would never change. But having Mr. Harrison as a husband terrified her. She would rather work in the mines until her dying days than marry that beast.

Yet her dreams were so close. She could not discard them like a torn piece of fabric!

"You have my money," she called after Thomas. "You run this home as you see fit. But I'm not returning to the workhouse tomorrow, and I'll certainly never agree to marry that... that *man!*"

Thomas stopped and turned toward her. "Then whom will you marry? Do you believe a man like that *duke* would want someone like you?"

Anna looked away, for that very question had been on her mind. Every sensible part of her told her that he would not, but she held to that tiny scrap of hope.

"It was apparent by your state of undress that he sees you as a plaything," Thomas said with a snort. "Perhaps you truly are like our mother and have already allowed him to have his way with you."

Rage bubbled up inside Anna as she marched over to her brother, pulled her arm back, and placed a well-positioned slap on his cheek. "How dare you say such a thing!" she cried. "Don't speak of Mother that way!"

She pulled her arm back again, but Thomas grabbed her by the wrist, turning it until she cried out in pain.

"Leave her alone!" Christian shouted as he came running toward them to push Thomas away. "Anna's our sister, not one of the horses to be trained and bartered. What're you thinking?"

Tears rolled down Anna's cheeks as her brothers turned on each other like wild animals.

"You always take her side," Thomas snapped. "But both of you are fools. Can't you see what our lives could be?" He reached into his pocket, and Anna recognized the sack of savings she had given him. "You act as if I wish to make your lives miserable. Have you ever considered that what I do is for all of us? Of course not. All either of you does is complain! There's only ever just enough money to maintain the house and to feed the four of us. Have you any idea how many times I'm tempted to sell it and just be done with it all?"

A wave of guilt washed over Anna. "Oh, Thomas, I'm sorry."

He thrust the bag toward her. "Here. Take the money and do as you wish in life." When she did nothing more than stare, he added, "Go on. Take it."

"I don't want it."

Thomas grabbed her hand, opened it, and poured the contents of the bag into it. "Take the deuced money. You're in such a hurry to destroy your life, so, by all means, do so. But when you fail, don't come crying to me."

Anna shook her head as shame filled her. She pressed the money back into his hand. "Please, don't make me return to work just yet. I know I'll have to marry soon, but not today. Please, Thomas. If this is to be my last summer here, then at least allow me to spend it the way I want."

Thomas drew in a deep breath, returned the money to the sack, and placed it in his pocket. "Fine. But I'm also telling Mr. Harrison that his offer of marriage is still under consideration just in case you back out on your promise."

Swallowing hard, Anna nodded. Thomas turned and walked back toward the house.

Anna turned to Christian. "Does he not realize how thankful we are to have him?"

"I've no idea what he thinks anymore," Christian said, giving her a hug. "I know he cares for us, but he's just got a funny way of showing it."

When the embrace broke, Anna gave Christian a weak smile. "Thank you for defending me."

He shrugged. "You're my sister. I'll protect you from any man, including Thomas if I have to. Or your boss or even that duke you met."

Anna hugged her brother once more. Although she knew Christian would always protect her, he had no need to worry about Colin. She was certain he would never hurt her.

Chapter Ten

Since his arrival at Redstone Estate, Colin had enjoyed his time spent with his cousins. Evelyn had remained in good form, causing his first memory of seeing her to fade. He, Evelyn, and Caroline spent many hours discussing a variety of topics, from who was courting whom to which members of the gentry were having affairs.

Or rather, that was what the women discussed. Colin found gossip boring. As long as it did not disrupt his life, who cared what others did with theirs?

Then the conversation turned to the vast number of Remingtons, all considered cousins regardless of how far back their roots went. Of course, with so many spread across England, Colin had not heard of, let alone met, many of them.

What fascinated him most was the strange feud his cousins had with the Silverstones., which stemmed from ownership of the river. From Colin's limited understanding of the situation, the Silverstones had sold various parcels of their property to the Remingtons over the years. At some point, that included the land through which the river ran. Later, however, a disagreement about the terms of that agreement erupted, leading to the dispute between the families ever since.

Although he was a Remington, Colin felt no animosity toward the Silverstones, especially when it came to Anna. They were to meet soon, and he spent a great deal of his time with his cousins glancing at a clock whose hands moved far too slow to be correct. Yet when he checked it against his pocket watch, he realized it was nothing more than his anticipation slowing the time.

The Duke Who Loved Me

When Evelyn complained of a headache and Caroline excused herself to lie down, Colin went to his rooms to change into his riding clothes. Stopping at the mirror beside the front door, he studied his reflection. Dark tan knee-high leather riding boots, beige pantaloons, a crisp white shirt beneath his waistcoat, and matching riding coat made up the ensemble. He carried his coat draped over an arm.

It would have been near sacrilegious for any gentleman, let alone a duke, to ride without a coat, but he preferred the freeness of wearing only his waistcoat and shirtsleeves.

He chuckled. Dear Aunt Mabel would have cried at his "nakedness" and called for a vicar if she could see him now.

Anna had asked him to forgo the coat and considered deferring to her wise council. Yet acting upon a thought was far different from simply considering it.

He glanced down at his hand. The ducal ring mocked him. How could an insignificant coat cause him such turmoil? The truth was, as much as he complained about his life, he knew he had a role to fill. His title was one of honor, and he wished to keep it that way.

If he wished to be Colin rather than the Duke of Greystoke, even for a few days, he would need to take small steps. Seeing neither the butler nor his cousins, he hung the coat over the back of a nearby chair covered in red fabric and walked out the door.

"Colin?"

He stared. Evelyn sat beside Caroline at a small round table in the grassy area in the middle of the drive. "Well, hello," he said, giving them a smile. "I thought the two of you had gone to lie down."

"We did," Caroline said as she closed her book, her finger acting as a placeholder. "But we don't enjoy wasting away our days in bed."

"And do you often spend time in front of the house?" Colin asked, amused. "You've such a lovely back garden."

Caroline shrugged. "I don't like bothering the gardeners while they're working. They always believe they must leave if we decide to spend time outside, no matter how often we tell them that it's unnecessary. So, we began coming out here." She looked up. "Plus, we have more shade beneath this lovely laurel tree than we have at this time of day on the veranda."

"Where are you off to, Colin?" Evelyn asked.

"I thought I mentioned that I was going riding this afternoon," he said. "I'll not be gone long."

The door opened, and Davis emerged from the house, a silver tray with a large pitcher of what appeared to be cordial water and two glasses in his hands.

"His smile tells me that he's meeting Anna Silverstone," Caroline said. "And I think that's wonderful. Perhaps it will be Colin who ends this silly ongoing feud between our families." She gave him a mischievous grin. "Dare I say that this can be accomplished with a kiss?"

"Caroline!" Evelyn snapped. "My goodness, what's come over you? I'm of a mind to have Davis burn every romantic novel in the house!"

Caroline raised her chin. "Evelyn just doesn't understand that the stories I read are genuine. My dear friend Miss Sally Perkins told me that women sell their true accounts to writers in London. Who would print lies?"

"Miss Perkins also told you that removing your gloves in a married man's presence is the same as adultery," Evelyn retorted.

Fearing the two would drag him into their argument, Colin said, "Well, I'm off to enjoy this fine day. I'll see you soon."

"Wait, please," Caroline said as she pushed back her chair. "It's been three years since Miss Anna and I have spoken. Perhaps you can invite her to tea this afternoon."

The butler, who stood beside one of the portico columns, grunted as if someone had struck him in the stomach, but his stoic stance returned within moments.

"Are we not a peaceful family?" Caroline asked, that mischievous grin deepening. "No Silverstone has been at Redstone Estate for a very long time. Is that not right, Davis?"

"Forgive my boldness, Miss Caroline, but I cannot in good conscience remain silent. Your dear father would never have allowed a Silverstone to come for tea."

"But Father is no longer here," Caroline pointed out. "What would you suggest?"

"Perhaps a nice letter would suffice, Miss Caroline," the butler said. Poor Davis had gone so red, Colin worried the man was having an apoplectic fit.

Caroline, who seemed to find Davis's discomfort amusing, shook her head. "No. I believe tea would be far more pleasant." She turned to Evelyn. "What harm can it do? We can have it on the back veranda. It's not as if I'm inviting her to stay in one of the rooms."

Colin was uncertain if this was a good idea. He did not believe Anna unworthy of sharing a cup of tea with a Remington nor being invited inside the house. The differences in positions, however, made him fret. It simply was not done. If Evelyn, or even the old butler, were to gossip about it, the rumors would send Colin's head to aching.

But was his time here not meant to allow him the opportunity to do many of those things a duke would likely never do?

"I must go," Colin said. "Perhaps we can discuss this at another time."

Caroline went to say something, but Evelyn spoke first. "Bring her here for tea if you would like. Do what you wish, Colin. There will be no judgment from either of us. But if you choose to invite her, it must be today. Remember, Markus arrives tomorrow afternoon, and he'll not be as receptive as we."

"I'll give it some thought," Colin replied, although he was still uncertain if he should broach the subject with Anna. To not offer sent a pang to his heart, but he simply could not abandon everything he had been taught. He had already moved well beyond what was appropriate by spending as much time with her as he did.

A stable hand waited with a chocolate brown stallion with a beautiful glossy coat and finely brushed mane. The boy bowed to him and said, "This's the finest 'orse in the stable, Your Grace."

"Thank you," Colin said, placing his foot in the stirrup and swinging his other leg over. Then he took the reins from the boy and heeled the horse's flanks.

Once his cousins were out of sight, Colin let out a sigh of relief. He had been unsure how Evelyn would handle the fact he was accompanying Anna on this ride, but her assurance of doing what he could before Markus arrived had eased his worries.

A laugh erupted from deep inside him. A duke having tea with a woman as poor as Anna? His mother would have had a fit. The newspapers in London would fill their pages with all sorts of wild speculations. He had family members who would shun him for consorting with someone like her. To them, it was one thing to bed a woman of her station and quite another to treat her as if he had designs of marrying her.

Yet, as Anna came to view at the crest of the hill, Colin found he did not care about any of that. She had pinned back her hair, and her posture was graceful and alluring as she stood beside her horse in the same blue dress she had worn before. In her raised hand, she held a blade of grass, and as she had done during their initial meeting, she released it and allowed it to float away on the light breeze.

His gaze returned to her dress, and his heart clenched. If anyone deserved a new dress, it was she. He suspected that she owned no more than two, and it had not escaped his notice how she admired the food packed by Mrs. Montgomery for their last meeting. She had even said as much.

Despite her need, he had seen the universe in her eyes that day—dreams, hopes, and an appreciation for something as basic as simple food. All was pure without a hint of greed.

Transfixed on her feminine form, a strange feeling came over him, one he could not explain. It was not that same primal urge he had felt when they had wrestled on the ground during that first encounter. No, this was far different. He felt an overwhelming duty to protect her. To fulfill her every need in life. To hold her and tell her how her beauty humbled him. Where had these unusual thoughts come from?

Well, he would dwell on that another time. Now he wanted to go to her lest he lost even one precious moment in her presence.

The top of the knoll offered a fantastic view of luxurious rolling hills of green dotted with blue and yellow wildflowers, a spattering of thatched cottages, and white clouds touching the horizon. He doubted he had ever seen anything so spectacular.

Except when he looked at Anna.

"How kind of you to come," Anna said as she looked up at him, a twinkle in her eye. "I was just considering leaving. I see you left behind your coat. Was it difficult?"

"Of course not," Collin lied. Then he chuckled. "I suppose it was. It feels unnatural to be in such a state of undress. But if I'm to be Colin this week rather than the Duke of Greystoke, then I should be willing to set aside such restrictions."

That, of course, made little sense. Even poor men wore coats out of doors. Then again, Colin had seen many working with the sleeves of their shirts rolled up and their coats tossed aside. It was nice to learn that it was as freeing as he had suspected.

"You really should be careful," Anna said. "If you get too carried away, you may begin wearing clothes made outside of London. How could you ever continue on such a shameful path?" She gave him a wink, placed a booted foot in a stirrup, and threw her leg over the saddle, unabashed by showing her stockinged legs.

"Can you imagine?" Colin asked, unable to keep from grinning at her good-natured banter. "I think I would fall over in shock and never recover."

When Anna laughed at this, Colin realized no sound on earth could match its heavenly tone. "I don't wish to spend another day listening to you complain," Anna said with a defiant jut to her chin. "Now, show me what an accomplished rider you are, duke."

Before he could respond, she snapped her reins, and the horse galloped down the hill.

Accepting the challenge, Colin dug his heels into the horse's flanks and followed after her.

"I assume a man of your standing has had training by expert riders," she called with a quick glance over her shoulder.

"I've had the finest instructors who serve only those wealthy enough to pay their fees. Why? Are you jealous of my skills?"

She snorted. "Skills? Do you mean your rigid and slow riding? Those are not skills. Henry rides the same, and he's just seven."

Drawing his horse beside her, Colin pointed ahead of them. "If you are so good a rider, then I say we compete. That lone tree there. I'll race you to it."

"Don't hurt yourself just to try to impress me," Anna said. She glanced down. "And do mind your saddle. It's not secured properly. I'd hate to see you fall."

Colin leaned over, looked up, and roared with laughter when he noticed she had taken off without him. "You'll pay for your trickery!" he shouted, heeling the horse and lying low over its neck.

It was too late. Her distraction had the effect she wanted, for she had already circled around the tree and was riding past him back to their starting point long before he reached the tree.

Dismounting beside the tree, Colin tied the reins to one of the branches.

Anna returned, laughing. "Do you find losing so distasteful that you refuse to complete the course?"

"Not at all. I simply see no reason to continue with a lost cause."

"I find that very unlikely," Anna said with a sniff. "Only those upset about losing refuse to help a lady dismount."

"I would never refuse you anything." Colin placed his hands around Anna's waist and lowered her to the ground in front of him, and that overwhelming desire of wanting to hold her returned.

"Forgive my forwardness," he said, forcing his breathing to remain calm when she placed her hands on his arms. "Yet, I cannot help but wonder why a woman as beautiful as you is not spoken for."

"Because men see me as an object they wish to conquer," came her reply. "You're the first man to see me as something more."

How pleasing to know that he was better than most men she had encountered. Not because of his station, but because of who he was as a man.

He searched her face. If he never released her, he would be happy the rest of his life. "You're an enigma, Anna. You're beautiful, intelligent, and have the ability to do anything. Surely there is nothing you cannot achieve. But I cannot help but wonder if there is more about you to discover."

Her smile faded. Had he offended her in some way?

That thought faded when her smile returned. "Enough about me," she said, pulling out of his embrace. He would have preferred she remain there forever. "I wish to know more about you." She walked over to the tree and leaned her back against it. "How long have you been a duke?"

"Six years," he replied, glancing down at the ring. "My father fell ill and never recovered. He remained strong, even in the face of death."

"So, that is where your strength comes from," she said with a smile. "Besides your resounding propensity to tell everyone that you're a duke, what else do you enjoy?" The laughter that followed was a melodious sound. "Your expression was well worth me offending you."

Colin squared his shoulders. "I was not offended. Well, perhaps slightly." He gave her a wink, causing her to laugh again. "But to your question, I've not had time to do much else. Of course, there is the odd hunt and parties, which I've mentioned before. And I do enjoy a bit of reading from time to time, but otherwise, my days are filled with meetings followed by more meetings." He approached her at the tree. "And what of you, Miss Silverstone? What do you enjoy?"

"Everything in life that I can. Cooking breakfast for my brothers to admiring the stars at night, I find that it's the things we cannot purchase that should be cherished most. Those moments are what bring me enjoyment."

"Once again, you've amazed me," he said.

The Duke Who Loved Me

Desire took hold of him and all he wanted to do was pull her into his arms. She had indeed amazed him.

Oh, why could you not have been born to a different family? he thought. For the first time, he found someone whose face he could have looked into for eternity if given the opportunity.

Chapter Eleven

Anna found herself lost in Colin's gaze. Unlike the previous times they had met, this time felt different. Oh, her legs still turned to jelly, and her head could have floated away on the breeze. But now her heart ached for him, a most unusual phenomenon but one she welcomed all the same.

As he looked down at her, a single thought came to mind. Colin was a duke, and she was a Silverstone. She wanted him to kiss her but feared the day when there would be no more kisses from him.

"Anna," he whispered. "Look at me." He placed a finger beneath her chin and lifted her face to look at him. "What's wrong?"

"I'm just reminded that I'm a simple woman and you're a—"

"Never speak of yourself that way again," he said. "You're worth far more than any titled society believes you to be. You're Miss Anna Silverstone, a woman who should be proud of who she is." The way he said her name was like a soft caress and sent shivers down her spine. "And I'm far more than a duke. That's why I came here. To be the man I am inside, the man I'm trying to find. I know that, somehow, you'll help me in this endeavor. I'm sure of it."

"I'm happy to help you, Colin," she whispered. "Not because you're a duke, and not for anything you could do for me. But rather because I've come to have a certain regard for you."

The words came with no hesitation. Despite the fact they had known one another only a short time, she did care for him. To what extent remained to be seen. But as the world stopped around them and they stood staring into one another's eyes, she saw nothing but Colin.

With the speed of a fox leaping at a hare, Colin took hold of her waist.

Anna's heart skipped a beat. Before she could respond, he pulled her against him.

"You're beautiful, Anna," he whispered. "I must confess that your lips have pleaded with me for far too long." He rested the back of his hand on her cheek. "You know what they ask." It was not a question but rather a statement of fact, and the boldness of his words sent a thrill through her body. "And to that," he continued, "I must oblige."

He lowered his lips to hers. She had thought her first kiss would be gentle, but that passion behind the way he had said her name now burst through. It took every bit of strength she could muster to not collapse. She abandoned herself to that kiss, to him. Yielded herself to the urgency behind it. A tide of warmth surged through her, sending an enjoyable tingling down her spine. The trees no longer existed, nor the grass, nor the breeze. Only they two, locked together in a world all their own.

When the kiss came to an end, Anna placed her head against his firm chest. Strong arms wrapped around her and drew her closer.

"That was wonderful," she whispered. "I've never experienced such feelings before."

"Nor have I. If I could hold you forever, I would."

For the first time in as long as she could remember, she allowed her guard to drop. No man, no beast, no problems could hurt her. "I could wish for nothing more."

She savored his embrace, relished the feel of his arms around her. But they could not remain there forever— no matter how badly she wanted it.

As though reading her thoughts, Colin released his hold and grasped her hand. Leading her to the horses he stopped.

"Now, we must return to Redstone Estate. Caroline has invited us to tea."

"Tea?" Anna asked. "Surely, you must be teasing! I'm to be allowed over for tea?"

She and Caroline had been friends as children, but no Silverstone would have ever set foot on Remington property as a guest. A servant perhaps. A courier, definitely, but never a guest for tea.

"I'm not teasing," he replied. "I've been asked personally to bring you to the house." He lifted her onto the horse as if she weighed no more than a sack of flour. "Trust me, I was as surprised as you. With Markus now living elsewhere, the women have become comfortable in the running of the house. Therefore, the decision is theirs. I, for one, would not argue with them about such an invitation."

Despite his reassurances, panic welled up in Anna. "But I'm not dressed for tea at Redstone Estate!" She touched her head. "And my hair! It must look a sight! And what if I break a teacup?"

"What you're wearing now is satisfactory," he replied with a grunt as he mounted his horse. "Have I mentioned that I rather like the color blue? More so when you wear it."

Anna's throat went dry. Not only had she received her first kiss, but she was also receiving an invitation to tea with a duke!

No, he was not the duke. He was Colin.

"Regarding the teacup. If you break one, I'll insist you sell the coat you stole from me to pay for the damages."

This made Anna laugh.

"Whether it be a horse race or a broken teacup, nothing you do will change what I feel for you."

Her face burned as an image of Colin holding her and peppering her face with small kisses came to mind.

An image of which, this time, she did not want to be rid.

***

Anna bit at her lip as the horses moved at a leisurely pace. The rays of the sun highlighted Colin's strong jawline and perfect nose, somehow making him even more handsome.

"Before we arrive at the house," Colin said as he brought the horse to a stop. "I have a question I would like to ask. Caroline mentioned a feud between the families. What can you tell me about it?"

Anna brushed a stray strand of hair from her face. "My family owned a great deal of property at one time, including our side of where the log crosses the river and the river itself. Over the years, the land was parceled out, most of it sold to the Remingtons. When the land touching the river was sold, an agreement was made that we would be granted use of the river. So it's as much ours as theirs." She shook her head. "But I don't think it matters, not really. It's all rather silly if you ask me."

Colin moved his horse closer to hers and took her hand. She could not help but marvel at how small and delicate hers appeared in his. "I could not agree more," he said.

When he released her hand, she was left with an empty feeling. She could have him hold her hand forever!

"We should go," Colin said. "If we don't get to the house soon, I suspect Caroline will see a new feud started."

Once Redstone Estate came into view, the worry returned. Anna was going to make an utter dolt of herself, she was certain of it! What did she know about drinking tea at a noble house? Not a single thing!

Anna had not been to the estate house before. Oh, she had seen it from the main road on many occasions, but there had never been reason for her to be within its boundaries. Besides at the river, of course. This close, it appeared far larger. Built of deep red stone, the front of the house showed more than five times the number of windows on the entire cottage in which she lived.

Miss Caroline came bounding out the double front doors, her yellow dress flowing around her ankles, and Anna tensed.

"You've nothing to fear," Colin whispered.

He was right. When had Anna become so concerned about what others thought of her? She had never cared before about such trivial matters.

"You're right," Anna said, glancing at Colin. She smiled. "It's good to see you, Miss Caroline."

It had been three years since Anna had last spoken to Miss Caroline, but she had not changed one bit.

"It's been far too long," Miss Caroline said. "We may no longer be young girls secretly swimming in a river, but we can still be friends."

"I suppose so," Anna replied. "I admit I miss those times we shared at the river and think of them often with great affection."

"I'm so pleased you're here. We'll have tea and sandwiches. I've had Davis set up a table on the veranda out back." She turned to an older man in livery. "Davis, this is my friend, Miss Anna Silverstone. Davis has been awaiting your arrival with great anticipation, have you not, Davis?"

"I dare say I have, Miss Caroline," the butler replied, although he sounded as if he were reaching deep into his throat to pull out the words. "Welcome to Redstone Estate, Miss Silverstone."

"We are ready for our tea, Davis," Miss Caroline said. "And please be sure you provide us with the best we have."

"Yes, Miss Caroline," Davis replied with a bow before leaving to do her bidding.

"Come. We'll go around to the back. You've not been to the house, have you?"

Anna shook her head. "But it's very lovely."

The back gardens were far more extravagant than she could have ever imagined, with cobbled pathways weaving through various flowerbeds and between carefully trimmed hedgerows. Someone spent a great deal of time pulling every weed and tending every plant. Anna could imagine herself spending hours exploring there.

On the veranda sat a table already set with drinking glasses, plates, and utensils. Would they be eating a meal? Anna lowered herself into a chair Miss Caroline indicated, and Colin hurried over to push it in for her. Then he did the same for Caroline.

Anna wrung her hands beneath the table. Why was Miss Caroline staring at her? She reached up to pat her hair. Was it out of place?

Of course it was. Had she not just returned from a ride, one on which she had chosen to go without a head covering? What had she been thinking?

"I cannot believe how lovely you've become, Miss Anna," Miss Caroline said. "You always were, of course, but have you any idea how many women strive to have a fraction of what you have naturally? Lady Craven, a dear friend of mine, would give up her husband's estate for a tenth of what you have."

"Thank you," Anna said, her cheeks heating at being so thoughtfully compared to one of the area's loveliest baronesses. "You're too kind."

I doubt that tenth includes my leaky cottage, she thought ruefully.

Miss Caroline continued to study her. "I can see why Colin is so smitten with you."

The heat in Anna's cheeks deepened, and when she glanced at Colin, he had suddenly become consumed with studying a nearby hedge.

"Oh, don't give me such looks of innocence, either of you. I'm a reader of romance novels, and I can see what's in front me as easily as a banker can see money."

Anna found herself unable to respond and was relieved when Colin asked, "And where is Miss Remington? Will she not be joining us?"

Miss Caroline shook her head. "I'm afraid she's gone into seclusion again and will remain so for several days."

Seclusion? Anna thought. *What an odd choice of words to use. Well, it has nothing to do with me, so I'll not inquire.*

She wrung her hands in her lap once more. Despite the warm welcome, never had she felt so out of place!

A door to the house opened, and Davis emerged carrying a silver tray laden with a silver tea service. He filled three matching red teacups with gold rims and displaying the Remington family crest— a crown flanked by two ravens facing inward. Behind him came two footmen, each carrying a tray filled with tiny triangular sandwiches and a variety of tea cakes.

Anna's mother had spent many hours teaching her about proper table etiquette, but she could not stop tea from nearly sloshing over the rim of the teacup when her hand trembled so. Yet she managed to take a sip without incident.

"So, was your time with my cousin pleasant?" Miss Caroline asked. Anna nearly *did* spill her tea. "I imagine you enjoyed yourselves." She wore a grin that made Anna wonder if she suspected the kiss they had shared.

The Duke Who Loved Me

"Anna is a very skilled rider," Colin said. "Today I learned that my childhood instructor exaggerated when he praised my abilities. Which does not surprise me." Anna was not certain she was meant to hear the last.

"I saw your brother Christian in the village three weeks ago on Sunday," Miss Caroline said.

Anna stifled a groan. Christian had been in a fight with another boy recently. Had Miss Caroline witnessed that altercation? Anna prayed not.

"Sadly, he did not see me," Miss Caroline continued. "I would not have minded saying hello to him."

Anna studied the young woman. Was that a dreamy expression on her face? Did Miss Caroline have an attraction to Christian? No, Anna was reading far too much into the situation.

"I'll tell him to make sure to look for you the next time he's there," Anna said.

"Please do," Miss Caroline said, beaming with pleasure. "It would mean much to me."

So, she *had* read Miss Caroline's expression correctly! The thought of Christian and Miss Caroline together pleased Anna, but she knew it would never come to pass any more than she and Colin.

The conversation continued on to other matters, and Anna found herself relaxing. She used all her mother had taught her about proper etiquette— tea with the likes of Miss Caroline was far different from dining with her brothers. Soon, they were laughing together as if this was a regular occurrence.

"A word alone with you, Miss Anna, if you please," Miss Caroline said, hooking her arm through Anna's after they had finished their tea. "Give us a moment, Colin."

Colin bowed. "Of course."

They descended the steps to the garden level. "Although the last time we spoke we were children, we're now adults. Or you're an adult and I'm nearly there. Therefore, I would like to ask something if I may."

"Yes, of course," Anna replied. "What would you like to know?"

"My cousin... do you have romantic notions toward him? Oh, I'm sure the question is not proper, but I don't care. We're both women— and friends— and so we may speak of such things."

Anna could not help but laugh. Miss Caroline's immediate family may not have been titled, but they were quite wealthy with close ties to the aristocracy. Then her gaze fell on Colin, who leaned against the parapet wall that enclosed the veranda. She had no artistic skills, but if she could paint, she would have chosen him as her subject.

With a sigh, she replied, "I had not realized until today that I do have feelings for him, so yes, I do. I can't name them, nor can I describe them, but I can admit that something is there. What I can't seem to fathom is how it came about so soon after we met." She shook her head. "It's all rather strange if you ask me."

"Oh, how romantic!" Miss Caroline said in an excited whisper. "Don't worry. Markus will never know. Evelyn already suspects, but I don't believe she cares. I know I certainly do not." She embraced Anna. "We'll meet again soon, I promise. I've forgotten how much I enjoy your company. Perhaps we can even go swimming together again like we did when we were children. This time, however, we'll not need to keep it secret."

"I'd like that."

Miss Caroline turned them around and headed back to the veranda. "Well, I'll give you and Colin a moment alone. I do look forward to seeing you again."

"I'll not ask what she said," Colin said once Miss Caroline had gone inside. "I suspect I would die from embarrassment if I knew."

Anna smiled. "It was quite horrendous. I would be surprised if you appear in public after what she told me!"

Colin barked a laugh. "Why do I choose to keep company with a woman who wishes to torment me?"

"Because you enjoy it," Anna said, adding a mischievous grin. "Now, I have a request. Tomorrow at midnight, I wish you to meet me at the river.

"Midnight?" Colin asked as he led her around to the stables where a stable hand waited with her horse. "What exactly do you have in mind?"

"That is a secret," Anna replied. "Meet me if you wish to know more." She raised herself onto her toes and kissed his cheek, not caring who was around to see. "I'll see you then."

Once she was on her horse, she waved goodbye and headed down the drive toward home.

Today, two of her dreams had become reality. She had experienced her first kiss, and the gentleman she had always mentioned to Betty had finally arrived. His name was Colin, Duke of Greystoke, but she knew him simply as Colin— a man unlike any other. One who made her heart act in ways it never had before.

Chapter Twelve

With her eyes closed, Anna replayed the kiss in her mind. She had done so the night before, after returning from Redstone Estate. She had done so in her dreams. And she had done the same as she performed her chores around the house. The idea of seeing Colin again excited her. But a problem stood in her way.

Thomas.

She had managed to sneak about these last days and avoid raising his suspicion. But her luck would soon run out, and Thomas would become wise to her dishonesty.

Yet, she wanted to see Colin again. No, she needed to be in his arms. To learn more about him. To spend every waking moment with him. No matter how short lived it turned out to be.

For any of that to happen, however, she would have to be able to leave the house, and convincing Thomas to allow her to go would be nearly impossible.

Opening her eyes to the reality of her situation, she placed the cleaning rag on the counter. Thomas had taken Henry into the village for the day, leaving Anna to clean. Why did men believe housework was a duty meant for women alone? Then again, when one of her brothers did deign to see to the housekeeping, the job was never done properly, leaving her forced to see to it all over again. How did they stand living in such disarray?

Reaching for a teacup, she counted the small chips along the base and rim. How no tea leaked through the long crack down the side amazed her. She set it next to three others and smiled. None shared the same pattern. Yet she and her brothers had shared in many good times drinking from them, and that was what was most important.

Still, if there was any money left of what her father gave her once they met, she would see about purchasing a new set of teacups, all with a matching pattern. Nothing too fancy, just something nice.

She wiped her brow with the back of her hand and walked outside to find Christian sitting beneath a tree.

"Is this how you work when Thomas is gone?" Anna teased as she sat beside him. Usually, Christian would return her good humor, or at least laugh, but he did neither. "What's wrong?"

"It's Thomas," he grumbled. "That chestnut stallion we purchased last month? He's taken it with him today."

"He rode it into the village? But why would that upset you?"

He picked up a small stone and threw it. "Because he's selling it to a man he hopes to impress, which means, at best, we'll barely break even again." He stood, brushing dirt from his trousers. "That's why we struggle, Anna. He doesn't seem to realize that those men will never accept him. They must be laughing themselves silly at how he practically gives them everything we own."

Placing her palms in the dirt, Anna pushed up and stood. "What he does may be reckless, but I've come to see he means well. But none of that matters. I'm going to see that our lives are improved." Although she believed the words, she did not know how she would keep them.

Christian grimaced. "Please tell me the duke hasn't made an unsuitable offer for you."

Anna placed her hands on her hips and gave him a glare. "Christian! You know better than to think I'd do such a thing!" she sighed. "Has Thomas been filling your head with his worries?"

Kicking at a clump of dirt, he nodded.

"And you believe him?"

"No, of course not. I know better than that. But I know you worry just as much as I do."

She touched his arm. "Don't fret. I'm not so desperate that I'm willing to do that. But I do have a problem. I wish to see Colin again, more so over this coming week. We both know Thomas will never allow me to do so, so I must devise the perfect story to ease his suspicions each time I'm away from the house. Going to the market can only allow so much leeway."

Christian rubbed his chin. "Yes. A good excuse for you to be gone."

They stood in silence, and Anna contemplated every possible pretext for her absence. She could say she found another position. No, Thomas would ask far too many questions. Plus, she was not very good at lying.

Perhaps she could simply leave and face his wrath upon her return. Yet, that, too, felt wrong.

"'Ello! Whatcha two up to?"

Anna turned and smiled as Betty Voss came walking up the drive. Living no more than two miles away, she often dropped by unexpected every few weeks.

"There's your answer," Christian said with a grin. "I should get back to work."

He gave Betty a smile and a wave. Her cheeks turned a deep crimson, and she patted her dark hair, turning to stare after him with far too much appreciation.

Anna laughed all the same. "Did you not have to work today?"

"Oh, I did," Betty replied. "Mr. Harrison let a few of us go early. Should be more work next week, so I ain't worried none. So, what've you been up to?"

Anna laughed again as she snaked an arm through Betty's. "You'll not believe what I've been doing. Come inside. I believe a nice cup of tea is in order. And I need your help."

"Well, I never turn down a nice cup o' tea and a bit o' gossip. I take it it's good."

"Oh, it's wonderful," Anna replied.

Soon they were sitting at the kitchen table with two mismatched teacups in front of them. As Anna shared her story, Betty remained silent, only nodding from time to time, but it was clear she was keeping her excitement at bay with difficulty.

"So now, I only need to find a way to see Colin without angering Thomas." She poured them each another cup of tea. "What do you think?"

Unsurprisingly, Betty's first question burst forth. "When the duke pinned ye to the ground, did he kiss ye? Ye can tell me. Was it nice?"

Anna laughed. "After all I told you, that's the question you ask? What type of woman do you take me for?"

"One who'll get a kiss from a duke," Betty replied, making them both laugh.

"Well, he didn't kiss me that day, but he did yesterday."

"I knew it!" Betty squealed. "Bein' kissed by a duke. I can only imagine what that was like!"

Anna sighed. "It was wonderful, truly magical. Do you think poorly of me for wanting him to do it again?"

Betty gave an adamant shake of her head. "I'd be disappointed if ye didn't."

Anna glanced toward the door in hopes that Thomas would not be returning anytime soon. She directed the conversation back to the matter at hand. "I need your help to think of an excuse to leave the cottage. Do you have any ideas?"

Frowning, Betty smoothed her burlap dress. Then she sat up straight. "I've an idea! We'll send Thomas a ransom letter demandin' a thousand pounds for yer return!"

"A ransom? We don't have a thousand pounds. I doubt Thomas has more than two."

"That's the point. Since he don't 'ave it, 'e can't pay. Then, when ye come back, ye'll tell 'im ye managed to 'scape."

Anna shook her head. "I could never do that to Thomas. Nor to poor Henry. The thought of them believing I've been kidnapped is far more than I'm willing to do."

"That's 'bout the best I can do." Betty stood. "I'm sorry I couldn't come up with somethin' better. I've gotta run. Mum's needin' me help. Me Auntie Muriel's stayin' with us, and she ain't easy to please with all her wantin' this an' that."

Anna bolted from her chair. "That's it! I'll tell Thomas that I'm going to your house to help with your aunt."

No sooner than the words left her mouth than Henry came hurrying into the kitchen. "Anna! Thomas bought me a sweet!" He grabbed her around the waist and gave her a quick squeeze.

Anna ruffled his hair. "How wonderful!" she said.

Thomas entered the kitchen, and when he caught sight of Betty, a scowl crossed his lips. Why did he believe himself better than her, or anyone else equally as poor?

"What are you two doing?"

"Betty came to tell me about her sick aunt," Anna said, her heart thudding in her chest when Thomas narrowed his eyes at her. "I've agreed to call over to her house every day so I can help while she's at work."

"Since when do we offer charity?" Thomas demanded. "I'm sorry, Betty, but Anna's needed here."

"Charity?" Betty asked. "This ain't charity. Me aunt's rich. And generous, too." She shrugged. "But if Anna's not able, I guess I'll jus' haveta ask someone else. Someone who can use the money."

Thomas reversed his frown in an instant. "Your aunt, you say? I must have misheard. Of course, Anna would be happy to help. For how long?"

Betty glanced at Anna.

"At least a week," Anna replied. "Perhaps longer, but I have a feeling she'll mend quickly."

"Well, I see no issue with you going," he said. "Henry, go and prepare for your lessons. I must speak to Christian."

As soon as Thomas was gone, Anna hugged her friend. "I don't know how to thank you!"

"It's no bother," Betty replied. "But be sure to tell me all 'bout it once he's gone."

Promising she would, Anna walked her friend out. When Betty was gone, Anna sighed and leaned her back against the door. Tonight— and for every day thereafter— she would meet Colin.

Upon hearing Thomas's grumble outside, she returned to her cleaning, but her thoughts remained on the night ahead.

And oh, how she could not wait!

***

Colin had never been more excited. Tonight at the stroke of midnight, he would meet Anna. He had no idea what she had planned, but he looked forward to it, nonetheless.

Another thought entered his mind, one that made him lean back into the plush chair in the drawing room of Redstone Estate. One he had done all he could to ignore. If he put off the inevitable announcement of his intentions to marry Lady Katherine any longer, his mother would be far worse than displeased. Why could he not find a gentlewoman who was more like Anna? Or preferably Anna herself.

Turning the ring on his finger, Colin considered— not for the first time— the importance of bloodlines and how they determined one's path in life. They decided where they lived, to which parties they would receive invites, and worst of all, who one could marry.

Colin considered his own path. He had been given every available luxury in life. He owned more estates than he would ever need and could purchase whatever he wanted without a thought or worry for the cost.

Yet Anna could not afford a new dress.

Although Colin had never gone without, it often bothered him that so many did. Not the drunkards stumbling out of pubs after throwing their wages into mugs of ale. Nor a man who gambled away his fortune. Rather, he lamented for those like Anna, born into poverty and destined to die in it despite the long hours of hard work to earn just enough on which to live. Those were the people who he thought were wronged.

Their bloodlines told a different story from his, a tale of hope for better days. He had often heard servants speak to one another in hushed tones, wishing for what they called a "turn of fortune". Much like Anna hoped for. Those in his employ earned a reasonable wage. Most lived in the servants' quarters and ate from the servants' table.

But what of those who worked twice as hard as his servants only to earn far less?

If he had his way, he would take care of Anna for the rest of his life. Whatever she needed, he would give to her. She had already gifted him far more than anyone ever had given him in his life— the freedom to be Colin Remington and not the Duke of Greystoke. For that, she deserved to be cherished, and he was willing to do just that.

Yet bloodlines impeded his way. She could never become his wife, nor was she the type of woman to accept the position of mistress. Making such a request of her would only disgrace her, and he was unwilling to do that— no matter how much he wanted her in his life.

"Where's my cousin?" he heard a harsh voice bark.

Rising from his chair, Colin made his way to the foyer where Markus stood with the butler. His cousin was six years Colin's elder and carried himself like a grumpy man of sixty. He had dark eyes and matching hair that showed patches of silver. His tall, thin frame was much like Colin's.

"There he is," Markus said. "My cousin, the duke. It's been far too long." The stench of liquor rolled off Markus as if he had drenched himself in it.

"You look well," Colin said as they shook hands. "How is Tabitha?" Markus's wife was a small woman with red hair and ivory skin who had a constant look of terror on her face.

Markus shook his head. "Ungrateful, as always." He turned to the butler. "Davis, I'm hungry. Have food brought to the parlor."

"Yes, my lord," came the reply before Davis hurried away.

Before Colin could say more, Markus marched ahead. "Where are my sisters? Why are they not here to greet me? Have they become that accustomed to my absence? I'm here so rarely, one would think they would have the decency to be waiting for me at the door. I do pay for all they have, after all."

"Caroline is reading in the library," Colin replied, hurrying after his cousin. "Evelyn is in the parlor, or she was earlier."

It did not escape Colin that his cousin wobbled with each step. A bronze statue teetered to and fro, threatening to topple to the floor when Markus collided with it.

Evelyn was indeed still in the parlor, appearing as she had upon Colin's arrival the week before.

"Oh, Evelyn," Markus growled. "How dare you embarrass me. Stand up at once and greet me and your cousin!"

Colin took a step forward. "There's no need. She and I have shared in some wonderful conversations since I arrived. I'm sure I've bored her enough already with my various tales."

Markus scowled. "That may be so, but I'm sick of these childish games she plays." He reached down and snatched something from her hand.

"Give that back to me!" Evelyn said, leaping from her chair. "Markus, return it to me at once!"

"What is this? A ring? You're no better than Caroline, sitting at home dreaming all day."

During his short stay, Colin was well aware that something was not quite right with Evelyn. One thing of which he was sure was that this was no act. The anger in her eyes coupled with the sorrow in her features could not have been matched by the best actors on a London stage.

"I've warned you about seeking others' attention," Markus said. "Why must you insist on embarrassing me?"

Evelyn lowered herself back into the chair and said nothing.

Markus tossed the ring into her lap. "Take it. Now get out of here so the men can have a drink without being forced to endure your constant state of melancholy."

With a sob, Evelyn grasped the ring in her hand and hurried from the room.

"Have you any idea how humiliating it is to have a sister like her? When my friends inquire about her, I've no idea what to tell them. I certainly cannot reveal that she's going mad! What would they think of me then?"

Colin sat in one of the chairs. "I doubt she's mad, Markus. She and I have had several conversations over the past week, and she appeared and spoke as we are now."

Markus heaved a heavy sigh and fell into one of the chairs. "Which proves my point that it's all a ruse. She has been this way since Father died."

The butler entered with a tray filled with fruit and cheese and set it on the table.

"Pour us some brandies and leave us, Davis." He gestured toward the food, but Colin waved a hand to decline.

Once the butler was gone, Markus raised his glass in a toast. "To our freedom away from women. How marvelous it is." He downed the entire measure in one gulp and rose to pour himself another. "I've one sister who acts like a child, and the other has her nose stuck in books all day. Do you see why I only return twice a year?"

Colin suspected his cousin had other reasons but said nothing. Rumor had it that Markus had as many mistresses as he had coats. It was a shame he had chosen to drown his sorrows in liquor after the death of his father. At least he had not lost his sharp mind for business.

"So, I hear you're to announce your engagement to Lady Katherine Haskett soon."

"I am," Colin replied. "But the announcement will be delayed a bit longer. The fact is that another has caught my interest. I may consider remaining a bit longer than I had planned. If your sisters will have me." An image of Anna came to mind. He was in no hurry to return home as it was, but having her nearby only made it that much more difficult. "I also must go to London next week."

Markus chuckled. "A bit of fun before you're forced to tie yourself down, eh? I don't blame you. Don't think of marriage as the end of your life but rather the beginning. We're men, even more, we're Remingtons. It's our right to indulge ourselves with any willing female. Especially you being a duke and all."

Although he would never admit as much to his cousin, Anna was the first woman he had ever kissed. To him, such intimacies should be saved for marriage. Now that he had shared that special moment with Anna, the idea of kissing any other woman repulsed him.

His cousin knitted his brows in thought. "Does the idea of marrying Lady Katherine not appeal to you?"

"If I'm honest, it does not. She's a lovely young lady, but she has no mind of her own. She refuses to share her own opinions but, instead, has been taught to agree with everything I say. Is it too much to ask for a woman with whom I can converse?"

Markus chuckled. "I've seen Lady Katherine on occasion, and a woman such as she is not meant for conversation. Have you not noticed her beauty? The swell of her bosom? She's meant to please you in the ways of the flesh as a proper wife should. Trust me, you don't want a woman with her own opinions. They only cause trouble."

Any arguments would be futile, so Colin simply replied, "Lady Katherine is appealing to the eye, any man can see that. But I've no desire to marry her."

He did not say aloud that Anna was quite different. He could listen to her thoughts all day. Whether they rode horses or attended balls together, it did not matter. He needed her.

Markus frowned. "This other woman... There's something about her that says she may not be appropriate for you. I can see it in your face. Is she ruined? Is her father bankrupt?"

Colin took a drink of his brandy to give him a moment to think of a response. "I barely know her, so the thought of marriage is too far off to consider. Plus, even if I did decide she's the one with whom I would enjoy spending the rest of my life, I could not marry her. She is not of titled blood nor the gentry."

"Then you would be as mad as my sister if you wasted your time with her. I take it you find her attractive."

"Quite," Colin replied. "But she's also intelligent."

Markus gave a derisive snort.

"I know you believe it senseless, but I find conversation with her to be intriguing. It's her deuced bloodline that keeps us from being anything but friends."

"Friendship alone with poor stock is risky," Markus said. "Nevertheless, there is a solution to your problem. Marry Lady Katherine, but put up this other woman in paid accommodations. When the need arises, go visit her. That's how I keep my sanity."

So, he finally admits aloud his indiscretions, Colin thought. "And what about your wife? Do you not fear she'll learn about this other woman? Will it not cause her a great deal of pain?"

Crossing one leg over the other, Markus rested his glass on his knee. "Women are here to serve certain purposes— to warm our beds and to bear us children. Her feelings on the matter do not trump my God-given rights as a Remington." He finished off the last of his brandy. "Tabitha's well aware of the situation and makes no argument. You'll find a good wife who'll learn to remain quiet about such matters, just you wait and see. Especially since you can make her a duchess. Any woman in her right mind would be willing to give up everything to live such a lavish life."

Irritation nipped at Colin. His cousin was all too much like so many other men when it came to his opinions on women. Colin did not know Mistress Tabitha well, but he could not help but pity her.

I pray I have more integrity once I'm married, he thought. Yet, he could not help but agree to the fact that most ladies aimed for a marriage that offered a title rather than love. That, too, was a pity.

When Markus eyed him with clear suspicion, however, Colin added, "I'll consider your advice, Cousin."

"Good. Now, have you been approached about certain investments in Oxford?"

It was a relief to have the conversation turn to business, and Colin and Markus shared in what news they had heard.

When Markus offered to pour Colin a fourth glass of brandy, he waved him away. Colin had consumed far too much already— the idea of a measure to Markus was far different from his— and he preferred to keep a clear head.

"My ways are often the topic of gossip," Markus said when the discussion of members of the *ton* arose. Colin went to interject, but Markus waved him away. "Don't worry. I hear many of the rumors bouncing about and have no reason to dispute most of them. You must understand. I'm a practical man. We're Remingtons, Cousin. You're a duke, and although I may not be titled, our name carries a great deal of weight. Those who have tried to challenge that fact often find themselves up to their necks in trouble. Let the ring on your finger remind you of that."

Markus leaned forward and refilled Colin's glass, although Colin had refused.

"Do whatever you wish," his cousin said. "Continue seeing this mysterious woman. I only make one request."

"What is that?"

"That you put the name of Remington before your own desires. We have all faced many scandals, but you're a duke and therefore represent the entire family. If you fall in any area, we all fall with you— my sisters, all the cousins spread across the country, and I— all of us shall be hurt. I don't mean to dishearten you, but it's who you are."

The reality of what his cousin said did not sit well with Colin. After all the absurdity of which Markus had spoken over the last two hours, this single point was true. Whatever choice he made, he had to consider what it would do to his family's reputation.

His gaze dropped once more to his ring, a symbol of who he was and whom he represented. The journey to Redstone Estate was meant to learn who he— Collin Remington— truly was. Now he feared the very man who had left Hemingford Home at the beginning of this journey was who Colin truly was.

Chapter Thirteen

Anna was excited. No, ecstatic. Tonight, she would be meeting Colin after what felt like years. She had chosen one of her burlap dresses and wore the coat she had taken from Colin over it.

Stopping for a moment to look at the peaceful form of Henry, who often slept in her bed, she leaned over and kissed his forehead, praying he would not awaken.

"Sleep well," she whispered and then added the promise she had made every night since the death of their mother. "And know that life will soon be better."

The hinges on the door creaked when she opened it, and she paused to listen for any changes in Thomas's snores. The fact that he snored was a blessing, for it created enough noise to make Anna's escape from the cottage that much easier. Given that it was also ten minutes before midnight was also helpful.

Once outside, she drew in a deep breath of fresh air. She could not have hoped for a better night. The moon was full, allowing for light to wash over the ground and making her walk far easier.

With her heart thudding in her chest, Anna scurried to the forest's edge. In just a few minutes, she would be with Colin once again!

It seemed an eternity since they last met, and she had so many things she wished to talk to him about. So much more she wanted to learn about his past, his present, and his future. No matter the topic, she did not care, just so long as they had time to be together.

And, perhaps, he would kiss her again. If she was lucky.

She sighed. Why did thinking of kissing Colin make her entire body tingle in anticipation? Every time she imagined herself in his arms, it was as if her heart felt lighter than the blades of grass that she often threw to the wind. She had never been one for lewd thoughts before, yet here she was having notions only harlots would have!

Life certainly had a strange way of changing directions without warning.

As she approached the log bridge, she scanned the opposite bank for any sign of Colin. Where was he? Perhaps he had been held up somehow. Well, he would come, she was sure of it.

Partway across the fallen log, she glanced down at the reflection of the moon— as bright as her future— on the smooth water of the pool below.

As Anna stepped off the bridge, she paused. What was that noise? Besides the odd deer or stray dog, no animal existed that would make that much racket. No, the deer would have been far quieter.

"Where's the bloody path?"

Anna burst out laughing as Colin emerged from the trees. He was devoid of a coat, and leaves and small twigs clung to his clothing and hair.

"Perhaps you should hire some men to build you a path," she called out to him. "Or better yet, have them build you a road so you may bring your carriage with you. Then you'll not be forced to stumble through the woods."

Colin started and then barked a laugh. "I didn't realize my voice carried so far." He brushed at his breeches. "My apologies. I must look a fright."

She walked over and looked him up and down. "I'll not lie. The word unkempt has taken on an entirely new meaning." When he frowned, she rolled her eyes. "Here, let me help."

His firm, muscular form beneath her fingertips made heat rush through her body, and it was not long before she had to move away or catch fire. "That should be good enough," she managed to croak.

"Thank you," he replied, clearly oblivious to his effect on her senses. He glanced around them. "This is beautiful. The moon, the stars, what a perfect night."

"My thoughts exactly," she said. "And now you're here, which only makes it more perfect. Follow me. We'll only be a moment." She led him to the fallen tree. When he gave her a skeptical look, she added, "Don't worry. If you take your time, you'll not fall."

"Of course you would say that," he said. "You spend a great deal of time doing this sort of thing. I, on the other hand, have had little practice with crossing fallen trees. I suspect your true motive is to watch me fall."

Anna feigned a gasp. "Are my thoughts that evident?" She reached out to him. "Here, take my hand, so you can take me with you if you fall."

He did as she bade, and they shifted along the log until they were halfway across.

"Let's sit here," she said.

"What a wonderful—" Colin gasped as he wobbled, and his grip tightened.

Anna held her breath. If he fell, he would indeed drag her in with him!

His faltering came to an abrupt stop, and he grinned at her. "You're not the only one who can torment, Miss Silverstone."

Anna laughed as he sat beside her. "I should push you in for that!" She glanced at their intertwined fingers, pleased he had not released her hand.

Colin turned to look at her. "You told me the first time we met that you enjoy coming here at midnight to swim. Why is that? Why midnight?"

Anna looked up at the stars. "There's no feeling like it," she replied. "To be free and alone with only the stars watching. I don't have to worry about whether Thomas will be angry at me. If Christian has sold a horse. Or if Henry's stomach is grumbling with hunger. I can imagine everything is perfect, even if it's just for a short time."

"If there were ever a woman who deserved the very best, it's you. I believe that, one day, the world will repay you for your selflessness."

Squeezing his hand, she said, "I believe it already has."

The sound of the flowing river had always been a peaceful experience. How lucky she was to now share it with Colin.

The Duke Who Loved Me

"What about you?" she asked. "How will the world one day repay you?"

Colin snorted. "You assume I'm as selfless as you, but I assure you, I'm not. Oh, I'm not a horrible man, but I would never describe myself as magnanimous."

"I'm sure no one would ever consider you horrible," Anna said. "I mean, look at this fine coat you gave me. Is that an act of a selfish man?"

"I don't recall that I *gave* it to you," Colin said with a laugh. "I believe it was taken from me through blackmail. Or was it coercion? Either way, I didn't simply give it to you." He winked at her. "Do you find it comfortable?"

Anna nodded. What she found was that it reminded her of being wrapped in his arms. Would he hold her tonight before they went their separate ways? Perhaps she could see that happen. "It's a very fine fabric, but I do feel a bit cold." She glanced around as if in search of something. "Now, how can I warm up more?"

Colin frowned. "Cold? I find it quite warm. You're not falling ill, are you?"

Anna laughed, which only made Colin's frown deepen.

"Oh!" he gasped. "I'm as dense as the trees around us." He placed an arm around her shoulders.

Sighing, Anna snuggled closer. She felt protected, comforted as she laid her head against him.

"Tell me about your mother," he said. "Was she like you?"

"She was so beautiful," Anna replied. "She radiated happiness no matter how life treated her. I learned from her to be thankful for all we have. And to dream. Mother often said that dreams are what we're made of. I never truly understood what she meant until now." She lifted her face so she could look up at him. "Our dreams are what compel us to act as we do. To search out what may seem foolish or unlikely to others. I suppose I'm saying that we should allow our dreams to guide our steps because they lead to what we want."

Colin smiled. "Again, you've given me much to consider. My father always said that our paths are already set for us, by our parents

105

and by society as a whole. That dreams outside what is planned for us are a wild-goose chase. For most of my life, I believed that, but I've come to see things in a much different light over the past few months. I've begun asking whether or not I should be allowed dreams, and if so, what dreams do I have? In truth, I believed what my father had told me, that I am not allowed to have aspirations outside of the dukedom. Because of you, however, I've come to realize that I don't have to limit myself to my title. Therefore, I plan to go in search of those dreams."

"Tell me one," Anna whispered, leaning against him again. The sound of his heartbeat was soothing. "Just one dream that you hope to see realized while you're playing the part of Colin."

"You'll just think me silly. I would hate to have you laughing so hard that you fall into the river."

"Never," she said, smiling. "Tell me. I wish to hear it."

"I want to go to a public house," he replied. "A proper tavern with filthy windows and glasses filled with suspect drink. With patrons who care nothing for station, who may be chimney sweeps or miners. Where the men may not be able to read but greet a stranger like a long-lost family member. To share a drink with them and have them speak to me honestly. That's what I dream of."

Anna could not help but smile as Colin ran a hand up and down her arm. "I'd like to see you achieve that," she said, snuggling even closer to him. "I bet we can find all sorts of taverns like that." Then a thought came to mind. "But what if a man wishes to pull me aside to buy me a drink? Or asks for a kiss? What would you tell him?"

"That you're there with me," he replied, his hold becoming firm. Possessive. "And that if he values his life, he'll walk away."

"So, you'd protect me?" she asked, her heart soaring.

"No one will ever harm you if I have anything to do with it," he said. He placed a hand on the side of her face and turned her toward him. "For there is no one like you. The gods themselves sent their most prized beauty to me. You are a treasure of wonders, Anna." His eyes searched her face. "There's so much I wish to explore."

Their lips met in a passionate kiss, one that was firmer and hungrier than the one they had shared before. With trepidation, she placed a hand on his arm, enjoying the firm muscle beneath the thin fabric of his shirtsleeves. Her heart pounded, her body heated, and soon she felt as if she were floating away.

Then, much to her disappointment, the kiss came to an end. Yet his strong hold on her did not.

"If I may be honest," he said as he looked down at her. "I find myself thinking of kissing you quite often these days."

Anna nodded. "You're not alone, I assure you. I've had the same thoughts." She placed her hands on either side of his face. "It would be far too improper for you to do so again."

"You're right."

"That's why I'll kiss you instead."

This time the kiss was soft and sensual, and Anna considered throwing herself into the pool below to cool her blazing skin. Reluctantly, she pulled away lest their kiss continued until dawn.

For some time they remained quiet. Then he said, "When we had tea, I was surprised how well you conducted yourself. I've seen other women fail where you succeeded." He turned a warm gaze on her. "I speak not just of tea but of everything."

Anna smiled, enjoying his touch, his words, his very being. "My mother was unlike any other. She taught me that being poor is no excuse for bad form."

For a moment they listened to the current of the river. With the bright moon, she could see their watery reflection in the pool. What a beautiful sight to behold.

"This surprise," he said waving his arm to encompass their surroundings. "You, the scenery, I have never had a surprise quite like this."

Anna smiled. "I also had hoped we could swim together as I've often done. Would you consider such a thing?"

Her heart sank as he shook his head. "I'm afraid not. That is much too bold for someone like me. Not at such a late hour, and certainly not without the benefit of a chaperone. After all, we are taking an extreme risk being here alone in the first place."

To say she was disappointed was not strong enough. Sadness would have described her current reaction to his response."

"Allow me to help you up," Colin said, rising and nearly toppling over before he righted himself and put a hand out to her. "Beginning tonight, I wish to be free by choosing your ways. But don't worry. Only you and the stars are watching."

Anna frowned. "Free? Colin, what're you doing?"

He pulled his shirt over his head to reveal a well-defined torso that appeared even better than she could have imagined. Every sensibility told her to look away, yet that battle lasted all of half a breath. His body was a work of art, a sculpture with details that made her breath catch. The firm ridges on his stomach were an alluring sight.

Removing his boots and stockings and setting them beside him, he stood there in nothing more than his breeches like an Adonis brought down to earth solely for her personal inspection. A privilege she would honor. When he ran a hand through his hair, the muscles in his arms tightened, and she could not stop a gasp from escaping her lips.

"How deep is the pool below us?"

Anna had to force the words through a dry throat. "I'd say your height and half again. What are you planning to do?"

He grinned down at her. "Experience the freedom of which you spoke," he replied and then leapt from the log into the pool below.

"Colin!" Anna cried in shock when he rose to the surface. "I thought this was beneath you! You're unbelievable!"

"This is so wonderful!" he shouted as he wiped water from his eyes. "I'm free! Swimming out here beneath the night sky, knowing that at any moment, you may join me." His smile was devilish. "There's no feeling like it in the world, is there?

Laughing, Anna removed his coat and her shoes and stockings. When she reached around to unbutton her dress, Colin turned away. With quick movements, she stepped out of her dress and stood only in her shift.

The water rippled around his broad back, and she knew then that she had been correct. She had been given an invitation to not only inspect him but to also join him.

"I want to be free with you," she whispered, looking down in the water below her. "Forever, if possible."

Then she jumped.

Chapter Fourteen

Colin had never felt more liberated than he did now. He swam toward Anna, separating the water in front of him. Her idea to swim this night had been magical. Made more so with the bright moon and countless stars that joined them.

Anna pulled back wet hair from her face as he drew closer. "I'm too short," she said. "I can't touch the bottom."

Without a word, he took hold of her waist and pulled her to him. A small gasp emitted from her as he locked his hands at the small of her back. With her so close to him, with the power that came from holding her, his breathing quickened.

"Colin—"

He silenced her with a kiss.

She clasped her hands around his neck as their lips danced together. All he wanted to do was to carry her away, to have her all to himself. When her hands trailed over his arms, he ceased the kiss. Still holding her, he searched her eyes. How could a woman he had known such a short time have such a hold on him?

"What are you thinking?" she asked in a whisper.

"About you. How you consume me. I could gaze upon you all day and never wish to see anything else. To kiss you for the rest of my life." When she bit at her bottom lip, desire rushed through his body. Leaving an arm wrapped around her, he reached up and moved a strand of hair from her face. "You asked me about my dreams, and I responded with the truth. Why not now share yours?"

Anna looked away. "I cannot reveal them to you."

Her words pained him. Did she not see he could be trusted? "You can tell me anything."

She looked back up at him. "This night has been far too marvelous to ruin with such things."

Did she not see that he was consumed with her? "I swear to you," he said, searching her eyes, "no matter what you say, I'll not hold it against you. Tell me, and if there is any way I can see your dreams realized, I'll do it."

She sighed. "I wish to journey to London."

"London?" he asked. "What's in London?" Did she wish to place an order with one of the renowned dressmakers there? Perhaps she had a cousin there she wished to visit. Either would be easy for him to see happen.

Still she did not respond. Was it far more complex than he realized?

"Anna, what is it?"

She dropped her gaze once more. "It's far too embarrassing to say. Or too embarrassing to say to someone like you."

"Why? Because I'm a duke?"

She nodded. "That is part of it, yes."

"But I'm not the duke at the moment, remember. I'm Colin, at least for another week. See me as nothing more than a simple man, as one of your friends equal in station."

When she looked up at him, he was surprised to see the pain in her eyes. "That may be true for now, but when you return home next week, you'll return to being the duke. I'll become nothing more than a woman you found attractive." She sighed. "I'm just a Silverstone. We're easily forgotten. So why burden you with my troubles now?"

What she said was true, at least in part. There would be no inviting her to his home for tea or to take a stroll through his gardens. Bloodlines and the ring on his finger made certain of that.

"I'll not argue, but I'll say this." He took her hand in his. "No matter what happens, I can never forget you."

Her smile warmed him far more than the heat of their closeness. "My father— or the man I suspect to be my father— is an earl. All I know is his name and that he resides in London. It's been my dream to search him out."

"An earl?" Colin asked in surprise. "Are you certain?"

Anna nodded. "Don't you see? Finding and presenting myself to him can open a whole new world. No longer will Thomas and I worry late into the night about our lack of funds. Everything will change for me, for my entire family."

Colin was not so sure. If what she said was true, more problems would arise the moment she stepped foot on this earl's doorstep. Few men of title claimed a child born out of wedlock, and those who did rarely publicized the relationship. How that fact had escaped Anna concerned him. She was far too intelligent to believe that the man would simply open up his arms to her and her brother.

When he peered into her lovely blue eyes, however, he found he could not bring himself to explain this truth to her. How could he cause her such heartache?

If it was money she hoped to gain from an introduction, he, Colin, had more than enough to provide for this journey she so desired. Or anything else she wanted in life. He would have to do so out of the prying eyes of the aristocracy, of course. If word got out that he had aided her in this strange endeavor, his name could be tarnished. Plus, how could he put a peer through such an accusation?

Yet, as he searched her face, his heart ached. "What's this man's name?"

"The Earl of Leedon," she replied.

Colin's brows rose. "Leedon?" he repeated with enthusiasm. "Why, I'm well acquainted with Leedon. We've done business together on at least two occasions in the past. Are you certain he's your father?"

"Oh, yes, quite certain," she replied, her grip tightening around his neck. Mother told me, and I swore to never forget his name."

Colin frowned. "He's now married with children. They're younger than you, but it could be possible if he and your mother had an affair."

"Mother said that she knew him before moving here. He was forced into a marriage of convenience and, because of her common status, was unable to marry her. I don't wish to intrude on his life nor cause his family distress, for what happened is long over. Nothing can change the past. But I must meet him. Do you think you could arrange a meeting between us?"

As a duke, the likelihood of anyone refusing to see Colin was slim. Few would deny such a request, and their reasoning had to be sound.

Yet could he do this? The risk would be great.

"I'm sorry," she said, looking down. "I can see that I've overstepped. You're a duke and I'm a Silverstone. And a bastard. Just forget I mentioned it."

The pain in her eyes told him a story far more than the callouses on her hands. It was the story of a woman who likely had missed many meals. A woman who labored in a workhouse as she dreamed of better days. This journey she wished to take should not be denied her. And certainly not by him.

"I'll take you there myself," he found himself blurting out before he could put a clamp on his tongue. "Together we'll go to London."

Once the words reached his ears, reason intervened and he closed his mouth. What was he doing making such an offer? It was ridiculous!

Yet, as she tightened her arms around him and whispered thanks in his ear, that worry began to fade.

"How will we get there?" she asked. "And when can we leave?"

He pulled her into the shallows until she was able to stand on her own. "Markus will leave Monday. I'll hire a carriage to take you the following day. I have my own, but it would not do for us to travel together unchaperoned." That was a humorous thought given where they were now, but he had to hold to some sort of decorum before losing himself completely. "I'll then send word to my mother to inform her that I'll be returning home later than expected."

He had promised to attend a function for a cousin on his mother's side of the family.

"I'll finally be able to meet him!" she said. "Once I do, everything will be made right. Henry needs new shoes, and Christian could use a new coat—"

"Anna, I must warn you to tread lightly." Watching her smile fall saddened him, but he had to be as truthful as he could. "You're not certain that he's your father, which means there is a chance he is not. And even if he is, he may choose not to acknowledge that fact."

"I do believe I'm his daughter but thank you for your concern. Trust me, my mother never lied. If he's a decent man, he'll accept me. I'm sure of it. Now, before we leave, I have an idea of what we can do while we're in London." She swam past him to return to the middle of the pool. Then she raised her eyebrows at him. "Will you join me, or do you prefer to watch me drown?"

Collin laughed, and just as before, she wrapped her arms around his neck. "If you wished for another kiss," he said huskily, "you only need to ask."

Anna feigned a gasp of surprise before placing a hand on the side of his face. "Tomorrow morning, I want you to meet me here early. No later than seven."

He frowned. "Seven? Why?"

She pressed a finger to his lips and leaned in close. "That is another surprise," she whispered. "Do you wish for another kiss before we leave?"

Colin smiled. "I would love nothing more."

She gave a great push against his chest. "Then you'll have to catch me!" she shouted. "You're a slower swimmer than you are a horseman!"

Overcome with happiness, Colin chased after her. Whether it was because he swam faster or because she allowed him to catch her, he did not know, but she was right where she belonged. In his arms once more.

And as they kissed again, Colin hoped that many more times together like this would follow. Yet, he could not shake the truth that, one day, because of their bloodlines, those kisses would have to come to an end.

Chapter Fifteen

As sunlight broke over the horizon, Colin made his way back to the very river in which he had swum only hours before. His time with Anna had been wonderful, and soon both would set out to London.

After returning home, he had written to his mother, informing her that he would once again be delaying his return home. Oh, but she would be irate with him!

Let her be, he thought.

He had also already sent word about the need for a hired carriage for Anna. That they would not have one available for his use never occurred to him, for they would. At least being a duke gave him some privileges of which he would make use.

Although doubt about Anna and Lord Leedon still attempted to impede his thoughts, Colin could not bring himself to deny her request. If this was what she wanted, he would see it done, and that was all there was to it.

When he reached the edge of the tree line, he smiled. Anna awaited him, a sack in her hand.

"I'm glad you came," she said as he approached. "I debated whether I should leave." The last was said with a mischievous grin. "Here, this is for you."

He took the offered sack and frowned upon opening it. A shirt, trousers, and cap lay inside. "What are these?"

"You said you wished to be Colin this week. Do you still want that?"

"I do," he replied, still unsure what the contents were for.

"Then you must look like Colin and not a duke. That is, if you still wish to visit a tavern with dusty windows. Those belong to my brother Thomas, so they should fit."

Realization crossed his features, and he smiled. "What a fantastic idea! I cannot believe I didn't think of it. Thank you. But surely your brother will miss them." He was not about to say that he knew few of her class had more than two sets of clothing.

She waved a hand at him. "He spends most of his time wearing his better clothes to meet with people and rarely wears these anymore. There's no need to concern yourself." She stood on her toes and kissed his cheek. "I need to leave and speak with Betty. It occurred to me that in order for me to leave for London with you, I need a sound reason, and Betty's sick Aunt will be the perfect excuse. Well, she's not truly sick, but that doesn't matter."

Colin went to speak, but Anna gave him a quick kiss on the lips and hurried back into the woods.

Smiling, he returned to Redstone Estate, careful not to disturb anyone, lest he arouse their suspicion.

After placing the clothes Anna had given him in the bottom of the wardrobe, he returned to bed, hoping for a few more hours of sleep.

And many dreams about lovely flaxen hair and deep-blue eyes.

***

Bright sunlight shining through the open curtains woke Colin far earlier than he had hoped. As he stretched, he barely noticed the smooth silken sheets as memories of the previous night came tumbling into his mind.

He had to admit that he surprised even himself by jumping into the river. How long had it been since he had experienced such a thrill? Far too many to count. And, to his delight, Anna had leapt in after him. It was as if the world had stopped for them. That nothing could keep them apart.

In two days, he and Anna would set out for London. He regretted not being able to travel with her by his side, but it was necessary to arrive apart. Even in the commoner clothes she had given him, he was acquainted with far too many people to take the chance. At least he would save both their reputations with this arrangement.

Whether he could keep the visit covert once they arrived remained to be seen. Yet being among many was a far easier way to hide if the need arose than being found alone in a carriage. Perhaps he was being far too cautious, but he wanted to do what was right by Anna—whether she was noble or not. She deserved the same courtesies as any lady as far as he was concerned.

Once their time together in London came to an end, what then? Lady Katherine and his mother still waited for him to return to announce their engagement. Parties would follow, where members of the *ton* raised their glasses to toast his name. "The duke will be married!" they would say. "How fortunate for him!"

Yes, for the duke it would be a great day. For Colin, it would be one of misery.

Rising, he was glad he had insisted that his valet remain at Hemingford Home. How was he to be simply Colin if he was being dressed like a duke? What a battle that had been! Newbold, his valet of ten years, had been as shocked as his mother. In the end, however, the duke got what he wanted despite the irregularity of the situation.

Pulling on a fresh pair of breeches, he gazed at himself in the large standing mirror and attempted to flatten his hair. He chuckled. Some water from the pitcher would have it back to normal. Or perhaps he should leave it this way. Would fewer people recognize him if he did?

He walked over to the window. Past the gardens was the thick nestle of trees that blocked his view of the river beyond. And farther, a cottage he had yet to see. Yet it was not the cottage that held his interest but rather the young woman within.

The idea of not seeing Anna again after the following week made his heart clench and his stomach knot. But what if he came to visit his cousins again? He could easily slip away for an hour if the need arose…

No, if he were married by then, which he suspected would be the case, meeting her alone would be out of the question. Whatever he felt for Lady Katherine, he would not allow himself to be tempted by another woman. Not even Anna.

"There must be a way to avoid this marriage," he whispered.

He glanced at the ring on his finger. The precious gem mocked him. Becoming Colin for an entire week had been easy enough, but once that time came to an end, he had a duty to uphold. He would not become the duke who ruined the Greystoke dukedom. Nor the Remington name.

A knock on the door startled him. "Yes?"

The door opened, and Markus entered the room. By his appearance, he had risen some time ago. "I thought you would sleep until sunset," his cousin said with a laugh. "You certainly returned home late. Davis says your clothes were drenched. Did you go for a swim?"

For a moment, Colin considered lying, but for what reason should he deny it? "I did." He pulled a shirt from a dresser drawer, choosing not to expand on his response.

"And did you see her?" Markus asked.

Colin turned. His cousin sat on the edge of the bed. "Her?" Colin asked.

"Anna. The penniless girl from across the way."

Fearing his voice would betray his annoyance, Colin shook his head in reply.

"Pity. She's quite attractive for a woman of such low birth. If you do see her, I say you should have some fun with her."

This made Colin pause, his shirt over his head. "Are you implying that the woman has loose morals?"

Markus snorted as he rose from the bed. "How can you be so naive?" he asked. "Did you not know that all poor women can be easily wooed with just the promise of a few coins?" He paused and tilted his head. "How can hearing this cause you discomfort? Everyone knows it's nothing more than reality for people like her."

Colin refused to believe Anna capable of such behavior, but he also could not allow Markus to know the truth. "Why would it bother me?" he asked as he tucked the hem of his shirt into his breeches. "I'm not acquainted with her, and I doubt I'll ever meet her."

Markus grinned. "You just may, Cousin. If we see her today during the luncheon, I'll be sure to introduce you to her."

Colin frowned. "Luncheon? What luncheon?"

Markus walked over to the door. "I thought I told you. A dear friend of mine and her sister are awaiting us downstairs. We are to take them to the river for a picnic. There's nothing like sharing a meal al fresco with a lovely lady."

Colin could not go on an outing! And certainly not to the river. Anna might see him! "I don't think that's wise, Markus. After all, you're married." When his cousin gave no reaction, he added, "Think of your sisters. I'm sure they would raise a fuss."

"Evelyn's blubbering in her room, so I doubt we'll see her for the rest of the day. And Caroline is at the home of a friend and will not return until dinner. Now, hurry. We mustn't keep the ladies waiting." Then he left the room.

Dread filled Colin as he finished dressing. How could he be suffering from this guilt? He felt as if he were betraying Anna, but that made no sense. They had shared in a few kisses, to be sure, but they were not courting. If he was betraying anyone, it was Lady Katherine, not Anna.

Nevertheless, the guilt remained. He prayed Anna would not make a sudden appearance and that the outing would be quick. Contrary to his words, he did not judge Markus. Many of his male relatives were unfaithful in their marriages. He did not understand such a decision, but neither did he judge it.

As Colin descended the staircase, he entered the foyer to a chorus of laughter. Two women, one a brunette and the other blonde, stood on either side of Markus. They wore fine dresses, and jewels glinted on their necks and fingers.

"There he is," Markus said when he caught sight of Colin. "My cousin, the duke. These are my friends. Lady Fanny Helton." The blonde woman dipped her head. "And her sister, Lady Deborah." The younger woman also acknowledged the introduction with a nod.

"Their father is the Earl of Pearson. I believe you're acquainted with him."

"I am," Colin replied. "I believe we met several years ago during a party of some sort."

Lady Helton smiled. "Father will be pleased to hear you remember him. I'll have to inform him once he returns from Dover."

Colin forced a smile. Was there anyone in all of England who would dress him down if he admitted to forgetting him or her? If so, he would see that person received an entire estate for showing a bit of honesty and backbone!

"Markus has spoken much about Your Grace," continued Lady Helton. "I must admit that my sister and I have looked forward to this outing."

Any belief that this outing had been planned to introduce Colin and Lady Deborah evaporated with the provocative looks Lady Helton gave Markus. Despite the fact they both wore wedding rings.

"Oh, yes," Lady Deborah said. Then she batted her eyelashes at Colin, and her cheeks turned pink. Perhaps that first belief was not gone altogether. "I've never met a duke before, Your Grace."

"Yes, yes, we're all excited that a duke is with us," Markus said in a bored tone. "Now, do you ladies need anything before we leave?"

When Colin glanced at Lady Deborah, he was startled by her admiring smile. He prayed Markus had not filled her head with any ideas.

"Now, we'll take a short stroll," Markus was explaining as he took a basket and a blanket from the butler. "But don't worry, it's not far, so you'll not dirty your slippers."

The sound of the ladies tittering at this grated on Colin's nerves.

The things I'm willing to do for my cousins will get the best of me one of these days!

***

Anna had awoken that morning to a thin ray of sunlight that glinted through a hole in the thatch. At least it was not the *plop* of water droplets on the covers that often woke her when it rained. Repairing the roof was one of the first things she would see completed once she returned from London.

She had not gotten much sleep but seeing Colin again had made the early rising well worth the lost hours. If she had to give up all her sleep to see him, she would.

The feel of Colin's lips on hers remained as she hurried to speak to Betty, who had been more than happy to agree to her plan. Now, all she had to do was convince Thomas.

Entering the cottage, she went straight to the kitchen. The boys were just rising, so she prepared them a breakfast of eggs and potatoes. Their finances determined whether there would be sausages or rashers, and as the money was scarce, they would have neither. Their next meal would not be until much later, leaving a long period without sustenance, but they had to save what little food they had. This left them with no midday meal nor the tiny sandwiches the rich enjoyed in the afternoon.

When she called that the food was ready, she leaned against the kitchen counter to watch as her brothers ate. Henry enjoyed whispering to his potatoes before stabbing them with a fork and eating them. Christian sat hunched over his plate, shoveling his food into his mouth without taking a single breath. To him, time was wasted on eating when he could be out working a horse.

Then there was Thomas, who sat with a week-old newspaper open in front of him as he sipped his tea, ignoring the food on his plate. Living in a house full of boys had never been easy, but Anna loved each of them as they were.

Well, she could think of at least a few things she would like to change about Thomas.

"Thomas," she said, "I went to Betty's to check on her aunt this morning." Her heart pounded in her chest. Oh, how she hated the lies! "Her health has taken a turn for the worse and Betty's asked if I can stay the week with her so I can help out at night. It's so difficult for her family to be up so late and then have to leave for work early the next morning."

Thomas heaved a heavy sigh from behind the week-old newspaper. Fearing he would deny her request, she quickly added, "Of course, they've agreed to pay extra for the time."

"Fine," Thomas grumbled. "Now, let me read in peace."

Anna let out a sigh of relief. He had bought the rather hastily put-together story far better than she had believed.

As the boys continued to eat, Anna thought about her journey to London the following day. She had been to Town only twice in her life, both times with her mother and only for a day. She recalled shops lined up by the dozens, women in dresses so luxurious that she felt smaller than any insect that crawled the pathways.

The streets had been lined with all sorts of carriages— white, black, brown, some with the curtains drawn closed, others open to allow everyone to see its occupants.

London offered many things, but Anna cared nothing for any of them. She would be there to finally meet her father.

Would he be as handsome as her mother had been beautiful? Would he be willing to allow her to meet her half-siblings? Would they accept her? Yes, of course they would. She was a likable person, and she certainly did not begrudge them the fact they had been able to have their father with them while she could not.

Closing her eyes, she imagined that meeting. He would be overjoyed with their encounter, embracing her tightly like a father welcoming his prodigal child. They would discuss their separate lives to ready the mutual path they would follow therein.

Once they had become acquainted, he would invite her to his home to meet and dine with her new siblings. There, she would hear more stories, of which she refused to be resentful. They were not at fault for their circumstances any more than she or Thomas were.

Nor were either of her parents. Events happened as they did. The past could not be changed, so there was no reason to lament what could have been.

After dinner, her father would ask if there was anything she wanted. Anything she needed. That would be when she would request money. Just a little to get the house in order. Enough to fix the roof and replace the broken windows. A possible business contract for Thomas. Their home would be safe and warm, and the quarrels over money would cease.

Lowering his newspaper, Thomas let out a heavy sigh. "Don't forget that you're to do the washing today before you leave for Betty's tomorrow. There's no need to forget your duties here while seeing to someone else's needs."

Christian snorted. "The basket's right there beside her. Are you going blind in your old age?"

Henry hid a laugh behind his hand but stopped when Thomas shot him a glare.

Anna grabbed the old wicker basket. "I'm wondering if I'll return only to find you all dead from starvation," she teased. "After all, it's quite clear none of you is capable of doing anything around here, including the cooking. Henry, I suggest you run away if you become hungry."

This had them all laughing. Well, except Thomas. His scowl said he was not pleased by her comment.

Once outside, she sighed. "Just one more week and I'll put everything to rights. None of us will go hungry again."

That was taking their situation a bit too far, for they had never truly starved. But they had been forced to skip one meal or another when the funds were low.

During one of those lean times, Christian had taken it upon himself to steal from one of the stands at the market in the village. Thomas had been furious, and an argument had erupted between the two brothers. Anna had sided with Thomas in that instance. There was never a reason to steal, not even in hunger.

As she walked down the path that led to the river, her thoughts turned to the journey she and Colin would be making tomorrow. Soon, she would meet her father, and it was all because of the man she had kissed the night before.

She still felt a bit of shame for her actions. What had she been thinking undressing in his presence and then joining him in the water? What kind of woman did that make her? Then again, Colin had done it first.

Approaching the woods, she came to a stop. Colin had been the first man she had kissed, but how many women had he kissed before her? The thought bothered her far more than she had expected it would, sending an uneasiness rushing through her body.

No, that was silly. Even if he had, it did not matter. He had kissed her, and she suspected he would do so again. And likely very soon.

For a moment, she imagined them walking together, Colin in his fine suit and she an equally fine dress purchased from the money her father would give her. It would be blue, for Colin had commented that he liked her in blue.

They would talk and laugh as they strolled, enjoying their time together. Then, they would come to a stop at the crest of a hill, where he would grab her and pull her against him. They would express their admiration for one another and finish with a kiss so enchanting, so wonderful, it would leave them breathless.

Sighing, Anna continued her walk. Was she deceiving herself by allowing her thoughts to create such images? That world could never exist outside of her mind. But had they not grown closer despite their short acquaintance? Had Colin not sworn to protect her?

And what about the jealousy he had exhibited when she merely mentioned another man propositioning her? Did that not all say there was a chance, as slim as it might be?

Chapter Sixteen

A number of clouds dotted the sky, but none seemed threatening. Hopefully, the good weather would persist into tomorrow, allowing Collin and Anna to travel without incident.

As Markus and Lady Helton walked ahead, Colin looked at the younger lady at his side. Should he warn her now that he had no interest in building a relationship with her?

No, raising such a subject would only cause issues with which he did not wish to contend. This was a simple outing and nothing more.

Lady Deborah came to a stop. "My apologies, Your Grace, but I cannot walk as quickly as my sister, not on such uneven ground. I'll find my way alone if you would like to remain with Fanny and Mr. Remington."

Colin held back a frown. The path was as smooth as the sheets on his bed. But some ladies were more delicate than others. "Here, take my arm."

Her cheeks went pink again. "Thank you, Your Grace. You're very kind."

They resumed their stroll, but at a much slower pace. It would take them an hour to reach the river at this rate!

"So, are your sister and my cousin well acquainted?" Colin asked.

Lady Deborah nodded. "For a number of years now. Five or more, I believe."

"And her husband does not mind their friendship?" Colin winced. It was not this young lady's duty to speak ill of the actions of her sister. For all he knew, Lady Deborah was like Colin— forced to be here. "My apologies. I did not mean to imply that anything improper is taking place between them."

"No need to apologize, Your Grace. My sister is often lonely with Richard away on business, sometimes for weeks at a time. I'm thankful she has a friend to keep her sadness at bay."

Colin gave the Lady Deborah a sideways glance. He could not decide if she was naive or playing innocent. "And are you not married?"

"Not yet, Your Grace. Father wishes me to attend the coming Season, so I can meet any potential suitors."

As they entered the woods, their conversation turned to other, rather mundane topics. When they reached the river, he could not keep back a sigh of relief that the river was devoid of any Silverstones. Markus had already spread out the blanket, and he was helping Lady Helton to sit.

Markus removed a bottle of wine from the basket. "This wine was procured from a vineyard in France of which I'm quite fond." He poured them each a glass. "Now, tell me that it is not the finest you've tasted."

Colin took a sip. "It's quite good," he said. "Opulent with just a hint of oak." He took another sip. "Interesting. The taste lingers just long enough to tempt you with another. Yes, quite good, indeed."

"Much like a kiss from a particular woman," Markus said.

Lady Helton giggled, and judging by the color in her cheeks, Colin knew who that particular woman likely was.

"I find it lovely, as well," Lady Deborah said. "I must be careful, however. I don't drink wine very often."

She took another sip and proceeded to bat her eyelashes at him, which only left Colin feeling awkward. The lady was clearly flirting with him. He would have to speak to Markus about this arrangement once they returned home. He would not embarrass the ladies by mentioning it now, but he wanted nothing to do with his cousin's dalliances.

Colin allowed the others to continue with idle conversation. Markus refilled their glasses several times, and the laughter became easier to all. It was not long before his cousin laid out the platter of cold meats and cheeses. By all appearances, it was a perfect setting.

Except Anna was not there to enjoy it.

Lady Deborah leaned in and whispered, "Your Grace, have I offended you in some way? You've been very quiet. I hope the wine has not loosened my tongue and thus made you angry."

"What?" Colin asked. "No, of course not."

The young lady shifted to move closer to him. He could not also move, for doing so in front of Markus would seem odd, but he had to keep her at bay somehow. "I was just thinking of my fiancée, Lady Katherine."

Lady Deborah's smile fell, but only for a moment. "I understood that you're not yet engaged, Your Grace." The woman was persistent, he would give her that.

"Not as of yet, no," he replied. "But I'm to propose soon."

Rather than repel her, Lady Deborah leaned in and whispered, "Markus says that you don't wish to marry. If you'd like to discuss this in private, I promise to keep any secrets you tell me. I'm sure I can come up with an excuse that will allow us to slip away alone."

How dare this woman be so bold! He should push her away from him!

But before he could, Markus bellowed, "Well, hello, Anna! Would you care to join us for a drink?"

Colin's heart leapt to his throat as he turned to find Anna standing on the opposite bank. She wore a simple dress, and her hair was tied back with a kerchief. On her hip was a basket of clothes.

Even from this distance, he saw the blush that crept into her cheeks. His worst fears had come true. Here he was, appearing to be enjoying himself in the company of another woman. It would be a wonder if she ever spoke to him again.

Rather than retreating, Anna raised her chin and walked to the river's edge. Removing a pair of trousers from the basket, she dipped them into the water."

"Is that one of your servants, Markus?" Lady Helton asked. "Why does she ignore you? That's quite rude of her."

Markus snorted. "She's not my servant, dear Fanny. Just a scorned lover."

Colin noticed Anna's lips thin, but she did not look up from her task.

Lady Helton clicked her tongue as she slapped Markus's arm. "Oh, come now. You're such a scoundrel!"

"I'm teasing," Markus said with a laugh. "Anna's nothing more than one of the poor wretches who plies her trade of washing the clothes of men during the day and entertaining them at night. It's quite a brilliant scheme if you ask me. She's devised two ways to earn money from the same man!"

"You mean she's a harlot?" Lady Helton asked with a gasp. "Remind me to stay away from the water. I'm sure she's dirtied it far too much for my delicate skin."

The sound of their laughter had Colin's blood boiling. How dare they speak of Anna in such a way! But if he defended her honor, it would only raise suspicion and have these women wagging their tongues for a year. Furthermore, Colin had no doubt his cousin would relay his attempt at gallantry to everyone he encountered.

"Anna!" Lady Helton called. "Will you clean my boots? I'm afraid I've muddied them.

Suddenly, Anna rose, threw the wet clothes into the basket, and marched away.

"Come back here, you worthless girl!" Lady Helton snapped.

This had the others roaring with laughter once more.

"Enough!" Colin growled as he leapt to his feet. "That woman did nothing to deserve such treatment. I refuse to witness such harassment any longer."

He turned to call after Anna, but she had already disappeared into the woods.

"You know," Markus said, "he's right. There's no need to step on the already downtrodden." He reached into his coat pocket and tossed a coin to Colin. "Why not go and make use of her services?"

"I'm returning to the house," Colin said through a clenched jaw as he tossed the coin back at Markus. "Good day to you."

"I only meant for her washing services," Markus called out after him, followed by another bout of laughter.

Storming through the woods, blood pounded behind Colin's ears. How had he allowed them to carry on as they did? And for so long? He should have spoken up sooner!

With a glance down at the ring on his finger, he realized why. Colin would have put a stop to such blatant disrespect far earlier, but the duke could not, lest he raise his cousin's suspicions.

Anna had been humiliated. And what had Colin done? Withdrawn and allowed the duke he had always been to emerge.

The very man he detested.

***

So lost in her thoughts was she, that Anna was startled at what she found upon exiting the woods beside the river. Across the way sat Colin, looking as handsome as ever in his dark coat. But it was the young lady who sat beside him, her lovely chestnut hair pulled up in an intricate coiffure and her wrap dropped into the crook of her elbows to reveal a deep neckline on her white dress. She was whispering something in his ear. Or was she kissing him? Would he kiss her back?

Anna's arms began to shake, and she gripped the basket tight against her hip to keep from dropping it. Thomas had warned her about titled men and their propensity to use women such as her for their own pleasure. Had Colin duped her? Did he see her as nothing more than an object of lust with which he could pass his time? She did not want to believe such a thing about him, but what she saw now made her question whether or not it could be true.

She went to turn to leave, but Master Remington called out to her. "Well, hello, Anna!"

Humiliation at their banter tightened her insides. A servant? How dare they call her a servant! And what did Markus mean by accusing her of having a tryst with the likes of him? Rage boiled inside her. Well, she would not allow the wealthy to ruin her day!

Holding her head high, she walked down to the riverbank. What others thought of her had never bothered her, so why should it now? She washed in the river every week, and these people— Colin included— would not stop her.

Six months earlier, she had come to the river to swim. Markus Remington had found her there and offered her twenty pounds for what he deemed as her "services". Anna, of course, had refused him, which had sent him into a fit of rage. The names he called her were worse than any she had ever heard from any man.

It was his accusations of how she made money that had her at the end of her tether. Stuffing the still-dripping clothes into the basket, she stood. Anger and shame coursed through her at their laughter. She had been humiliated and degraded before, but she had always endured the harsh words. She could not do so when it included Colin. Why had he done nothing to come to her defense?

Because he's a duke, that's why, she thought. He cannot admit that he's in any way acquainted with a woman of her low station.

"Anna!" one of the ladies called out to her when she reached the line of trees. "Will you clean my boots? I'm afraid I've muddied them."

Ignoring the taunt, Anna hurried her steps. The further away from the disgrace she could get, the better. Colin's voice rose behind her, but she could not make out what was said. Had he decided to join in with their mocking? Perhaps it was better she could not hear him.

Back at the cottage, she began hanging the wet laundry. Yanking a pair of trousers from the basket as if it were the cause of her anger, she threw it over the line that had been stretched from a corner of the cottage to one of the nearby trees. Not only was she angry about what had occurred, but now she was also unsure how she would make it to London. She certainly could not go with a man unwilling to champion her.

"Anna!" Christian called, "I'm going to take one of the mares out. Do you want to go with me?"

"No, thank you. I'll remain here." She had not meant for the words to be so harsh, but she could not help herself.

A shadow fell over her, and Christian placed a hand on her shoulder. "What's wrong? Thomas is surely ugly, but it's no reason to be so upset over it."

Letting out a choked laugh, Anna turned to face her brother. "It's nothing. I'm fine, really. Just a little dispirited is all."

"You're worried about London, huh?" Christian asked as he handed her one of the wet shirts. She had woken him the night before, too excited to keep such wonderful news to herself. "Well, I'm not worried, so you shouldn't be either. You're going to meet your father, and he's going to love you. How could he not? When you're done eating all that fancy food, you can come back here and share the wealth."

Anna could not help but smile at his wide grin. He was right. Her journey to London had nothing to do with her feelings for Colin. She was going to meet her father and find a way to improve the lives of her brothers. She had lost sight of that.

Drawing in a deep breath, she said, "You've become quite wise, did you know that? Yes, I'll succeed. And soon, everything will change."

Christian helped her hang the remaining clothes before leaving to train the mare. With the basket now empty, Anna looked over the tiny cottage. Come tomorrow, she would set out on a path that would change their lives forever. If Colin thought she would allow him to use her for his pleasure, he was mistaken.

He had his place, and she had hers. All he had offered her was protection for the time they were in London, not before nor after. No matter how much it hurt, she would allow him to help her and then they would go their separate ways.

Although she knew it was the right course of action, for some reason it left her with knots in her stomach. And in her heart.

Chapter Seventeen

Mary Ann, Duchess of Greystoke, read over the letter one more time. It had arrived the day before, and its message was simple. And infuriating. Colin wished to delay his return home. What matters of business could her son possibly have that would make him go to London on such short notice?

Colin had always been a well-behaved boy, one who listened to her wise counsel. Yet as he had grown into a man, her advice was no longer needed. Thus she felt useless, cast aside. But her worries for the dukedom remained. He had met with carefully selected women, whether for small excursions or afternoon tea.

By all appearances, he seemed pleased with the various ladies with whom he spent time. But once the topic of potential courtship arose, the excuses began. Either they were too plain or spent far too much time on their looks. They lacked the ability to hold a decent conversation, or they were far too talkative. Their fathers were a nuisance or lacked wealth. Never was he satisfied. Their fathers were a nuisance or lacked wealth. Never was he satisfied.

Folding the letter once more, she set it on the window ledge and peered out into the gardens, but the sight of her own reflection gave her pause. Although she had been told from a very young age that she possessed great beauty, she no longer saw it. Silver now invaded her once coal-black hair. Small lines in the corners of her eyes marred the otherwise smooth skin. If her beauty disappeared, what would she become?

"You must remain beautiful for as long as you can," her mother had advised as Mary Ann prepared for her wedding day. *"Once that is lost, you'll have nothing."*

To her mother, even a homely woman could have a title that brought her prestige and power, but handsomeness placed her above all others.

Pushing aside the thoughts, another beauty came to mind— Lady Katherine Haskett. Like herself, Lady Katherine waited for the engagement announcement. They had far too many preparations to wait much longer. There were cards to be sent to distinguished peers, parties to be planned, the reading of the banns, and finally, the wedding breakfast to celebrate the occasion. How could she possibly see it all finished in a timely manner if her son delayed with the proposal? Lady Katherine was quite a catch, which meant that if Colin waited too long, she might be caught by another, more attentive, fisherman.

Plus, Mary Ann had spent far too much time convincing Colin that Lady Katherine would make a perfect duchess. The last thing she wanted was to begin the process anew!

She nearly screamed when a face appeared in the reflection beside her own.

The devil himself had arrived.

"Mr. Keats, you startled me."

With silver hair and numerous pale scars on his face, Mr. Keats seemed older than time itself. She despised needing his assistance, but she had little choice. He had served various members of the Remington family over the years, acquiring rare items or gathering information unavailable through standard channels. If a price could be agreed upon, even a person could disappear.

Yet there were consequences to dealing with the devil, which was why she took great care on the few occasions that she had required his services.

"Your fear is not my problem," Mr. Keats said, his voice devoid of emotion.

Turning to face him, Mary Ann said, "What have you learned?"

"It appears that Markus has several mistresses, which I had already suspected. His actions as of late have made him more than one enemy. And your suspicions were correct, he's seeking a divorce. Who he plans to marry next, I was unable to determine."

Mary Ann frowned. The granting of a divorce would send shame rippling through the family.

As much as that worried her, however, she feared for his wife, Tabitha, a frail woman who flinched whenever a voice was raised above a whisper. And she knew why. It was difficult to say what Markus would do to Tabitha if the divorce was not granted, but there had already been enough funerals in the last year. They did not need another.

"Go to their home and speak to Tabitha. Relay to her what you've told me. I want her prepared for his desire to seek a divorce." She removed a bundle of notes from the bodice of her dress. "This should suffice."

"I've other matters to see to first."

"Mr. Keats," Mary Ann said firmly, "you'll go there immediately. You work for *me*. It would be wise you not forget that."

Mr. Keats brushed the sleeve of his dark coat. "You know very well that I keep my own schedule, Mary Ann."

The use of her given name was a means to provoke her, she was sure. Yet what could she do about it? He knew too many of her secrets and was far too valuable for her needs. So she said nothing.

He counted the notes she had given him and smiled. "But you've always paid me better than most," he continued, "so maybe I'll be inclined to hasten my journey. Is there anything else I can do for you?" His tone was mocking now. Oh, how she wished she could find someone else for these unpleasant tasks!

"No," she snapped. "Just see this completed as soon as possible."

She heaved a sigh of relief when the man was gone. Pushing him out of her mind, she returned her thoughts to Colin. He had been acting strangely as of late, and she had to puzzle out what was going on in his thoughts.

She was unsure how long she stood staring out the window, but the sound of the door opening made her turn.

"Your tea, Your Grace," the butler said as he placed a tray on the table and began to pour.

"Thank you, Pendleton." She walked over and sat on the sofa. "Pendleton? Has my son confided anything to you as of late? Something of which I should be aware?"

The butler pursed his lips. Why was he hesitant to speak? Well, Mary Ann had no patience for those in her employ keeping secrets from her.

"No, Your Grace, he has not."

Mary Ann sighed. Her husband had one particular reason to go away for several days at a time, especially to London. She had never been foolish enough to believe the man she married, the former Duke of Greystoke, had remained faithful. The Remington men had more mistresses than they had children. Although she did not wish such a life for her son, she would turn a blind eye if that was how he chose to live it with Lady Katherine.

"Surely he's mentioned a mistress? Or perhaps another woman who's caught his fancy?" She clicked her tongue in vexation and mumbled, "I see no other reason for him to rush to London when he is supposed to return here to propose to Lady Katherine."

A gasp made Mary Ann turn to find her future daughter-in-law standing at the doorway.

"Oh, Katherine, don't start with the dramatics," Mary Ann sighed. "We've already discussed this. You know perfectly well that men indulge themselves when the opportunity arises. We, as women, simply must accept that fact."

Lady Katherine was indeed a lovely young lady, the daughter of an earl who had trained since an early age to marry a man of Colin's rank. She spoke with grace, walked with elegance, and was trained to be a dutiful wife. All about her was perfect. Except for her naivety. And Mary Ann had grown tired of it more so over the last month.

"I recall such a conversation," Lady Katherine said as she walked over to sit in one of the beige chairs. "But I did not realize you meant the same for your son."

"Well, who else could I have meant?" Mary Ann asked with no care for her harsh tone. "Did you think I was confiding in you about the gardener? Or Pendleton, for that matter?" She returned her attention to the butler. "Now, Pendleton, I want you to think carefully. He must have said something before leaving for his cousins' home."

The old butler furrowed his brow.

Having had enough of the stupidity, she rose and walked over to him. "Come now, Pendleton," she said, placing a hand on his arm. "After all these years, you would not deny me what I must know, would you?"

"Never, Your Grace," he exclaimed. "It's just that I don't wish to upset you."

Mary Ann chuckled. "I'm the Duchess of Greystoke. Nothing can upset me. Now, tell me what you know."

Pendleton sighed. "He did happen to mention something about what it would be to live a commoner's life. He asked my opinion as to whether he could be a blacksmith or a cobbler. I refused to entertain such notions, Your Grace, I assure you. A Remington— nay, a duke!— living as a common man? It's absurd and outright bordering blasphemy to even consider such a thing!"

Mary Ann sighed. "Your loyalty to this family has been noted for many years. With a future daughter-in-law with few wits about her, and a son asking brainless questions, I'm thankful for the stability you bring. The sense of reason. So, thank you. You're excused."

Pendleton gave her one of his stiff bows and left the room.

Mary Ann turned her attention to Lady Katherine. The girl was staring at the rim of the cup in her hand.

"I will ask you a question," Mary Ann said, "and you are to answer truthfully. Three weeks ago, Colin took you on a carriage ride."

Lady Katherine nodded. "He did. It was a lovely outing."

"And what did you discuss?"

"We discussed the small farms he owns and other affairs pertaining to the estate."

Walking over to where the young lady sat, Mary Ann smiled. "And did anything happen?"

"Your Grace?" Lady Katherine gasped. "Please tell me you are not implying what I believe you are!"

Anger bubbled in Mary Ann. The girl was as thick as custard! "I'm not implying anything. I'm simply asking a question. Did anything happen between you two?"

"No, of course not. I had a chaperone with me. And I'm not—"

"Wise in the ways of men?" Mary Ann asked. "I can see that now. I knew you were naive, but to this extent shocks me. Your mother has not done her duty in training you properly." The girl's pained expression made Mary Ann roll her eyes. "Katherine, don't give me that look. The next time the opportunity presents itself, you must take advantage of the situation."

Lady Katherine's eyes nearly popped out of her face. "You wish me to—"

"Of course not, my dear. That's what harlots do, and you're no harlot. Simply allow him to kiss you, and then ask for another. He will only want you more if you do this." She tapped her lips with a finger. "Now to decide when. Yes, that's it. I'll plan a small gathering of friends once my son returns. This will give you the perfect opportunity to be caught in a compromising position. Colin will then be left with no choice but to propose marriage that very night."

Lady Katherine frowned in thought. "I'll do as you suggest. You'll find that I'm a woman of great dedication."

Mary Ann smiled. "You're very much like me, my dear. A very beautiful woman. That is who you are and who you'll ever be. Do you understand?" Lady Katherine nodded. "Good. We must work together to see my son fulfills his duty by marrying you. I'll do what is necessary to see the opportunity created. If you play your cards right, you'll have him caught in your net." She turned a stern gaze on the young lady. "Let me make myself perfectly clear. If you're unwilling to do your part, you'll not be invited to return again, and I'll find a woman who is willing to do as she's told."

With a determined look on her face, Lady Katherine replied, "I understand. I'll do whatever it takes."

Mary Ann nodded and brought her teacup to her lips, her thoughts on Colin's sudden journey to London. Had he truly become his father? The first time she learned of the reasons for her husband's journeys— of his sordid affairs— it had hurt deeply. She had cried herself to sleep and woke feeling numb and asking, "Am I not pretty enough?"

It was not long, however, before she came to understand that men such as the Remingtons were allowed their fleshly desires. The pain from that first night reared its head from time to time, but she had hidden it from everyone. In return for being an obedient wife, she had been given a healthy allowance, fine jewels, and wonderful country estates in which to spend her days as she pleased.

Yet all that paled in comparison to the looks of admiration she received from everyone she encountered— rich and poor alike. And who could blame them? She was a duchess and had married a Remington. Her life as a duchess had been well worth what she had been forced to give up. As the future dowager, her life would go in a different direction, and she had to prepare herself for the inevitable.

The door opened, and Pendleton entered. "Evan, Lord Westlake, Your Grace."

Mary Ann gave a single nod, and Evan entered. The young man had broad muscles and unruly blond hair, a true Remington in looks and intellect. He was the epitome of the Remington name.

It was no secret that many articles in the gossip columns of London spoke of him. He had a mind as sharp as a sword, a tongue doubly so, and whatever his eyes fell on, he took it for his own, always to increase the Remington fortune.

Although he had gone so far as to step on a few of the lower Remingtons to get where he was today, he had never used or mistreated Colin. Nor Mary Ann. Which was why Colin trusted him. And why Mary Ann had sent for him the day before.

"Dear Cousin Mary Ann," Evan said. "Your letter sounded quite urgent. My apologies for not being able to come sooner, but I'm afraid I've been a bit... preoccupied with other matters."

His eyes fell on Lady Katherine, raking over her in a way he might not have done in Colin's presence. If she left him alone with Colin's betrothed, Mary Ann worried the man would have her in a bed within the hour. Engaged or not.

"I'm grateful you came," Mary Ann said, directing him to an extra chair. "Pendleton, bring us more tea, please." Once the butler was gone, she turned to Evan. "I've come to learn that Colin has been acting oddly. Apparently, he's been speaking of living another life as a cobbler, or other such nonsense."

Evan laughed as he unbuttoned his coat. "Truly? Has he been drinking too much? It is a family trait, after all."

"No," Mary Ann replied. "He's been delaying the announcement of his engagement to Lady Katherine, and now he's set off for London for no apparent reason. I've got my suspicions, of course, but I cannot be certain."

Pendleton returned with a new tea tray, removing the old when he left.

"Has Lady Katherine offended him in some way?" Evan asked. "I mean no offense, but these things do happen."

Mary Ann went to reply, but then Lady Katherine said, "I may have upset him the day he left for Wilkworth." She turned to Mary Ann. "I'm sorry, but I didn't think to mention it until now."

Could all of this have been avoided? Lady Katherine was beautiful, but she was not very intelligent. "It's too late for apologies," Mary Ann snapped. "Now, out with it. What did you do to upset my son?"

"He asked me to address him informally, and I told him I would if he required me to do so."

Mary Ann clicked her tongue in exasperation. "That's it? Good heavens, I thought you had something worthwhile to say. Don't interrupt us again with such nonsense."

The girl nodded as tears welled in her eyes. Not this again! Mary Ann rose and pulled the bell cord. When Pendleton entered, she said,

"Please escort Lady Katherine to her room. I believe she needs to rest." She wished she had not invited the girl to stay while Colin was away!

"Of course, Your Grace," Pendleton replied. "This way, my lady."

Waiting until she and Evan were alone, Mary Ann turned to Evan and said, "Something is amiss with my son, but I'm not certain what it is. I would like you to help me in this matter. Will you be willing to go to London?"

"To spy on my cousin?" he asked in mock affront. "Why, Mary Ann, I don't know if I'm capable of such underhandedness."

Evan might not have ever chosen to deceive her or Colin, but that did not mean he would not. Flattery would get her nowhere, so Mary Ann chose something far more useful— a bribe.

"Lady Katherine has a sister, two years younger than she. If you help me, I'll arrange for you to meet her."

A sly grin crossed his lips. "You mean to cast off her sister? What sort of disfigurement does she have?"

"None at all. One would believe they are twins." The idea of throwing the lovely younger sister of Lady Katherine to this wolf sickened her, but her son's future was at stake.

"I admit that I'm intrigued," Evan said. "What is it I'm to do exactly?"

"Find him," Mary Ann replied. "I'm sure he'll be staying at his estate there. Learn what you can about this nonsense about wanting to work as a cobbler. And also learn why he keeps delaying this engagement. He trusts you, so use that. This will ease my worries."

"Your timing is impeccable, as always. I already planned to journey to London this week. An old baron is hosting a party on Friday, and I've been invited. I'll ask Colin if he would like to go, as well, which will be the perfect opportunity to find out what he's up to."

Mary Ann sighed with relief. The idea of her son laboring in any position would shame the Remington name for a thousand years! "Thank you. I do hope it's nothing more than just frightful imagination running amok. I fear what will happen if he does something foolish."

"Oh, Cousin Mary Ann," Evan said as he rose and walked to the door, "we are Remingtons and therefore must watch out for one another. And I know that in the future, if I ever am in need of your help, you'll heed my call. Am I right in my assumption?"

"Do you mean with Lady Katherine's sister?"

Evan chuckled. "Oh, she's only a deposit and nothing more. There may come a time when I must collect in full for this favor."

If that was what it took to see Colin back on the path he should be on, Mary Ann had no choice and thus gave a nod.

With a half-smile, Evan walked out of the room.

Mary Ann returned to her tea. Whatever her son was doing, she would know soon enough. And if it was anything that could harm him, the dukedom, or the Remington name, she would see it stopped.

Whether Colin agreed or not.

Chapter Eighteen

Although the events of two days earlier still pained Anna, she pushed them aside to allow a sense of excitement about her journey to take over as she made her way to meet Colin. She owned no luggage or bags, so what meager items she brought with her she had placed into a bundle, tying the corners of the fabric to keep it all together. She had never been embarrassed by what she did not have, and she would never allow herself to be so now.

As she crossed the fallen tree, a new thought came to mind. What if Colin already left? Could the women who he had been with yesterday have enticed him away? That concerned her far more than if he had simply gone without her.

Well, worrying before one knew the truth never got anyone anything but a sour stomach.

Ignoring the path she typically took to work— the one that led to the river— she followed a separate, less-used trail that snaked through a large field and came out at the front of Redstone Estate.

Two black carriages sat in front of the house, each with its own driver. Colin paced back and forth in front of one, his hands clasped behind his back and mumbling to himself.

As if he should be the one perturbed, she thought with annoyance. It was not he who caught her with a man whispering honeyed words in her ear!

Regardless, she needed him if she was to meet her father. She despised the idea of using him in such a way, but he clearly wanted to lend his aid despite the fact he had no romantic interest in her. Not anything lasting. Which was perfectly fine. Falling in love with a titled man only to be left alone with two children as her mother had was not the future she wanted.

The Duke Who Loved Me

Colin looked up as she approached. "Oh, Anna, I'm so glad to see you. I cannot tell you how sorry I am about yesterday. If you'll just give me a few moments before we leave, I can explain."

"There is no need, Your Grace." He winced at her formal address, but she ignored it. This was all for the best, anyway. "You're a duke. Who am I to think you'll not be spending time with your kind?"

An image of the lady leaning in to whisper in Colin's ear came to mind. Oh, how she would enjoy teaching that chit a lesson if their paths crossed!

Then she shook her head. No, she was the one learning a lesson here. She was not foolish enough to believe that he would fall in love with her and then propose marriage. Dukes simply did not marry women like her. And what kind of duchess would she be?

One who would be mocked by Colin's friends, that's who. At least she finally had her head out of the clouds and her feet firmly planted on the ground.

"If you're still willing to take me to London, your carriage is most welcome. I have no money at the moment, but if you're willing to accept payments, I'll send you a set amount on a monthly basis until it's repaid. With interest, of course. I don't accept charity."

Her breath caught when he took her hands in his. But he wore such a contrite look, she did not pull away.

"Please, listen," he insisted. "Markus arranged that outing without my knowledge. I didn't know about it until he introduced the ladies, and by then, I could not simply decline without being rude. Have no doubt, I did have words with him about his behavior and went to call after you, but you were already gone."

Anna considered his words. She did recall hearing his voice.

Then she glanced down as Colin gave her hand a gentle squeeze. "That will never happen again," he said.

Many men had promised Anna the stars and moon for a chance to call on her. Every time, she could hear the insincerity in their words. Yet, as she looked into Colin's eyes, she could see he was different.

She believed him. Why, she did not know, but there it was. Her anger and sadness dissipated, and a certain calm replaced them. Her worry over the last days had been for nothing. Colin did care and that was enough for her.

With her hand still in his, she said, "Thank you for coming to my defense."

"I always will," Colin said. "Now, we should go before it gets too late." He took her bundle and led her to one of the carriages. "You'll be taken straight to your hotel. I'll be staying in my London home. I say we meet for dinner." He explained their plans for the day ahead.

When he was finished, Anna went to speak, but Miss Caroline approached them.

"Colin, will you excuse us? I wish to speak to Miss Anna for a moment."

He frowned. "But we really should be on our way—"

"What I wish to discuss are matters of a feminine nature," Caroline retorted. "If you wish to hear what I have to say, then by all means, remain."

His wide eyes and clearing of his throat said it all. "I'll be in my carriage." He placed her bundle in the vehicle assigned to her before stepping into his.

"You do have a fine way with words, Miss Caroline," Anna said with a light laugh. "So? What did you want to discuss?"

Miss Caroline took her by the arm and walked several paces away from the vehicles. "I simply wanted to tell you how pleased I am."

"Pleased? And why is that?"

"Last night, I saw a rare side of Colin. I doubt I've ever seen him so angry, and the fact his anger was directed toward my brother only made it all the more exciting."

"Oh?" Anna asked. Miss Caroline had not been at the river, so how did she know?

"Indeed. I came home Sunday afternoon to find Colin and Markus shouting at one another. Apparently, Markus said something quite terrible about you, and Colin defended your honor!"

Anna had to suppress a smile. "Did he tell Master Markus that we've been spending time together?"

"Well, no," Miss Caroline admitted. "He just said that no woman should be treated as you were. It was all very chivalrous. I thought for sure Colin was going to strike Markus!" Her gaze dropped. "I heard what my brother said. I want you to know that not all of us believe as he does. He's a simpleton with too little sense. And he's a man." She grinned at this. "I wish you could have seen it! Colin defended you with such passion, I'd say he's a bit enamored with you. Even if he denies it!"

Anna was stunned. Colin had said his cousin's words had angered him, but he never mentioned how close to violence he had become! "I appreciate you saying so."

"Well, it's true," Miss Caroline said. "Now, regarding this journey to London. Colin refuses to tell me why you two are leaving. I don't suppose you'll tell me, either."

"I'm afraid I can't," Anna replied. "I don't want you to think it's because I don't trust you, but it's a personal matter that I'd rather wait to reveal. I hope you understand."

Miss Caroline patted Anna's arm. "You have the right to your privacy as much as anyone," she said with a smile. "I'm not sure what I should think about you traveling alone to London with any man, even if he is my cousin, but at least he's thought far enough ahead to see you have your own carriage. I do hope whatever business you have in London works out as you hope. But keep an eye on my cousin. I would hate to hear he got himself into some sort of mischief."

Anna could not help but laugh. Colin and mischief were certainly not two words she would pair together. "I'm sure he's quite capable of taking care of himself, Miss Caroline. But if it makes you feel better, I'll do what I can to keep him out of trouble."

Bidding Miss Caroline farewell, Anna approached her carriage. Riding atop a coach during her two journeys to London with her mother had been far from enjoyable, and Thomas's cart was no match for the luxury of this carriage. The cushions on the benches were comfortable enough she would have preferred them to the straw mattress on her bed!

Colin poked his head through the door. "This is it, Anna. Are you excited?"

"I am," she replied as she ran a hand across the velvet fabric. "I can't believe that today has finally arrived. I've waited for it for so long."

"I'll see you tonight," Colin said before moving to close the door.

"Colin, wait."

He leaned back inside. "Yes?"

Anna studied his handsome face. Surely there was no kinder man in all of England! "Thank you again for helping me."

That familiar smile came to his lips. "You're more than welcome, my dear Anna. If anyone deserves to see her dreams come true, it's you."

When he closed the door, she leaned back into the seat. His dear Anna? Now, that had a marvelous note to it.

Oh, she had no delusions of fancy. Crossing societal lines were almost unheard of. But if they remained friends through it all, she could accept that. She would not be added to any guest lists for parties, nor did she expect it. But if he saw her as a woman before he saw her as poor, she would be happy.

The carriage moved forward, and she sighed with pleasure. If she were in Thomas's rickety cart, her bottom would have already been sore from the hard wooden bench. How often had she returned home with aching arms from the tight grip she had to keep so as not to be tossed from the seat? All too many.

When the carriage reached the main road that led to London, her thoughts turned to her father. How many carriages did he own? Would he offer her one for her return journey? Yes, she would think so. What man would wish to see his daughter suffer any more than she already had in life?

Once he learned of her troubles, he would do the right thing. She was certain of it. Perhaps he would even join her for the journey home.

She could not help but laugh as an image of Thomas appeared in her mind. How surprised he would be! Then their father and he would talk as men did, allowing Thomas to put aside his animosity and opening up the opportunity to build what they had missed for far too long.

Amid these thoughts, another came to mind, one that excited Anna so much that her skin pebbled. Once she and her father were reunited, proof of her bloodline would be established. In time, she would adapt to the ways of the *ton*. People like Markus would no longer look down on her.

But more importantly, gentlemen would no longer be afraid of being seen in her company. Colin would not need to hire a second carriage. Oh, he said he did so to save her honor or some other sort of rubbish, but she could see the truth. She could not blame him. Even with a chaperone, dukes simply did not ride alone in private carriages with unmarried women. And certainly not those from the working class. Not without fear of repercussion.

Indeed, it would be she and not Lady Deborah who would be at his side. The fact was, he would have no reason not to ask to court her.

That had her swooning more than the sudden rut they hit on the road. With the money her father would give her, she could purchase a new dress. Nothing too expensive, of course, for the repairs on the cottage had to come first. But to go to a seamstress and have a dress made for her would be a far cry from the uneven stitches she created.

Yes, a lovely blue dress that would make Colin fumble his words. With such a dress, and her newly established family, Anna would no longer be seen as less than who she truly was.

As the minutes became hours, Anna watched the changing sea of landscape. Thick forests became rolling hills. Tiny villages became small, which became larger, and several hours later, they arrived in London

Despite the fact she had been to Town in the past, Anna could not stop herself from gawking. She had forgotten how crowded London was, how busy. There seemed to be more shops, more people, than before. The buildings bore down on her like a dense forest with thick underbrush. The air was thick with soot, making her cough. But the excitement remained, for this was London!

The carriage came to a stop in front of a brown brick building with a sign above the door that said, "Fairweather Inn." She had to rein in her desire to leap out of the carriage.

"May I assist you with your things, Miss?" the driver asked with a glance at her bundle.

"No, thank you," she replied.

The man frowned but then nodded before closing the carriage door.

Once inside, Anna studied the place that would be her home for the next couple of days with a sense of excitement. It was a modest inn with a simple counter, a handful of chairs, and not much else, but it was absolutely fantastic! The carpet that ran from the door to the counter was free of stains, and although there was a bit of dust on the windows, light shined through.

The clerk smiled at her as she approached. "Good afternoon and welcome to the Fairweather Inn," he said. "I'm Gregory Thompson. Will you be needing a room?"

"Yes, please. I believe one has already been reserved in the name of Anna Silverstone."

Mr. Thompson opened a ledger and ran a finger down a list of names. "Oh, yes, here we are. It's reserved for a week, paid for in advance by the..." His brow knitted. "The Periwinkle Family? I've never heard of them."

"Yes, well, you likely would not. The baron is newly titled. I'm here to supervise the cleaning of various properties belonging to the family, and he was kind enough to put me up here until I've completed my work."

"Must be some housekeeper," the clerk mumbled as he reached for a key from the many that hung on a pegboard behind him. "The room's down the hall. Number fourteen. The tavern and the kitchen are both closed for the rest of the week. There was a fire last month, and they're finishing up the last of the remodeling. But there are several restaurants nearby where you can be served a decent meal."

"I appreciate you saying so," Anna replied.

She walked down the corridor the clerk had indicated and soon found herself outside of room fourteen. The sense of anticipation grew as she put the key in the lock. An inn! She was staying at an inn. In London! How wonderful it was to be on such an adventure!

When she stepped into the room, she glanced up at the ceiling. No cracks that would have water dripping on her in the middle of the night. The furnishings were modest— a simple bed, a single chair beside a small round table, a stand that held a bowl and pitcher. But the covers appeared to be clean and without holes. The chair was sturdy despite not having a cushion. And the table did not wobble although it did have several scratches on its surface.

Several pegs on the wall allowed her a place to hang the dress and extra shift she had brought with her. She placed the hairbrush beside the pitcher and draped her nightgown over the back of the chair. It really was a very nice room. Hopefully Betty would not become jealous when she told her about it!

Colin was not to come for her for another three hours, so she removed her shoes and stretched out across the bed. Soon, her eyelids began to flutter.

With the little sleep the night before, it was not long before she fell asleep, dreaming of the blue dress she would purchase with the money her father gave her. The dress in which Colin would be able to accept her. The dress in which all of her dreams would be realized.

Chapter Nineteen

Colin had not been to his estate in Mayfair for nearly a year. Standing before it now, he wondered for the first time if it appealed to him any longer.

There was nothing wrong with the building itself, for the red brick that made up its facade was appealing to the eye. Wrought-iron fences created a sense of privacy, separating the footpath from the front windows and keeping anyone who had no business at the home from entering the lower level. With Regent Street to the east and Park Lane to the west, the area was the most exclusive in London.

What troubled Colin, however, was who he had to be while here. He was expected to conduct himself in a certain way, to interact with particular people, to be someone he truly was not.

Yet this week would be different. He had informed no one of his arrival— besides his resident butler, of course— and, therefore, could hope for neither callers nor invitations. If the servants kept a watch on their wagging tongues, that is.

Dismissing the driver, Colin walked to the front door. It opened immediately to Harper.

"Welcome, Your Grace," the butler said as he took the bag from Colin.

"Thank you, Harper," Colin said as he stepped into the foyer. It was strange, but he found himself re-evaluating everything he owned. That blue and gold Meissen porcelain vase could have fed Anna's family for a year. The floral Dutch painting would have seen them all clothed in the finest fabrics. He sighed. "Any news since my last visit?"

"As a matter of fact, a letter arrived for you just ten minutes ago," Harper replied. "From your cousin. He delivered it himself, Your Grace. Apparently it's an urgent matter."

Colin laughed. "My cousin? Harper, you do realize that I have a number of cousins. Which one precisely was it?"

"Of course, Your Grace. It was Lord Evan." He walked over to a side table and retrieved the letter. "Your letter, Your Grace. Shall I see tea brought up to you in your study?"

"Yes. And the library will be fine," Colin replied.

The room was not as large as the library in his country estate, but it held nearly a thousand books. Sitting in a green leather chair, Colin crossed one leg over the other and stared at the correspondence in his hand. What could Evan want? And how had he known that Colin would be in London?

Opening the letter, he began to read:

Dear Cousin Colin,

I'm not sure what has taken you to London, but I was summoned by your mother, who is deeply concerned for your wellbeing. Although I imagine we have much to discuss, I don't feel comfortable doing so in writing for fear it will fall into the wrong hands. Alan, Lord Dundwhich, is hosting a party at his London home on Saturday Evening. I think it would be wise if we met there so we can speak, perhaps around seven?

Until then,
Evan Westlake

Folding the letter, Colin sighed. How could a single journey to London arouse his mother's suspicions? No, he knew very well what concerned her. And it was not him. He had delayed the announcement of his engagement to Lady Katherine for far too long. And his mother had never been a patient woman when it came to matters of the dukedom. To her, every word spoken, every plan developed, had a reason. There was no time for spontaneous decisions.

His curiosity grew concerning his cousin. Evan had never mistreated Colin, but he had been suspected several times of swindling others, including members of his own family.

Although Colin would have preferred to spend all his time with Anna, a short meeting with Evan would do no harm. Perhaps his cousin could give him advice on his current situation. After all, he was two years older than Colin and had been able to steer clear of speaking any wedding vows as of yet. It was not as if the expectations of a baron were all that different from a duke.

Harper arrived with the tea tray, poured a cup for Colin, and then left the room with a bow. As Colin sipped at his tea, he considered his current predicament. Even if he could continue to delay the engagement, what then? Eventually, he had to marry.

An image of Anna came to mind. How unfair it was that they could not be together. Yet, proposing marriage to her would shame his position, his mother, his family, and he could not do that. Not to mention what it would do to Anna. She had no formal training, no idea what the life of a duchess would entail. Thrusting her into such a world would be unfair.

If the situation changed, if expectations allowed and lessons could be put into place, he would marry her tomorrow. But life was what it was, and he saw no way around it. Why torment himself with what was forbidden to him?

His mind returned to this morning and the guilt that had plagued him from the previous day. He was pleased that Anna had forgiven him, for the pain in her eyes had been strong. Markus had no right to say what he did. The dresses she wore were made of cheap fabric and she worked in a workhouse, but that did not make her less of a person. To him, those who labored had a reason for pride, for they earned what they had. Men such as he and Markus never had to strain a muscle, for everything was done for them.

Rising, he made his way to his study. At his desk, he took a sheet of parchment and began his reply to Evan. When he was finished, he set it aside to allow the ink to dry and started a new correspondence.

This was addressed to the Earl of Leedon, the man Anna believed to be her father.

Colin paused. What was he getting himself into? How did one write to an earl about a woman who claimed to be his daughter? Had he gotten himself mired into muck from which he would struggle to free himself?

Anna had no understanding of how bloodlines worked. Many titled men had fathered children out of wedlock, and some acknowledged those offspring. If the truth were revealed, his family would be the topic of conversation at every salon and behind every fan.

Until the next scandal took its place.

But when Anna had spoken of the man, of what it would be like to meet him, Colin could not bring himself to contradict her. Perhaps not being forthright was unfair to her, but keeping the truth from her had allowed her to have her dreams. Her eyes had been so alight with hope, he could not be the one to bring the darkness to cloud them.

Then an idea came to mind. He could tell Anna he had sent the letter and that the man ever replied. Or that Leedon was away for business and was unreachable.

He shook his head. No, it was one thing to keep the truth that would shatter her dreams and quite another to outright lie so she never learned the truth.

Letting out a frustrated sigh, he began to write:

Dear Leedon,

I am writing to you today because I have a friend, Miss Anna Silverstone by name, who has a tale you may find of interest. I would call on your good graces to allow her a few moments of your time. Though you may not know her, from my understanding, you may have once been acquainted with her mother.

I am in London until Monday next, so please reply with an appropriate time for the two of you to meet. I'll consider this a personal favor, and, in return, we may discuss fully the hotel venture you mentioned to me the last time we saw one another.

Sincerely,
Greystoke

Colin had no interest in purchasing any hotels, but if it meant scheduling a time for Anna and Leedon to meet, so be it.

Once the ink was dry, he folded and applied his seal. He glanced at the mantel clock.

"Five to four?" he gasped. He was to meet Anna in an hour. Where had the time gone?

Taking the letters, he searched out Harper, who was in the dining room polishing the silver. He rose when Colin entered.

"Harper," Colin said as he placed the letters on the table. "I would like you to see these delivered today. I won't be here for dinner, so please inform the cook. And remember, I want no one to know I'm here, so please see the staff keeps a guard on their tongues."

"Yes, Your Grace," the butler replied with a bow.

"Thank you."

Colin returned to his rooms and removed the clothes Anna had given him. He was amazed at Anna's brilliant idea. The clothes would be perfect for getting lost in the crowds.

Once he was changed, he surveyed himself in the mirror. How did people wear such fabrics? The twill brown cap fit well enough, as did the shirt, but the coat was a tad tight across the back. It felt strange to leave it unbuttoned, but otherwise it would pull across his shoulders. The trousers had an array of patches in various places. He prayed the fabric would hold.

Then he looked at the ring on his finger. He was a duke, not some gardener or laborer. His week at Redstone Estate would pale in comparison to what he planned to do this week. The risk could be costly, but the reward was far greater. It was time he learned who Colin truly was. Or rather who he was not.

Removing the ring, he set it on the dressing table. Despite the nakedness he felt, he turned his back on the ruby to consider a problem he had not foreseen.

How would he get to the hotel where Anna was staying without drawing suspicion? Simply leaving the house was a risk in itself, let alone traveling across Town.

Drat his senselessness! If he were a commoner like Anna, he would have stayed at her inn and bypassed all this. Then an idea came to him. He barked a laugh and headed downstairs. Harper walked into the foyer just as Colin reached the bottom of the stairs.

"Your Grace?" the butler asked, unable to hide his shock. "Is... is everything all right?"

"Indeed it is," Colin replied. "You're not to repeat what I'm about to tell you. No one, not even the duchess, can know of this." Harper nodded. "I've taken on a small part in a play!"

The butler's eyes nearly covered his face, but then he smiled. "Your secret is safe with me, Your Grace. And may I say how daring it is of you to do something so bold? Shall I arrange to have the carriage brought around?"

"That won't be necessary," Colin replied. "If I'm to get a sense for this role I'm to play, I believe I should walk."

"Very good, Your Grace." The butler gave him a bow. "Truly there is none like you, Your Grace."

"I've been told that, Harper," Colin said with a laugh.

Rather than going out the front door like a duke, he left through the servant's entrance and was pleasantly surprised when no one gave him a second glance. He pulled down the hat to further hide his features and began to walk. With each step, the stress of the dukedom fell away, and the happiness of being Colin replaced it.

Chapter Twenty

A rumbling woke Anna with a start. Was the building shaking? Sitting up in bed, she rubbed her eyes as she wondered where she was. Then she recalled she was in London.

Then the sound came again. It was a knock on the door.

She hurried over and answered it. "Colin?" she asked in amazement. Although she had given him the clothes he wore, it took her a moment to realize who he was.

"These clothes are magical!" he said as he stepped into the room without invitation. "Not even you recognized me! Not a single person took any notice of me. I even passed a gentleman with whom I'm acquainted, and he turned his nose up at me! Can you believe it?"

"I most certainly can," Anna replied, smiling. The masculine display before her had been well deserved for her efforts. Everything fit him quite well. The trousers were snug and showed off a well-turned calf, and the coat allowed for a better view of his wonderful form. Likely, he thought it too tight, but she did not. Not at all.

"I'm afraid I just woke from a nap," she said. "Did you get the opportunity to sleep?"

"No, there was no time. But I did write a letter to the Earl of Leedon. I should expect to hear a reply in a couple of days."

Without thinking, Anna threw her arms around Colin's neck. "Oh, thank you! To think that my father will be reading your letter before the sun sets!" She kissed his cheek and took a step back to assess him once more. "I cannot believe how different you look."

Colin turned about. "I think I look rather handsome. And the cap suits me well. The clothes could use a bit of letting out, however. Do you think I should find something else that fits better?"

Anna shook her head. "No, you can't!" she found herself blurting. She liked the idea of seeing his muscular form so well. When Colin tilted his head and frowned, she added, "What I mean is that this is the style of the working class. No one will believe you are other than who you seem to appear."

That seemed to appease him. "I think you'll be happy to know that I'll be staying in the next room."

"Here?" Anna asked, shocked. "You're staying here for the night? I thought you had a house here."

Colin grasped her by the waist, and the familiar heat coursed through her body. "Not just tonight. Tomorrow night, too. In fact, I'll be staying here the entire week! So, what shall we do first? I would like to go out and explore London as Colin."

Anna was pleased with his sense of adventure. He reminded her of Henry when they planned a day out in the forest. "I suppose the first thing we should do is leave." She glanced down. "Unless you wish to kiss me, then remain holding me instead."

"Must you tempt me with such a decision?" he asked, grinning. "Both would please me greatly, and thus I can't decide which I would prefer."

Anna's breath came in short gasps. "Then why not do both?"

Colin honored her request, and they shared in a short yet powerful kiss. Once it ended, he took a step back.

She smiled. "Now that the matter's been settled, we should go. Have you not heard it's improper to be alone with a woman? And in her room of all places! Even those of the working class have their standards."

Laughing, Colin opened the door and allowed her to leave first.

They made their way past the empty counter. "I know this week is meant for you," Colin said. "But I cannot help but feel happy for myself, as well."

Anna stopped and turned to face him. "You have every right to be happy, Colin. This is our week, not just mine. Both of us are meant to seek out our dreams."

He puckered his lips in thought. "You know what? You're right. And we shall both realize them, won't we?"

"Indeed." For a moment Anna wondered if there was not a dream that they could both possibly share...

Colin looked first left and then right. "I say we go. I would hate for my stomach to rumble and draw unwanted attention."

She studied him for a moment. "There's one more thing." She walked over to a nearby flower pot, took out a handful of dirt, and rubbed her hands together. "You're far too clean to be a laborer." She placed the palms of her hands on his cheeks and finished with a finger alongside his nose. "There. Now you look proper."

Colin laughed as he peered into the bubbled glass of a nearby window. "Oh, yes, that is much better."

They made their way down the narrow lane and out to a busier street. The foot traffic had eased but some were still making last-minute purchases before the shops closed. A lone carriage ambled past them, a dog chasing after it.

Ten minutes later, they crossed over to another street. "There's a tavern up ahead," Colin said. "Should we see if they serve food?"

Anna went to reply that they should, but the door flew open, and a man came stumbling out. Behind him stood a large man with beefy arms and a red face. "Ye come back tonight an' I'll give ya a proper wallopin', ye 'ear?"

The patron pulled himself from the ground and swiped at his trousers. "Come'n fight me like a man!"

The larger man took a step forward, and the drunk turned and ran.

"How amazing," Colin said. "A proper argument in a tavern. I've never actually witnessed a man being thrown out before, but I've heard about it."

Anna understood that Colin wanted to experience the life of the lower class, but this would likely be far more than he could have handled.

"If you want my opinion, I say we stay away from there," Anna said when he started toward the pub. "It's your decision, but don't you think a tavern with the name 'The Polite Highwayman' may be a bad omen for trouble? Plus, we've just seen a patron bodily removed from the premises."

"This is exactly what I need," Colin replied. Then he turned to Anna. "You don't mind, do you?"

She laughed. "Not at all. As long as you don't mind."

He straightened his shoulders and drew in a deep breath. "Have you any advice for me before we enter? I don't wish to give away that I'm not one of them."

Anna took a moment to consider this. "First, if anyone asks, you work as a gardener. No one discusses the latest trees or what types of plants they tend. Oh, and don't make any mention of the *ton* or how you lost your coat to me. If you adhere to that, you'll earn their respect soon enough."

"Good advice," Colin replied. "This will be quite an experience."

"I imagine it will be," Anna said, hiding a laugh.

They pushed through the red double doors. The tavern was dark from the haze of smoke and the minimal light that filtered through the dirt-encrusted windows. A dozen or so men sat scattered among the line of tables along one wall, and three men sat at a polished bartop on the other. Two barmaids wiped off empty tables, and the beefy man they had seen from outside had joined a group of three others. All were men of the working class. No gentleman would likely enter today. Or any day, for that matter.

As they approached the bar, the first thing Anna noticed was the barkeep's bloodshot eyes. The second was the stench of liquor on his breath.

"What do ya want?"

"A claret sounds lovely," Colin said.

The barkeep squinted. "Come again?"

Anna let out a nervous laugh. "My friend's just teasing. Two ales, please." When the barkeep left, she turned to Colin, who wore a frown. "Cheer up. You did nothing wrong."

"What was I thinking?" he asked. "Perhaps when we order our food, I should leave it up to you. I don't want to start a riot."

When the drinks arrived and Colin had paid, Anna led them to a table near the front windows. Two men close to Anna's age sat three tables away, and one of them seemed to have taken an interest in her, for he had yet to drop his gaze. She would have to keep an eye on that one.

As they sat, Anna glanced at Colin and could not help but laugh. "You seem to be enjoying yourself," she said. "Is this everything you wanted?"

He grinned at her. "Oh, it is and more!" he replied. "My chair wobbles." He moved it back and forth to demonstrate. "As does the table." Ale splashed over the rim of their mugs. "Drat!" He glanced around them. "I've often wondered about those who choose to drink in such squalor. I don't judge them, however. In fact, there's a sense of authenticity to such a setting, and I'm pleased to join them!"

Anna sighed in relief. If he was ever given the opportunity to see her home, he would not find it far different from this tavern.

"If I'm able to converse with one of these men by the night's end, my dream will be completed."

"I'm sure you'll speak to many of them," she said, amused that he could be so excited over the idea of speaking to commoners. "Men do little else in such places— prattle on about whatever comes to mind."

Although she did not frequent taverns, she and Betty had on occasion visited the local pub in Wilkworth. Men there spent a great deal of time boasting about all sorts of things— fights in which they had participated. Schemes that would one day make them rich. Or the women they had supposedly conquered.

The last she found highly unlikely. Some of the names they mentioned were women who would not have given them the time of day! Regardless, she found most of their discussions silly.

If they were simply trying to impress their companions, she would have been less critical. But why did men believe that women were impressed by men who enjoyed fighting? It amazed her how little men truly understood women.

More patrons entered the establishment as they sat at their table. When their mugs were nearly empty, a barmaid with bright red curly hair walked up to them, her apron dotted with wet spots. She was not much older than Anna, and by her smile, she had eyes for Colin.

"Two more ales?" she asked, placing a hand on her hip. "And will you be eating, too? The stew's nearly ready. The cook makes the best in London."

"Indeed, Miss," Colin said. "I'm quite famished. The sooner I eat, the sooner I'll stop being quarrelsome."

"Miss, is it?" the barmaid asked as she placed an all too familiar hand on Colin's shoulder. "I'll make sure you're served first, handsome."

As soon as she was gone, Colin said, "You see? It's just as I told my cousin Paul. If you speak to those of the lower classes with respect, you'll be rewarded for it."

Anna leaned forward. "I don't think your manners are the culprit in this case. It appears you have an admirer."

Colin's eyes went wide. "Who?"

"The barmaid," Anna replied. "She's clearly smitten with you."

"Well, she'll be left heartbroken, for I have eyes for no one but you."

Anna's cheeks heated. Why did he continuously speak as if they had some sort of future together? Surely this week would be their last.

But what if he wished to take their future further? She refused to become any man's mistress, so if he had no intention of marrying her, they would be going their own ways once they returned to Wilkworth.

Summoning her courage to ask him outright, she nearly growled in frustration when the barmaid returned and slammed two mugs of ale on the table. A moment later, the same woman set down two steaming bowls of stew with a generous portion of bread. Well, her questions would have to wait.

"This stew," Colin whispered, his voice filled with awe, "I've never tasted anything as wonderful. I must request the recipe so my cook can prepare it for me."

Anna laughed. "It's a simple stew eaten in many homes across England every night. I often make it for my family."

As they ate, more patrons arrived until no more could enter. They picked up bits of conversation that included the usual with a few grumblings about prospective employment.

Anna stifled a laugh. Were these the same men who frequented the pub in Wilkworth? How odd that different men would have the very same topics of discussion.

Soon after their empty bowls were removed, Colin was working on his fourth ale. Anna feared he would become drunk if he were not careful. She was only on her second.

She started when the two men she had observed earlier pulled out the two extra chairs and sat across from her and Colin without so much as asking permission.

The blond man who had been ogling her lifted his mug. "Here's to better days and better pay. 'Cause if I don't get a pay rise soon, I'll starve." His nose was crooked, as if it had been broken at least once and not mended. A long, thin scar ran down the side of his neck, and one of his earlobes had a nick out of it.

His companion, a man with thinning brown hair despite his young age, lifted his mug and took a generous drink before wiping his mouth on the sleeve of his threadbare coat. The black around his fingernails and in his hair said he likely delivered coal.

Colin raised his mug. "May we all increase in wealth."

Anna took a polite sip, finding the blond man's gray-eyed stare disconcerting.

"Name's Johnathan. Johnathan Bowemont. This here's Alan Stickler."

Colin grinned. "I'm Colin, and this is my friend Anna."

Anna cringed, wishing he had not used that term for their relationship. Now this man would pester her all night!

"Friend is it?" Johnathan asked, his eyes raking her up and down. "I thought maybe the two of you were married or somethin'. You're far too pretty to be without a man." He scooted his chair closer to hers. "Are you sure you ain't married?"

Anna went to respond, but, to her joy, Colin stood to glare down at Johnathan.

"Perhaps my choice of words was poor. Anna is with me. Now, I suggest you move your chair back where it belongs before I decide to move it for you."

"Apologies," Johnathan said as the chair scraped the floor in his haste to return it to where it had been.

Winking at Anna, Colin returned to his seat and signaled to the barmaid. "Did you truly think that I would allow this lovely woman to fall prey to another man?"

Anna sighed and considered leaping into his arms right there and then.

The barmaid returned with four more mugs of ale.

"Ah, here are our drinks!" Colin reached into his pocket and pulled out a note. "This one's on me, gentlemen!"

The men clapped Colin on the shoulder, and soon the trio was speaking amicably to one another. After a while, his newfound friends excused themselves, much to Anna's relief.

Colin placed his hand atop that of Anna. "You're more than a friend. I'll choose my words more carefully next time."

If they were not friends, Anna wondered, what were they? Did his words mean that they were a couple? And if so, what sort of couple could they possibly be?

She went to ask him outright, but her words were drowned out as half a dozen men began to sing. Those around them broke out into deafening applause when they finished, making being heard impossible.

"What great people there are here tonight!" Colin shouted. "Even those two who sat with us were harmless."

Anna leaned in close to Colin and said, "Be careful they don't try to take your money. Men such as they are quite crafty in their ways."

Colin threw his head back and laughed. "Oh, you worry too much. I'm wise in the ways of men. My tutors taught me everything I should know." His words were slurred, and Anna wondered if he would collapse from intoxication before the clock struck nine.

When the barmaid lifted her skirts and began moving her feet to the beat of a man playing a lively tune on a fiddle, Anna could not stop her brows from rising. Not for the barmaid's antics, for she was doing what women in her position did. No, her surprise— and dare she say annoyance— came from the way Colin gawked at her.

Well, this was his first encounter with the livelier people of the lower class. Just because the redhead batted her eyelashes at him and showed off her stockings did not mean he would rush to her side.

"I must join her!" Colin shouted to be heard above the noise. "You see? She's calling me over!" Indeed, the barmaid crooked a finger at Colin. "Wait here. I'll return in a moment."

Anna frowned as she clenched her hands into fists in her lap as Colin stumbled over to the barmaid. How dare that woman be so brazen!

Her ire was short-lived, however, when Colin began to dance. If that was what one would call the way he moved his feet— in a most awkward manner— as ale sloshed over the rim of his mug. He moved from foot to foot using steps that nowhere matched the rhythm of the music.

But when his gaze met hers, her heart swelled. Time came to a standstill. For the first time, Anna truly considered if she were falling in love with him.

Chapter Twenty-One

Were there any people more friendly in all of London than those around Colin at this very moment? He gave this question a great deal of thought as he gulped down another mug of ale. The two men from the working class who had joined them were quite pleasant and had included him in their conversation. The tavern maid had been most welcoming and was attentive to Colin's every need.

Colin had made a mistake naming Anna as simply a friend. Yet how could he describe their relationship? She was a woman who captivated him. One whose beauty took a hold on him. But there had to be more to their association than attraction. His indecisiveness, however, had led Johnathan to believe Anna was available for the taking.

Never had anyone been more wrong.

Standing above the man, Colin had clarified that misunderstanding. Although he had not said it outright, he relayed a message with his tone.

She is mine. I'll do whatever it takes to keep it that way!

Johnathan had moved back so quickly, Colin wondered if the man would topple over in his chair. But once the drinks arrived, the laughter had returned. Anna was safe.

And he would always keep her safe.

"If ye can't find work in London," Alan was saying, "then ye can't find work anywheres. That's why me an' Johnathan came 'ere last month. Pay's better, but the rents're higher. But it'll all work out in the end. Or at least that's what I'm hopin'."

Colin nodded in agreement. What a wonderful opportunity to be one of them! "Better wages for us all, boys!"

The men roared their approval, much to his delight, and then left the table, leaving Colin alone with Anna.

Suddenly, the room burst out in song. Many of the patrons rose from their seats and clapped to the music as the barmaid began dancing.

Colin thought of the many balls he had attended in his life with their sophisticated food and drink and well-dressed orchestras. None of that compared to what he was experiencing this night. This was a working man's party, and Colin wanted nothing more than to immerse himself in it.

The barmaid smiled at him and, to his delight, motioned him to join her. She was pretty enough, but he was not attracted to her. Not the way he was attracted to Anna. Yet he was here to have fun, and fun he would have!

Leaping from his seat, he joined her in the festivities. Ale sloshed over the rim of his mug and onto the floor. "I'm terribly sorry," he said, nearly shouting to be heard over the din. "Send me the bill for any damages."

The barmaid roared with laughter. "Ain't you a funny one? What's your name, handsome?"

"Colin," he replied.

"I'm Elsie. How come I ain't seen you here before?"

The song ended— or at least the music came to stop. He was unsure what song had been played— and Colin came to a standstill. "This is my first time here," he said. "To be honest, it's my first visit to a tavern of this... caliber."

You dolt, Colin! came a voice through the haze that was his brain. *If you wish to remain incognito, you mustn't give away too much information about yourself.*

"What I mean to say is that this is my first visit to a tavern on this side of London."

Elsie barked another laugh and placed a hand on his arm. "I think you need another drink. What do you think?" Colin nodded. Then, to his surprise, she squeezed his arm muscle and smiled. "Mmm. I like that."

He downed the last of his ale and set it on a table full of other empty mugs.

"Are you having a pleasant time?" Anna asked.

A sudden rush of guilt came over Colin. Was she upset with him? "It seems like that barmaid plans to take you away from me tonight."

"Who?" Colin asked. "Elsie?" He gave a hearty laugh.

Anna's eyebrows raised. "Oh, so you're addressing her by her Christian name, are you? I can leave the two of you alone if you'd like."

Colin waved a hand at her. "She's friendly enough. You know, I believe she may be interested in me as more than a friend."

Anna gasped and put a hand to her breast. "No! Tell me it isn't so!"

Leaning in, he whispered, "Oh, but it is. She touched my arm in a most familiar way. I'm beginning to believe that her friendliness may be more than simple kindness." He frowned. Was he repeating himself? Ah, well, what did it matter?

"Oh, Colin," Anna said, laughing, "do you know how wonderful you are?" She placed a hand on his cheek. "The word adorable comes to mind."

"I'll take that as a compliment," he said as Elsie returned with two new mugs of ale.

Once the barmaid disappeared, Colin focused on Anna. "I should not have left you alone to go dance."

"No, you did nothing wrong. I understand why you did, but if you ever do it again, I'll beat you!" She pressed a fist into his arm.

When the music resumed, Colin placed a hand on her lower back. Her sigh sent a thrill down his spine. "I've no doubt you would. Just as Johnathon has no doubt of what I would do."

"Are you saying you'd fight for me?" she asked. When she bit her bottom lip, he had to restrain himself from pulling her into his arms.

"Anna, I'd do anything for you. If you wish me to defend your honor, I'll go search him out this instant."

She leaned in, and he found his heart thudding in his chest at her closeness. "What I'd like," she said, "is to spend the rest of the evening with you. Come, let's sit. Unless you plan to dance again."

"I think I've done enough dancing for the time being," Colin replied with a grin.

They returned to their seats, and Colin took a moment to look around the crowded tavern. What surprised him was the number of women who also were in attendance. They did not flaunt themselves as he would have first believed but instead joined in the laughter. Everyone seemed to be enjoying themselves.

"I cannot express how delightful this evening has been," he said. "I've drunk ale, danced to lively music, and spent time with the most beautiful woman in all of England." He turned and looked at Anna. "And I do mean that. I think I've developed...feelings for you."

She waved a hand at him. "You're just saying that because of the amount of drink you've had."

"No, I swear to you that it has nothing to do with the drink. From the moment I awoke beneath the tree and gazed upon your lovely face, I've been captivated by your beauty. I find the way you perceive the world fascinating. You see it with the honesty with which you speak, and I adore that about you."

Her cheeks went a delectable red. Then a glint entered her eye. "But I'm a bit curious about something, so I'd like to take advantage of your drunkenness."

Colin raised an eyebrow. "Oh?"

She nodded. "You said you have feelings for me. What did you mean?"

He took a moment to consider her question, which was quite fair in his opinion. "I've never cared for anyone the way I do you. But when one considers how we met and the short amount of time that we've known one another, it's ludicrous."

Anna laughed. "Ludicrous? Do you mean your belief that I stole your coat?"

"Why would I not?" he asked. "Is that not what you did?"

"Even if that were the case— and I'm not admitting to any wrongdoing— but, even so, it no longer matters." She jutted out her lower lip, causing his throat to go dry. "You see, I've come to have strong feelings for you, too."

168

Colin forced himself to take a drink. He had so much he wished to tell her, but he worried that what he had to say would only complicate matters. He wanted nothing more in this world than Anna, but he was also well aware that it could never happen. Which would only hurt her in the end. No, he could not do that to her.

"I say we explore our feelings for one another this week," he said. He refused to make any promises he would be unable to keep.

"I would like that," she replied. "Just promise me you'll not run off with the barmaid."

Colin glanced at the redheaded woman and laughed. Another man had wrapped his arms around her and was nuzzling her neck. "Alas, it appears the Baron of Missing Teeth has won her over. Never has a Remington felt as shamed as I do now."

Anna's laugh sent a tingling down Colin's spine. He could listen to that sound for the entirety of his life and be forever happy.

"I believe I'll have another," Colin said. "You?"

She glanced down at her mug. "I've not finished this one," she replied. "But you go on. This is your night."

Their conversation turned to a variety of topics, and Colin found himself imagining them as a couple. His days would be filled with joy and honesty, for Anna spoke her mind. Another trait for which he adored her.

"I've heard all sorts of rumors about the Remingtons," she replied in response to a question he had asked. "Most of them have to do with illicit affairs and dubious business practices."

Colin sighed. "If I could offer an argument, Miss Silverstone, I would. Sadly, what you've heard is true. Oh, there are a few of us with scruples, but not many. Caroline and Evelyn, for example, are kind souls who would never hurt anyone."

"And what about you?" she asked. "Are you a kind soul or a man who breaks women's hearts?"

Colin choked on his ale. Once he was able to breathe again, he replied, "I would never break a woman's heart. After all, I'm a duke." He added the last with a firm nod.

What he had expected was to make Anna laugh, but instead, she wore a frown. "It's not because you're a duke. It's because you're Colin. Never forget that."

He grinned at her. "Very well, I will not forget."

Elsie walked up and set two more mugs of ale in front of them. Then she winked at Colin and walked away.

Anna gave a dramatic sigh. "It appears I have indeed lost you to a barmaid," she said. "Miss Caroline will never forgive you, you know."

This had them both laughing, and soon their conversation moved to other subjects. It was not long before the room began to spin around him.

"Anna," he said through a tongue so thick he had to force the words, "I think... I wish to inform you that I'm quite drunk"

She stood and walked to stand beside him. "You certainly don't need to tell me that," she said with a wry smile. "I say we get you back to the hotel and into bed."

"I believe you may be right." Colin stood, and if he had not been using the table to steady himself, he would have fallen when the floor shifted beneath his feet. He placed a handful of coins on the table, and Elsie rushed over and scooped them up without counting them. Had he given her too many? Ah, well, what did it matter? He had plenty.

"Here, put your arm around me," Anna said. And to his delight, she placed an arm around his waist.

Somehow, he managed to stumble out the door and into the street.

"It's dark out," he said as he glanced around them.

"That's what happens when the sun sets," Anna said. "Does this aspect of nature fascinate you?"

"Oh, how you do torment me," he said around the tongue that had grown to twice its size. "You know, I think you enjoy torturing me. And don't deny it. You know it's true."

Anna sighed but did not respond.

"See! You're doing it again!"

She laughed and rested her head against his side. "Colin, we are in London. We drank a great deal of ale— or rather, you drank a great deal of ale. We laughed and talked and had a most wonderful evening. Thank you for everything that you've done for me."

At the end of the street, Colin came to a stop and turned to face her. "There's no need to thank me," he said as he touched her cheek with the back of his hand. Oh, but how soft her skin was! "It is I who am in your debt." Dipping his head, he kissed her soft lips.

He wished to kiss her for hours, but he had enough sense still in him to know better, despite his inebriated state. Therefore, he pulled back, took her hand in his, and they resumed their walk back to the inn.

When they arrived at his room— he was glad they had no cumbersome stairs to traverse— Anna helped him into bed. Not for the first time, he felt how rough her hands were. The callouses told a story of a life of hard labor. If he could change that for her, he would. She deserved to be served. To wear the finest clothes. And to never work again.

"Stand still," she admonished as she tried to remove his coat.

Colin frowned. "But I am standing still..." he glanced at the moving walls. "Oh, perhaps I'm not. Maybe I should sit." He dropped onto the bed and reached down to pull off a boot. "They're stuck," he grunted. The room shifted again, and the next thing he knew, he was lying on his side. "I can't get up."

"Oh, Colin, you're so funny. Here, lie down and put your feet up. I'll get these boots off for you."

"Perhaps I can get a kiss first," he murmured as he pulled himself up into a sitting position and puckered his lips.

"What you'll get is a right punch," Anna said as she pushed him in the chest, so he landed on his back. She lifted first one leg and then the other onto the bed, now bereft of their boots.

He closed his eyes to stop the room from spinning around him, and soon his lids became as heavy as sandbags. The mattress moved as Anna sat on the edge of the bed and took his hand in hers.

He wanted to speak, to tell her how happy he was, how spectacular the evening had been. How the feelings he had for her were difficult to explain but wonderful at the same time. But no matter how much he tried to move his lips, they refused his weak commands.

Before sleep overtook him, he heard her whisper, "When I first encountered you, you were nearly as drunk as you are now. This time, however, I find you far more handsome, if that is possible."

Once more, Colin attempted to say how beautiful he thought she was, but before he could, he was asleep.

Chapter Twenty-Two

Colin exited his Mayfair estate the same way he had two days earlier. With his head lowered lest his neighbors catch sight of him, he hurried past the row of grand homes. At the end of the street, he turned right. Anna was there waiting.

"Well?" she asked. "Is there a reply? Colin?"

"There is. Leedon has agreed to see you Saturday evening before he leaves for his country estate."

No sooner had the words left his lips than Anna threw her arms around him. "It's finally going to happen!" she whispered. "In just two days, I'll meet my father. Do you have any idea how long I've dreamed of this moment?"

Colin shook his head.

"Since I was a little girl. I prayed so many nights that we would come to know one another. Every time Thomas became angry over money, or when mother fell asleep weeping. The worries, the fears, all our troubles will finally come to an end!"

Colin felt a tightening in his chest. Saturday would likely resemble nothing like the dream Anna imagined, and he found his heart and mind once again battling over whether or not he should warn her. Was there a way he could protect her from the devastation she would surely endure without destroying her dreams?

He reached down and took her hand. "I want you to take care. You cannot be certain he's your father. Or that he will accept you."

"Oh, but I am," she said with a wide smile. "My heart has said as much! Now, come, we've more shopping to do."

They had spent the day going to the various shops on Fleet Street. She had not purchased a single item, but when he had asked her if she had enough funds to make any purchases, she had not responded.

Most of their conversation had been around Lord Leedon. "I'm sure he'll want me to share stories about my life, and that of Thomas, as well, of course." She came to a sudden stop. "Will you be going inside with me, or would you prefer to remain outside while I speak to him first?"

"I think you misunderstand," Colin replied. "As much as I would like to be there, I'm unable to go. I've a party that night I must attend. I meant to tell you sooner, but I didn't wish to ruin your week."

Although Anna assured him all was well, the disappointment in her eyes told another story. The idea of her going alone to see Lord Leedon did not sit well with him. Not because he feared the earl would cause her physical harm but rather how his words would hurt her. Speaking to Evan was far too important— his mother keeping tabs on him still annoyed him no end!— and Saturday evening was the only time he would be able to do so.

What if he did not see Anna again after this week? The idea left him with a vacant feeling in the middle of his chest.

"I've a marvelous idea," he said as he turned to her. "When you've completed your meeting with Leedon, why not meet me at the park near the party I'm to attend? We can go for a walk if you'd like, and you can tell me all about your time with your father."

"I'd like that," Anna said. "I can tell you all my good news, and you can bring me a piece of one of their extravagant desserts."

Colin laughed. "I believe that can be arranged."

When they arrived at Fleet Street, they maneuvered their way through the bustling crowd, filled with people from all walks of life. Shops lined the street, from teashops to millineries, to bookshops, every want could be had for a price. Children in tattered clothing ran between carriages as their drivers shouted obscenities at them.

"The footmen who're accompanying the ladies appear rather sturdy," Anna mused.

"They're far more than simple footmen. You see, there's a prison nearby. No gentleman would allow his wife to frequent the shops in this area without a proper escort, but neither is he willing to spend his time waiting outside shops. Therefore, they hire men to take on that responsibility."

As if to prove Colin's point, an unshaven man swaggered up to them, licking his lips and eying Anna. A stern glower from Colin sent the man away with a grunt.

They approached a large building with windows taller than Colin. The sign above proclaimed, "Thurston and Howell".

"A linendraper? What're we doing here?"

"Why, shopping for fabrics, of course," Anna replied. "I'll need at least a dozen dresses, and the sitting room could use a new set of curtains."

Colin frowned but made no comment as they entered the shop. Deep, circular shelves held large rolls of fabrics. Other styles of textiles stood on end, their ends hanging down like curtains.

Anna touched one of the displays. "I find it interesting that women like me created these designs," she said as she moved the fabric between her fingers. "But did you notice that only men work here?"

Colin glanced around. "I never gave it much thought, but you're right."

"Here, feel this." She held out the end of a roll of red fabric with gold threaded throughout. "Isn't it wonderful? I've never worked with such fine threading before." She looked at her fingertips. "And that's likely a good thing. I'd be too afraid to have the threads catch on my fingertips."

Taking her hand in his, he smiled. "Your hands tell a story, Anna. They tell a story of a woman who works very hard, who works in an industry that is very important to everyone, both rich and poor. You should feel nothing but pride for what you've done with your life."

He doubted her blushes would ever become tiresome.

She pulled her hand away. "Well," she said, resuming that false nasal tone of the upper class. "I believe this fabric will make fine curtains for the sitting room, do you not agree? And the purple for my bedroom."

"You'll purchase these?" Colin asked.

"Does the thought of such a poor woman owning such finery bother you?" Anna laughed. Then she lowered her voice and added, "This is how those of us who are poor spend our time shopping. Although we'll never be able to afford such luxuries, we pretend as if we can."

"And this is common?" he asked.

Anna nodded. "Quite common. If anyone says he doesn't pretend from time to time, he's lying."

"It is a novel idea, I suppose." He was not convinced, but neither was he willing to contradict her words. She seemed to be enjoying herself far too much for that.

"Here's what you must do. Act like you don't have two farthings to your name. Now, which would you prefer for your cottage?"

Colin looked over the choices and stopped before a roll of gold fabric. Just as he went to respond that he would like that one, a clerk approached them, and he did not appear pleased.

"We have no time for thieves or for charity," he said with his nose in the air. He was a rather thin character with beady eyes and a pinched face that made him look as if he were enduring some terrible odor. "I would like you to leave, please."

Colin's temper rose. Did this man not realize to whom he was speaking? He would have him thrown out of the establishment on his ear! How dare he speak to a duke in such a terrible...

He paused. No, of course the man had no idea who Colin was, not with his rumpled and patched clothing.

"My husband wishes to purchase some fabric," Anna said. "I'm sure we can come to some sort of terms."

"Terms?" the man replied, aghast. "Terms? Here are my terms. Leave now, lest you wish me to have you bodily removed. I'm certain you can find a shop that is better suited to your needs. Here, we have ladies from the best families." He looked them up and down, his frown deepening. "The last thing they want is to share a space with those equal to— if not beneath— their servants."

Every eye was on them. Two women pointed in their direction, and judging by the looks of terror, they thought he and Anna would rob them at any moment.

Yet their look was not foreign to Colin. Had he not witnessed this very behavior from his peers? He had never joined them, but not once had he stepped forward to berate them for their bad manners. Although he had not approved, now that he had endured such humiliation from the other side, he found the act despicable.

"Come, Anna," he said, offering his arm. "We'll go elsewhere." Before he left, however, he turned back to the clerk and added, "One day, I'll return, and you'll beg me to do business with you."

The clerk snorted. "And when that day comes, I shall fall on my knees and beg you for your forgiveness." Colin did not miss the note of sarcasm in the man's tone. "But until that day comes, I suggest you leave."

With Anna on his arm, Colin led her back onto the busy street. "I understand now what it feels like to be humiliated for one's status. This is just one of the many things I despise about being a duke."

A man stumbling past them stopped and chortled. "A duke? You? Well, I'll bet you know my cousin, the King!"

Colin sighed and turned to Anna. "Why must people treat each other so disgracefully?"

She laughed. "What does it matter? You're not like them, are you?"

Colin shook his head. "I would hope not."

"Then you mustn't allow such words to ruin your day. Now, cheer up. We're going to the dressmaker's next."

"The dressmaker's?" Colin asked with a yelp as she pulled him along after him. "Men don't join women in a dressmaker's shop no matter his station!"

Anna frowned. "You make it sound as if we're on our way to practice witchcraft. Trust me. All will be well."

Did she not understand that being forced to enter such a place would make him a laughingstock? Not to mention what the patrons would think of him being in what should be a sanctuary for women!

He would have been better off kissing a barmaid in front of his mother than to go there.

But when Anna smiled, he found he could not refuse. Therefore, with a sigh, he followed after her.

They came to a stop ten shops down. Several women browsed through large books or looked over a variety of ribbons and lace. One young lady turned in a full circle to show off her yellow dress.

"The two times Mother brought me to London," Anna said as she peered through the window, "I came to stand here, wondering what it would be like to be one of those ladies. To be able to walk in and order a new dress. To feel the soft fabric against my skin. To feel as if I were worthy." She turned to gaze up at him. "I know that seems silly, but it's what I've always wished for."

Colin felt a stirring inside him. It was not the passion of wanting to kiss her but rather a desire to see she had everything she wanted. To do whatever he could to make her happy.

"I see they have several dresses already made," he said, smiling down at her. "Go inside and select one. I'll purchase it for you. If you find three you like, then I'll purchase all three. I don't care. Buy whatever you wish."

To his surprise, Anna turned back to the window. "That's kind of you, and I'll admit that it's very tempting, but I think I'll wait. Good things are coming my way, and soon I'll have my own money to make such a purchase." She turned and smiled at him. "But I thank you all the same."

As he watched the young woman in the yellow dress, Colin wondered how many she had ordered. Would she be pleased with such a gift? Or would she be like countless others who took what they had for granted?

Then there was Anna, a woman who deserved it all and yet refused his offer.

"I wish I could be more like you," Colin said. "To speak my mind whenever I want. To see the world as you do. How wonderful it must be."

"And what stops you from doing the same?"

He laughed. Had she not learned after the time they had spent together? "You forget that I'm a duke."

"And I'm a woman who labors all day. If I can do such things, surely being a powerful duke shouldn't hinder you." She turned and smiled up at him. "The man before me is held back only by himself."

How much he wished to believe her words, but he could not make himself agree. The dukedom had certain expectations of him, and that did not include speaking his mind. Not fully. He had to choose his words carefully, present himself in a certain way. If he did not, he would only shame his position. And he refused to do that.

If anyone would have told Colin two weeks ago that he would be dressed as a commoner and peering into a dressmaker's shop on Fleet Street, he would have thought them mad. Yet here he was doing exactly that.

So far, he had slept in an inn that was more modest than the rooms in which his servants lived. He had danced with a barmaid and stumbled drunk to his room. And it was an experience he would enjoy doing again.

But not alone. No, he would need Anna at his side, for she was his guide, his escort.

As she peered through the window, speaking of the blue dress she would purchase, he thought about what his life would be with her in it. There had to be a way, and he prayed that Evan would have the answer he sought. After all Anna had done for him, for the hard life she had been forced to lead, she deserved a life of luxury. But, more importantly, she needed to be cherished. He had no doubt that no one but himself could do it.

And Colin vowed to do whatever it took to see that happen.

Chapter Twenty-Three

The day had finally arrived, the day when Anna's dreams would come true. A carriage would come for her any moment now, and she would be whisked away to meet her father. She had chosen her blue dress and spent the better part of an hour brushing her hair and using the few hairpins she had to pull it up into some semblance of a chignon.

Although her shoes had deep cracks in the leather from wear, she had asked Mr. Thompson for polish and was pleased when he obliged. The polish did not remove the cracks, but at least it helped make her shoes look less worn. A bit.

A knock came to the door, and Anna went to answer it. Colin stood there, once more in his tailored suit and clean cheeks. "I had forgotten how handsome you truly are," she teased. "Were you able to sneak past Mr. Thompson without him catching you?"

Colin nodded. "The front area was empty, so it was no trouble at all." He took her hands in his. "Are you nervous?"

"Nervous, excited, anxious," she replied with a laugh. "My stomach keeps churning, and I've spent a great deal of time fanning myself." She glanced down at her dress. "Do you think I look presentable? I worry my dress is too old. And these shoes!" She heaved a sigh. "What if he—"

"You're more beautiful today than you were yesterday," Colin said. "Leedon will have little concern for what clothing you're wearing, I assure you."

Anna's heart soared. "You're right. Once my father learns who I am, he'll send me straight to the dressmaker's." She laughed at her own humor, but Colin's expression did not change. "Well, I suppose we should go."

He nodded. "The driver's been instructed to take you to Portland Place once you've completed your meeting. He's to leave you at the park close to where the party is taking place."

They had spoken at length of this plan before, but Anna was thankful to hear it again. She had been in such a state of anticipation that she recalled only bits and pieces of it.

She looked down at their intertwined hands and said, "This week has seen our dreams realized. No matter what the future brings, I'll never forget it. Nor you."

He smiled down at her. "You would be impossible to forget," he whispered. "The woman who came into my life, who has shown me what it's like to live."

Anna's heart beat with such strong emotion that she wondered if it was love. The matter needed serious thought, for she would like to pursue it further. But she had a father to meet before taking such an important step.

Plus, once she verified that she was the daughter of an earl, their chances of moving forward would be far better.

Raising herself onto the tips of her toes, she kissed him. "We'll have another tonight as a way to celebrate. And do remember to bring wine with you when we meet."

"I'll be there waiting."

She smiled. "You go down first. We can't have anyone see us leaving together. The way you're dressed will be far too embarrassing."

Colin chuckled. "Good luck," he whispered.

Anna returned to her room to collect a wrap— and to give Colin time to leave— before going downstairs.

"Miss Silverstone," the clerk called out to her, making her start, "is all well?"

"Oh, yes, thank you, Mr. Thompson." Overcome with anticipation, she approached the counter and lowered her voice. "I'm off to meet my father, whom I've not seen in many years."

"How wonderful!" he said. "I do hope everything goes well for you. Will your mother be joining you?"

An image of her mother came to mind. How sad that she could not witness this wondrous reunion! "I'm afraid not. Oh, my carriage is waiting for me. I must be on my way."

"Good luck!" Mr. Thompson called out after her.

Anna gave him a grateful wave and exited the inn. Indeed, a nondescript carriage awaited, and the driver dipped his head as he opened the door for her. The interior was very much like that of the vehicle that had brought her to London, and she settled back into the plush cushion. She could become quite accustomed to this.

Soon, the carriage was on its way. Anna peered out the window without noticing the passing buildings. Once she and her father reconciled, no longer would she be a shadow everyone avoided. Instead, she would be the daughter of Lord Leedon, an earl and peer of the realm. Those who had turned their noses up at her would soon learn that she had worth.

One question that she had pushed into the back of her mind returned. Would she take her father's name or continue using her own? Still, she had no answer. Perhaps he could help her make that decision.

When the carriage came to a stop, Anna's heart thudded in her chest. She was grateful for the driver's hand as he helped her alight from the carriage. Her head was spinning so quickly that she had to stop and take a deep breath to put it back into order. Her mind barely registered that the driver said he would wait for her.

The houses here were enormous! Each had a feel of welcoming with their own tiny gardens consisting of perfectly trimmed bushes and flower beds filled with blue and yellow flowers or perfect red and pink roses. And so many windows! None showed a single crack and glimmered with the reflection of the sun. She could see herself living in such a marvelous place, enjoying the luxuries of such a life.

Well, that could not happen until she learned the truth about Lord Leedon.

The iron gate opened without the slightest creak, and the footpath that led to the front door had been swept clean. Both greeted her like a long-lost friend. Or perhaps a long-lost daughter…

Fear overtook her as she considered how worn her dress was. Even the garden was maintained better than she. Would her father look at her differently because of her bedraggled state?

When she rang the bell— a lovely note if she ever heard one!— the door opened to a man in formal livery. "Miss Silverstone? Lord Leedon awaits you in the drawing room. If you'll follow me, please."

"Thank you," Anna managed to whisper, although it came out more a croak. Oh, but how her nerves were as taut as a weft thread on a loom!

As she stepped into the foyer, it took every ounce of will not to gape. Fine tapestries of purple and gold hung from the walls, and the oak banister on the stairs gleamed. This was where she would greet her brothers when they came to meet her father. They would be as awed as she!

The butler led her toward a set of double doors. As she followed him, Anna thought her heart would explode. This moment had been a dream for so long, but what if she fainted before she and her father met?

"Miss Anna Silverstone," the butler announced before moving aside to allow her to enter the room.

A gentleman in a crisp suit rose from a plush chair covered in purple fabric. He had silver hair, and his smile had a certain glow to it that she was immediately drawn to. This man was an earl, her father, and he was everything she expected him to be. His eyes were dark like those of Thomas, but his nose was slender, much like hers. Thomas also shared his height, but this man's jawline was more pronounced.

"Thank you, Williams," the earl said. "See a tray brought up."

The butler bowed. "Yes, my lord."

"When His Grace sent word that I would be meeting Miss Anna Silverstone, I knew immediately who you were."

Anna's eyes went wide. "You did?"

"Of course. Your mother and I shared in numerous conversations." He extended his hand toward a set of chairs. "Please, sit."

For a moment, Anna could only stare. Which chair did he mean? She desperately needed to make a good impression, for she could not have her father think her uncivilized.

"Either is fine."

Anna smiled. He had sensed her thought, just as her mother would often do. Knowing this eased some of the trepidation she carried. It had a familiarity to it.

Choosing one, she found the red cushions even more luxurious, more comfortable, than the benches in the carriage. All around her spoke of great wealth, from the intricate paintings to the elaborate furniture. Marble columns flanked the large fireplace, each with an ornate carving of a cherub on its top end. Even the fabric of the drapes was far more elegant than anything produced at Mr. Harrison's workhouse.

Yet, although Anna admired the earl's possessions, she was not here for them. "My lord," she began, "I believe you know why I'm here. You see..." she swallowed hard. He looked at her with such consideration, that the words stuck in her throat.

You've waited far too long for this moment to act a frightened goose now!

Clearing her throat, she tried again. "I'm your daughter."

Everything went quiet. Should she rush over and hug him? Would he hug her? She was uncertain what to expect, but the sigh that came had not been it.

"Miss Silverstone."

"Please, call me Anna."

"Anna. Yes, well, I must ask. Who told you I was your father? Might I hazard a guess that it was your mother?"

"Yes, my lord." Then, like a sluice gate, her words began to tumble from her lips. "You see, she was on her deathbed when she revealed it to me. I'm sure you're already aware, but you also have a son, Thomas. Then there's Christian and Henry." She let out a nervous laugh. "Well, they are not your sons, only Thomas. Christian's a bit of a rebel but excellent with horses. Henry's just six, but he's well-mannered. I know he'll want to meet you, too."

"I'm sure he would," the earl murmured. His brows knitted, and his lips thinned. "Anna, I would like to tell you a story. About your mother."

Anna straightened in her seat. "I'd like that. I've often wondered what stories you would be able to share."

The door opened, and the butler entered with a tray laden with a porcelain tea set and two teacups. He poured them each a cup of tea and then bowed and left the room once more.

As she accepted the teacup the earl offered, she admired how different it was from the cracked ones at home. After taking a sip, she returned the cup to its saucer. Her hand shook far too much to continue to hold it. The last thing she needed was to spill tea down the front of her dress!

She studied her father, worry setting in. Her appearance had to be off-putting for a man of his station. Well, she would remedy that.

"I realize that this must be quite awkward for you, my lord. It's not every day that a daughter about whom you knew nothing suddenly arrives on your doorstep. But I can assure you that although my dress is worn, I'm a good, strong woman. I've done nothing to shame my name or that of any member of my family. You'll find that as your daughter, I'll be a boon to the Leedon name. Or rather the Braxton name, since that's your family name. That being said, I just want you to know that I'll make you proud."

The earl set his cup on the table and drew in a deep breath. "Anna. I'm sorry, but there is no other way to tell you this. I really must be completely upfront with you. You see, I'm not your father."

All the air seemed sucked from the room. Bile rose in Anna's throat. "I'm afraid you're mistaken," she said with a firmness she did not feel. "Mother gave me your name. She said you were forced to marry another woman instead of her."

Lord Leedon rose from his chair and walked over to lean against the fireplace. "Did your mother tell you how we met?"

Anna shook her head. Any verbal response was caught in her throat.

The Duke Who Loved Me

"I see. Well, if she chose not to share that with you, then perhaps it would be best that you don't know. I'd hate to resurrect a past she wished to hide."

With shaky legs, Anna stood. "But you are my father. Mother never lied. Not to me. She would never do that."

The pained expression that crossed the earl's features told her how untrue these words were. Her mother had lied. Even on her deathbed, she had been untruthful. How could she have deceived Anna in such a terrible way? What had she hoped to gain?

"I beg of you, tell me what you're unwilling to share. I must know the truth."

He shook his head. "Please, don't make me tell you. I don't want to hurt you any more than I already have."

"I've waited for this day my entire life," Anna said, forcing back the tears that threatened to fall. "And now I've come to realize that my life has been a fabrication. For far too long, I've believed a fairy tale. Please. I won't be angry with you, I promise."

"Very well," he replied. "But I believe we should sit back down."

Anna nodded and returned to her seat. With her hands clenching her skirts, she forced herself to calm.

When the earl was also seated, he began. "I was involved with numerous charities here in London. We worked with the poor and downtrodden throughout the city. One particular woman came to one of those charities, one who wished to leave behind the difficult life in which she found herself."

"I see," Anna said, wishing he would simply get to the point.

"So many of the women we aided were part of a particular profession, one that…" He shifted in his seat. "Well, one that is not discussed among those of stricter morals."

Anna stared at him. Was he saying what she believed he was saying? "You can't mean…"

He gave her a sad nod. "She was a prostitute."

"No!" Anna gasped. "No, it cannot be!"

"I'm sorry, but it is. The idea behind that particular charity was to teach the women who came to us how to find respectable work. They learned to sew or to create lace or what they would need to know to become servants of an estate. Your mother and I became friends, although I use the term loosely. Perhaps acquaintances would be a far better word to use. Either way, I found her resolve admirable. She had a great desire to better herself and leave her old ways behind. You should be proud of what she was able to accomplish."

Anna frowned. "So, the two of you spent time together? Perhaps a…relationship developed between you."

"I understand what you are alluding to, but the answer is no. We were not intimate in any way. We were never alone for even a moment for anything inappropriate to take place. Whenever I called on the home where your mother was staying, she would often tell me all sorts of grand tales. And I enjoyed hearing her stories. Then, during one of those calls, she told me she was with child. I assume that was the brother of whom you spoke."

Anna's stomach felt filled with lead. "Thomas," she whispered. "His name is Thomas."

"Rebecca never named the father," Lord Leedon continued. "And I didn't feel it was my business to ask. You must understand, we never met outside that building. Surely you must realize that an earl could never develop a relationship of any kind with a woman of her…background."

With tears stinging her eyes, Anna gave a dull nod. "I see that now, my lord."

Oh, how her heart ached! Her mother had lied to her. Molly had alluded to the fact that mothers such as she often made up stories to protect their children, but all it did was make her feel smaller, less significant than she had felt before knowing this information. Shame washed over her in waves. Her stomach roiled. How could she have ever thought herself worthy of being named an earl's daughter?

Did she deserve love, anyone's love? No, she did not. Not the daughter of a woman who used her body to earn a living. What she wanted to do was run far away where no one would be forced to set eyes upon her again.

Lord Leedon walked over and squatted beside her. "I can see how much this news has upset you, and for that, I'm sorry. I had considered lying to you, but I could not, not in good conscience."

"I admit this was not what I had hoped to hear," she said, wiping away the single tear that slid down her cheek. "I'd hope that we would be celebrating by now. That a new world would open up to me. That people would finally look past my clothing and my station in life. That had been my dream for so long, and now it's gone."

He patted her hand. "Although I'm not your father, Miss Silverstone, I do see past that. Before me sits a strong young woman. I may not know her, but I recognize strength when I see it, and yours shines brightly. I wish you the best in the days ahead. And I hope that, one day, you'll find your father, for he is a fortunate man indeed."

Anna stood. "Thank you for your kind words, my lord. I suppose I should be on my way." She looked around one last time. She had looked forward to being in this room, to remaining here to become better acquainted with the man she believed to be her father. And now, all she wanted was to leave. She had embarrassed herself long enough.

"May I offer you my carriage to take you to wherever it is you're staying?" Lord Leedon asked. "Perhaps some money? I have several notes if you'll accept them." He reached into his coat pocket. He counted out what appeared to be about forty pounds and held it out to her.

That much money was enough to purchase new window panes, teacups, blue dresses. Yet Lord Leedon had already done enough.

"I appreciate the gesture, my lord," she said, waving away the offered money. "But I've bothered you enough for two lifetimes. Thank you for agreeing to see me. And you've no need to worry. I'll keep this meeting between us. I'll see myself out."

Unable to hold back the tears of humiliation, Anna hurried out of the room and out the front door. The houses now glowered at her, hurling their rays of accusation at her through glaring reflections of the sun. The flowers turned away from her, reserved only for girls who knew their fathers. Even the carriage that awaited her was meant for ladies of good standing.

Not for the bastard daughter of a prostitute.

The driver opened the door and bowed. "Is there anywhere else you'd like to go before I'm to take you to your destination, Miss Silverstone?

"No," Anna said, looking down what she had first thought as a lovely street. "I believe I'll walk, thank you." Then she paused. "Although, I'll need directions."

"But His Grace instructed me to see you to Portland Place," the driver replied with an air of concern.

"Just directions, if you please."

Once she had a clear idea of where she needed to go, Anna lowered her head and began to walk. Her body felt numb, her heart felt vacant.

A couple was alighting from a carriage several houses away, and the lady sniffed. "I remember when servants had the decency to either wait until their betters went inside or crossed to the other side of the street so as not to be in our way. Much has changed."

"You've no need to worry," Anna said in a choked voice. "You'll never see me again."

At the end of the street, she paused. Everything had fallen apart, her world was crumbling down around her, and she felt more lost than ever. She was meant to turn left, but that led to Colin, and she was not ready to discuss what she had learned.

She headed to the right instead, uncertain where it would lead her. Nor did she care.

Chapter Twenty-Four

The London Estate belonging to Alan, Lord Dundwhich had a permanent dampness Colin found unsettling. Although every surface shined, and not a speck of dust settled on any piece of furniture, he pondered how often the viscount's servants opened the windows. Perhaps the man should see if the roof was in need of repair.

The party, which began an hour earlier, consisted of thirty or so guests. A five-piece orchestra played in the corner of the rather small ballroom, and several footmen circulated the area carrying trays of various types of drinks and food.

Colin had engaged in several conversations and came to the surprising realization that he was the youngest attendee by nearly thirty years.

Despite this fact, he smiled politely and nodded at the appropriate times, but he had trouble concentrating. His mind was on Anna and her meeting with Lord Leedon. He was due to meet her in half an hour, but first he had to find Evan. Once he had spoken to his cousin, he would wait at the designated place at the entrance to the park down the street.

He turned to find the old viscount approaching. With wild silver hair that stuck up in every direction and a terrible habit of rubbing his nose, Dundwhich could be defined as nothing other than a character.

"Well, Greystoke, I hope you've enjoyed the party thus far."

For a moment, Colin considered being honest and responding in the negative, but he would never do such a thing. Others seemed to be enjoying themselves well enough.

"I can't recall a more enjoyable evening," Colin replied.

"Excellent! I would be quite upset if you were not." He rubbed the side of his nose before taking a drink of his wine. "A pity the duchess could not attend. I sent her an invitation but received no response."

"I wouldn't take her lack of reply personally," Colin replied. "Mother's been quite occupied as of late with various projects, but I know she would send her regards."

Of course, his mother would do no such thing. She was the epitome of a duchess, looking down on everyone save her son. Though Colin sometimes wondered if he was not included in her snobbery.

"Well, it's still a disappointment," Lord Dundwhich said. "Sadly, I must make the rounds. If you'll excuse me."

"I understand," Colin replied.

Chatter rose from a group close to the entryway, and Colin turned to see his cousin Evan. With wavy blond hair and a mischievous grin, Evan had the ability to gain anyone's confidence in a matter of moments. Although it served him well in aspects of business, the *ton* was alighted with gossip about the various women he was said to have bedded— including a more recent tale of a baroness whose husband had been away to Scotland. Although Colin made a habit of dismissing such rumors, when it came to Evan, he did not doubt them.

Yet there was a kinder side to Evan that Colin had witnessed firsthand. Before his father died, Evan had been a kind man, often helping others in whatever way he could. That was the man Colin remembered. And the one from whom tonight he would gain insight.

"So, the Ninth Duke of Greystoke has graced us with his presence despite the fact that most of London is not here," Evan said as he approached. He pushed out his hand. "How are you, Cousin? It's been what? Six months? More?"

"Seven to be precise," Colin said, gripping the man's hand and giving it a firm shake. "The engagement party of Rosboat and his bride-to-be. If I recall, you and Balfour got into quite a heated argument. Did the two of you make peace?"

Evan snorted. "I told the old fool to watch his tongue. Ah, but what does it matter now? We're here, so let's just keep the past where it belongs and focus on the present. Which leads to us discussing your mother."

Colin glanced around them and indicated to Evan to follow him to a far corner where they would not be overheard. "Why did she send for you? And what exactly did she say?"

"I must admit that when I first received her letter, I thought you had gotten yourself entangled in some scandal. I cannot tell you what a relief it was to learn that it was not the case. No, she's concerned about how you've delayed the announcement of your engagement. Have you?"

"I have," Colin replied with a sigh. "But why she would complain to you about it is beyond me."

"You know how mothers can be, Colin. She fears you've come to London to get into some sort of mischief. She believed I would be a good person to counsel you against it. I told her that she should not worry, that you would never do anything to harm your title. Was I correct in saying so?"

Colin drank the last of his wine. It was as he had suspected. Well, now that Evan was here, perhaps his cousin could offer some advice. The question was, could he trust his own blood?

"If I tell you," he said in a low voice, "do you swear it will remain between us?"

Evan chuckled. "I'm your cousin, not a butcher." When Colin did not join in his laughter, Evan sighed. "My apologies, I did not mean to make light of your worries, whatever they may be. Rest assured, we are Remingtons and thus I'd never betray your trust."

"Good. The problem is that I've no interest in marrying Lady Katherine, but I feel as if I have no choice in the matter. Even if I dismiss her as a possible candidate, I'll still be expected to marry another. There's just no escaping the inevitable."

Evan snapped his fingers, and a liveried footman hurried over with a tray. New glasses replaced old, and when the man left, Evan said, "You cannot be more correct. You're expected to marry, more so than most men. What I don't understand is why you wish to avoid it. I've seen Lady Katherine. She's very beautiful. How could you not want someone as lovely as she warming your bed?" He frowned. "You've not set your sights on another woman, have you?"

Colin sighed. "You hit the nail on the head. The problem is that she comes from a family that is not of equal standing."

"Well, if she's of the landed gentry, that can be a sticky situation. Although, wealth can make up for status in some cases, though not for a duke. You're not speaking of Abigail Mullwood, are you?"

"Heaven forbid," Colin replied with a laugh. Miss Mullwood had a tendency to talk and never cease. Her mother had hired the best tutors and threatened to stop her allowance if she did not curb her tongue, but it did little to help. "The woman I've met comes from common stock. She's employed at a workhouse, and although she's poor, her heart is rich."

A look of surprise crossed Evan's face. "You know as well as I that the duchess will never condone such a union. The *ton* would mock you until the end of time if you married so far below your station. I respect you far too much to agree that this is acceptable."

"That's the problem," Colin said. "No one would give their blessing. Even if she proved who her father is, even if she proved her bloodline, it will not be enough."

Evan's brow furrowed. "I'm confused. What bloodline must she prove?"

"Perhaps if I tell you how I met this woman and how we got to this stage, you can help me devise a plan that may work." Colin explained everything, from meeting Anna at the river to agreeing to come to London so she could meet the earl. "So, you see," he said when he concluded the story, "even I know that if it were true and Leedon acknowledges her as his daughter, it would make no difference whatsoever. A woman born out of wedlock is often ridiculed, snubbed by those of the aristocracy. Yet, I cannot imagine marrying anyone besides Anna."

Evan had remained quiet throughout the tale, and Colin wondered if there was no solution. He glanced at the clock. The hour he was to meet Anna was drawing near and still he had no idea how to proceed.

"There are few solutions to your dilemma," Evan said. "You can marry Lady Katherine and then employ this woman as a housemaid to keep her close, so you may have her when the desire arises."

"No, I couldn't do that to either Lady Katherine or Anna. I'm also a firm believer in the sanctity of marriage. Furthermore, Anna would never agree, and I would not blame her."

"Let's suppose you dismiss the expectations of your mother— and that of the *ton*— and decided to marry this Anna. What do you believe would happen?"

"I'd become the laughingstock of the *ton*," Colin said with a snort. "My name would be ruined. It would draw unnecessary attention to Anna, for she would never be accepted into society no matter the fact she would become a duchess. I fear she would live her life shunned by everyone."

Evan gulped down the last of his drink and then handed it to a passing footman. "Colin, we're cousins. May I speak to you honestly, as if we're friends in a tavern rather than family?"

"Yes, please do."

"Your name will not be the only thing ruined, you know. So will be the Remington name. Do you realize what this would do to the rest of the family? Think of our many cousins, especially the women, for God's sake. Every eligible bachelor would run away! Footmen will think they can marry into— and forever taint— our bloodline." He took a step forward, his nose mere inches from that of Colin. "I mean no disrespect, but if you do choose to throw your life away because of this girl, you're being nothing short of selfish."

Anger rose in Colin. Selfish? He went to argue, but Evan spoke again, this time in a whisper. "The ring you wear represents us all, not just you. Please, I beg of you, think of the consequences before you decide to put the entire family at risk of humiliation and scorn."

Evan took a step back and then smoothed out his coat. "Although I have no solution to your problem," he said, his voice back to a normal volume, "I believe I may have a remedy. It may allow you the opportunity to delay your engagement without drawing suspicion."

"Out with it, then," Colin said. "I must admit that I'm quite desperate."

"When you return to Wilkworth, write to your mother and your business associates, whichever you choose. Tell them that we've decided to go into business together and that we'll be occupied for a while. This will give you the chance to consider the best way to handle this situation."

"What I'd like to do is have Anna with me for every day of my life," Colin said. Then he sighed. "Yet, even as a duke, I know it's impossible."

The orchestra began playing a new tune, and a sweet melody filled the air. "Have you heard the story of Lewis Remington?" Evan asked.

Colin shook his head.

"As I understand it, this was two generations ago, perhaps three, when he married a common woman."

"Yes, that sounds familiar, although I didn't know the name. So, what happened?"

"From what I recall, he married his cook. Immediately, the *ton* turned against him, and he never received another invitation to any parties or gatherings. Soon enough, his estate fell into bankruptcy because no one would do business with him. The point is, are you willing to give up everything for a woman you barely know? To betray your family for her? And think of Lady Katherine. Her future will also be ruined. Think of me lastly in this, but you must think of the other Remingtons whose name will be put into question by your decisions."

Although what Evan said was discomforting, Colin knew it was true. In fact, he had known it since he awoke beneath the tree and gazed into Anna's eyes. Some things in life could never happen, no matter how much he wanted them.

"I had hoped meeting with you tonight would help me solve this problem. That perhaps an answer had eluded me. What I've come to realize is that the truth is what I've already known."

"And what truth is that, Cousin?"

Colin sighed. "That Anna and I have no future together."

Evan clasped Colin on the shoulder. "I must go. I'll explain to your mother that she has nothing to fear. If you wish to do right, then I suggest you end whatever you have with this woman as soon as possible. Delaying the inevitable will only make matters worse."

As his cousin walked away, Colin rubbed his temples. Would this truly be the last weekend he would ever spend with Anna? Evan had not lied. If Colin were to marry her, it would not only harm him but also everyone he loved. To what extent was left to be seen, but he could not take that risk.

As he took drink of his wine, he took another look at his ring. He had a responsibility to his ancestors, the previous Dukes of Greystoke. To the Remington name.

Oh, how he wished the strong feelings he had for Anna were enough to secure their future together. Yet as much as he would have given it all up for her, the truth screamed at him like a banshee. He was a duke, and as such, it was his duty to put an end to all this. It would break her heart as much as his, but he had little choice.

There was no use waiting for the inevitable. Tonight, he would do just that.

***

Anna walked through the London streets for hours in an attempt to lessen the ache inside her. No one gave her a second look as she ambled through various neighborhoods and passed shopkeepers as they closed their shops for the night. More so than ever, she had a sense of insignificance, as if she were invisible. That somehow she belonged nowhere.

Loss pounded in her chest with a beat of its own, and it threatened to choke her. The realization of who she truly was mocked her. The knowledge of who she would never be made her want to scream until she had no voice left.

The daughter of a prostitute. Learning that she was not the daughter of an earl pained her, but the realization that she would never learn the identity of her father devastated her. Like a snuffed candle flame, all her dreams vanished in an instance. Had it been too much to hope to own a lovely dress? To have one night at home with her family having no concern for their situation? She had done something wrong, but she could not determine what that was.

Moving along the footpath, Anna approached the park Colin had described. More than a dozen carriages lined the curb, and the lights blazed inside one of the houses. That must have been where the party was taking place. For a moment, she considered turning back around and returning to the inn. Colin would eventually go there in search of her.

What she did not wish to do was to heighten her sense of shame, for once she revealed the truth to him, that would be her reward. Doing so here would only ruin what should be an entertaining evening for Colin.

Yet she felt a pull, a desire to remain. And so she did.

The windows of the ballroom must have been open, for she could hear the music even from this distance. The laughter of all the guests said they were enjoying their time together. For so long, she thought there was a chance of being a part of that world, to be seen as someone important. That dream had been dashed as easily as wash water.

Colin stood at the entrance to the park just as he promised he would be. Never had he looked more handsome as he stared up at the dark sky.

Tears welled in Anna's eyes. This weekend together in London would be their last. For a moment, she allowed herself to bring to mind the times they spent together. Their first encounter. Their shared picnic. Their night at the river. How they swam beneath the stars and expressed their anticipation for this journey to London.

"Anna?" Colin called as he hurried to her side. "Anna, what's wrong? I expected you hours ago. What happened?"

Doing her best to control her emotions, she replied, "Lord Leedon is a very kind man, and his home is quite lovely. Lovelier than I would have imagined." She could not stop a tear from escaping her eye and rolling down her cheek. "I had imagined my brothers going there to join us for tea. To be able to purchase a blue dress." She looked up at him, his features shadowed by the brighter lights of the house across the way. "Did you know that my house has windows we cannot afford to replace?"

"I did not."

"I had thought that after tonight they'd be fixed. That for once my brothers would have hope. Henry has been in need of new shoes for far too long, so I'd hoped to see he had a new pair so his toes would not hurt. But that can no longer happen, for, although Lord Leedon is a kind man and even offered me money, he's not my father."

"Oh, Anna, I'm so sorry," Colin said. "I had hoped for a different result, I truly did. I wish there was something I could have done, to learn the truth beforehand or to—"

"The fault's not yours," she said, wiping the tears from her cheeks. "If there is to be blame cast, it is on me. I'm a Silverstone. We're born into poverty and shall perish in poverty. It's always been the same for people like me and will remain so until the end of time."

"I'm sure there can be a way. You mustn't give up on your dreams."

"Dreams?" she asked in a choked laugh. "All my life, I've dreamed of meeting my father. Now, not only is Lord Leedon not that man, but I've learned that he'll never be found."

"Is he dead?"

Anna found she could not tell him the truth about her mother. It was one thing to humiliate oneself by having dreams that were far too lofty for one of her station and quite another to reveal how low she truly was.

"He's as good as dead," she replied. "I'll never know who my father is, and I cannot say why, for you'll be disgusted by me more than you are now."

Colin took hold of her arms. "You mustn't say such things. You don't disgust me in the least, nor could you ever."

Although she wished with all her heart she could believe his words, she knew she could not. For she was the daughter of a prostitute. Born out of a despicable act. The mere thought made her want to bathe for a week in an attempt to clean away the filth inside her.

"We came to London to seek out our dreams," she said. "And we accomplished that— in our way. You were able to experience a new life, and I learned the truth, which was really what I had hoped for. And now that we've fulfilled those dreams, we must return to the reality that is our lives. You'll return to your dukedom, and I'll return to the workhouse. Tonight must be our final night together."

"Don't say that," Colin said.

Anna shook her head. "I once believed that it was the river where we met that divided the Silverstones from the Remingtons. But I was wrong. Naive. It's our bloodlines that separate us. And you, a duke of all people, cannot argue that point, for you know that it's true."

Colin offered no argument, and although none could be had, she had hoped he would have made the attempt. Despite the shadows, the pain on his face was as clear as if the sun shone down on him. How she hated putting him in this predicament!

Unable to hold them back any longer, she allowed the tears to fall freely. Was she not allowed one last time to weep, to grieve for a dream that was now dead?

Although Colin spoke no words, he gathered her into his arms. The rhythm of his heartbeat accompanied the music wafting from the house, and Anna savored his hold.

"Do you remember asking me why I pluck a blade of grass from the ground and allow the wind to carry it away?"

"I do," he replied.

"It's something I've done since I was a little girl," Anna said. "I imagined that I sat upon that blade and the wind would carry me away from all my problems. That it would lift me up and take me to a place where I would never hurt again. But now I know that those are notions of a child. Tonight, a woman has emerged who knows better, who understands her place in life. That little girl has been put to rest."

She touched Colin's cheek. Oh, but how she cared for this wonderful man! "Do you know what I hoped for most meeting my father? That through his bloodline, I'd be accepted by you and your kind. For I deeply care for you. I may even love you. But now it will never happen. Whatever we thought we had is now over."

As she allowed her hand to drop to her side, sadness fell over her like a heavy blanket. Colin would agree and perhaps make an excuse to leave. This gave him the perfect opportunity to make a clean cut of it, to return to his life without remorse.

Yet to her surprise, he did not. Instead, he took her hands in his and said, "Now that you've told me all that, I too have a confession to make. Although I was truthful in saying that I was at Redstone Estate to find myself, I was there for another reason. I wished to escape an engagement I do not want."

Anna pulled her hand away. "You've a fiancée?" she asked, aghast. Had he been lying to her this entire time? Had he hoped to have one last frolic with a willing woman before he married? The thought made her ill.

"No," he replied. "I've been expected to propose and announce my engagement to a lady my mother selected for me. I've put off finding a bride despite the fact that many suitable ladies have been presented to me. The problem is that none of them held my interest. All were attracted to the idea of marrying the Duke of Greystoke, but they cared little for me— for Colin Remington. Then I met you, Anna. A woman who speaks her mind. One who has been honest with me from the moment we first met. The lady who helped me discover who I truly am beneath the disguise of a title."

"I've been called many things, Colin," Anna whispered. "The bastard child of an unknown man. A Silverstone. But a lady I am not. Look at my clothing. It names me for who I am. Do you remember the looks those ladies at the linendrapers gave me? They know me for who I am. We can't pretend any longer that I'm something I'm not."

"No!" Colin said in such a sharp tone that her heart jumped. "Your name and clothing tell not the true story. The way I cannot imagine a day without you speaks to who you are. For I care for you, more so than anyone in this world."

He pulled her to him once more, covering her gasp of surprise with his mouth. The music from inside the house filled the air around them, its melody the accompaniment to their embrace.

"You're more than beautiful, Anna," he whispered in her ear. "You are everything. I cannot exist without you in my life."

Still in his hold, Anna's heart beat with hope. "Do you believe there's a way for us to be together?"

Colin intertwined his fingers in hers as he pulled away. "You still have dreams that must be fulfilled. I don't know how, but I promise I'll do what I can to find a way."

Happiness coursed through her upon hearing his words. Somehow, Anna knew he spoke the truth, and she found herself believing him.

He leaned in and placed the smallest of kisses on her lips. "Tonight we dance as a couple, for that is what we are."

Anna smiled up at the man who had captured her heart. "I would like that."

As they swayed across the darkened path, the numbness Anna had been feeling receded. In its place settled a sense of euphoria. They were not in a fancy ballroom but a park. Her dress came not from a seamstress but was instead one that she had sewn herself. But none of that mattered. What did was the man with whom she danced beneath the stars.

"They speak of us," Colin said, and Anna followed his gaze to the heavens. "They come out to watch."

What he said was true. The curtain of night had been drawn back to reveal a host of stars too numerous to count. Their twinkles were like applause for the couple below them, and that radiated in her heart. In this way, they did speak, telling her all she needed to know.

"I belong in your arms," she whispered. "I know this now."

"As do I. That is why we dance until your dreams... No, until *our* dreams come true."

As they continued to dance, she thought of all that had been said this night. Despite the heartache she had been feeling upon her arrival, his kiss— and his promise— had pushed it away. Now, more than ever, Anna realized that her feelings for him had changed. Now, she suspected that she might have fallen in love with him.

As they continued to dance, however, a modicum of doubt crept into her mind as he glanced at the ring he wore. Was that concern in his eyes? He had made a promise to her, but she could not help but worry. Would his position as duke allow him to keep it?

Chapter Twenty-Five

Mary Ann, Duchess of Greystoke, had witnessed many forms of chaos in the years since she married into the Remington family. A nephew who collapsed at a ball to never stand again. A baron caught having an affair with the wife of a banker. Wives caught with footmen, husbands caught with maids, men and women both blackmailing their own blood. Despite the plethora of infractions of the many Remingtons, they had survived. It was as if an impenetrable wall surrounded the name, keeping it safe from destruction.

Yet, if what she had heard thus far was true, which she had no reason not doubt it was so, the entire family was in trouble. The walls that had so long held their empire in place were in danger of collapsing.

"It was then that Colin shared with me his true reason for going to London," Evan was saying. He heaved a sigh. "I'm finding it difficult to say, for the shock may prove to be far more than you can bear."

Mary Ann lifted the teacup to her lips only to find that the tea had gone cold. "If you're speaking of him finding some young chit with whom he is spending his time, I'm not surprised. Did I not say that it was likely the case? I'm not naive with no understanding of what men do while they are away from their wives. Or their intended."

Evan smirked, and Mary Ann had to fight back a strong urge to slap the boy. He was young and arrogant, and she wished to put him in his place. But she needed him if she was to learn the truth about her son. Despite his cockiness, she had yet to catch him in a lie. Not to her.

"This girl— Anna by name— has somehow convinced Colin that the Earl of Leedon might be her father," Evan said with a chuckle.

"What's worse is that he's arranged a meeting between the man and her."

The teacup clinked as she set it in its saucer. "Surely not!" She clicked her tongue in vexation. "What's come over my son? After this, Lord Leedon will believe he's an imbecile!"

How could Colin, a usually intelligent and perceptive man, be taken in by this girl? And worse, how could he allow himself to become entangled in these lies? He was the Duke of Greystoke— a Remington!

Rising, Mary Ann went over and pulled the bell cord. Pendleton entered within moments.

"Remove this tray and have fresh tea brought up."

The butler collected the still-full teacups and teapot without comment.

Once he was gone, Mary Ann turned to Evan. "So, my son has become smitten with a girl of questionable lineage? Her father's no earl, I tell you. More likely he's a farmhand or some other such laborer. But even if Lord Leedon is her father, even if he does acknowledge her as his daughter, she may be invited to a few events, but that does not make her a suitable prospect for a duke."

Her jaw ached with how tightly she clenched it. Colin was a grown man who could make his own choices, so using practical means to put a stop to whatever he had planned with this girl would do no good.

"I advised Colin to write to you as a way to gain more time," Evan said. "To say that he and I are discussing a business venture. I believe you may be able to use this to your advantage."

"Well, don't dally," she snapped. "Time is running out."

"It's quite simple, really. You must go to Redstone Estate and remain there until you're able to convince him that he's on a road to destruction."

Pendleton entered with a new tray, served the tea, and bowed out of the room once more.

Mary Ann pursed her lips in thought. "What if arguing with him only drives him into her arms? If he proves to be too stubborn to hear reason, what then?"

Evan took a sip of his tea and then set the cup down with a sigh. "I would appeal to his good nature. He cares far too much for the Remington name and the dukedom, so perhaps you can explain how his plans to carry on with this girl can harm all of us. Ask Lady Katherine to join you if you must. I don't care what you do, Cousin Mary Ann, but you cannot allow this to go on."

The corners of Mary Ann's lips twitched. "You're very sly, Evan. As crafty as a fox. It's no wonder that a hunter has not caught you."

He barked a laugh. "No one can best me, for I can outwit them all. You must adopt my way of thinking lest your name— no, our name— be dragged through the mud." He rose and buttoned his coat. "Now, concerning that deposit we agreed upon?"

Mary Ann nodded. "She's in the parlor with Lady Katherine and some companion their father enlisted. Inform Lady Katherine that I'd like to speak to her at once."

Once Evan left the room, Mary Ann walked to the window. She cared for her son, but she cherished the dukedom far more. Evan's suggestion to go to Wilkworth was sound, for Colin had a good nature about him. With her help— and that of Lady Katherine— she could exploit it.

"You asked to speak to me?" Lady Katherine asked as she entered the room.

Her red hair was pulled up into an intricate chignon, her natural tight curls hanging like tassels beside her ears. She really was a lovely young lady. Why Colin could not see it was beyond Mary Ann. Despite the white day dress and the purity it portrayed, Lady Katherine would have to forgo any semblance of innocence.

Whether she liked it or not.

Mary Ann walked over to sit on the sofa and patted the place beside her. "Come, sit beside me," she said, offering the girl a warm smile. "Don't look so worried, Katherine. You've done nothing wrong. But I cannot say the same for my son."

Concern filled the younger woman's features. "Is Colin in trouble?"

"Yes, my dear, he is in trouble. Yet he's too foolish to realize it." She took Lady Katherine's hand in hers. "You're to become my daughter-in-law soon, and that means we'll be a part of the same family."

"I'm honored, and dare I say excited, for it."

"As am I."

The girl blinked twice. "Forgive me, but I thought you didn't like me."

Oh, if she only knew the truth! "Like you?" Mary Ann said with wide eyes. "Oh, Katherine, I dare say that I care for you like the daughter I never had. That's why you'll be helping me see Colin returned to his rightful place."

"Whatever you wish me to do," Lady Katherine said.

Mary Ann smiled. "Tomorrow morning, you and I shall journey to Wilkworth, where Colin has been staying. We'll use whatever means we can to see he returns home with us, whether it be guilt or whatever you do to entice him. Of course, that will be a last resort, but we must be clear of the expectations before we leave. Will you agree to do your part?"

Lady Katherine frowned. "Guilt? What guilt?"

"The guilt he will feel knowing how much he has hurt us," Mary Ann said, patting the girl's hand. "Now, do you agree or not?"

"Yes, of course," Lady Katherine replied.

"Good. Listen carefully, for the future of all of us may rest in your hands."

Chapter Twenty-Six

Hope filled the air and the promise of better days guided Anna's feet as she walked home. She had asked the driver to stop a mile away from the house. It would do her no good to have Thomas see her in the rented carriage when she was supposed to have been caring for Betty's aunt all week. Her shoes sank in the mud, a sign that it had rained while she was away.

She and Colin remained for another wonderful day in London, with time spent exploring the city and visiting another tavern.

"I'm going to do all I can to see that we're together," he had told her.

And she believed him, despite the droplets of doubt that clung to her like moisture in the air. Although Colin spoke with assuredness, Anna detected notes of concern in his voice. Or were her own worries making her see what was not there? Regardless, she would remain positive until they met as planned beside the river tomorrow evening.

Her bundle clasped in her arms, Anna approached the house. Christian was on the roof, repairing another hole in the thatch. She had hoped to bring news that they could replace it, but that was not to be. Not yet.

Drawing in a deep breath, she silently repeated the story she would tell about the health of Betty's aunt. The door opened, and Thomas exited the house. The scowl he wore spoke volumes, and she came to an abrupt stop. She had expected annoyance, but not rage.

"Where have you been?" he demanded. "And don't lie to me!" He came to a stop in front of her, his face red and his fists clenched.

"I... that is..." She could not get the words to come. "Betty..."

"You disgust me," Thomas growled. "Go on then. Tell me Betty lied when she said that you've spent the week in London with a Remington."

Anna lowered her gaze. How could Betty have betrayed her? "I cannot," she whispered. "I was with him."

"Henry fell off the roof and broke his arm while you were gone. He cried, wanting to see you. So, like a dunderhead, I went to Betty's house in search of you. You can imagine my surprise when I learned you had never arrived!"

Poor Henry. She regretted not being there for him.

"I'm sorry for lying," she said. "If you'll just allow me—"

"Be silent!" Thomas barked. "I haven't finished. Not only did I not find you there, but I also found Betty's mother and aunt there, both hearty and hale. When I asked her aunt if she was feeling better, she looked at me as if I were mad. I then went in search of Betty, and after a bit of coaxing, she told me that my sister was in London sharing her bed with a Remington!"

Anger bubbled in Anna. "How dare you make such an accusation! Do you truly believe I'm that brazen? I went to London to better our lives!"

"Hi, Anna," Henry said from the doorway, his arm in a sling. "I missed you. Look, I broke my arm."

"I see that." Guilt tightened her throat. "Go back inside. I'll come and see you in a moment." Returning her attention to Thomas, she said, "I knew you'd never allow me to go. You never allow me to do anything except work."

Thomas snorted. "You think I'm vile because I don't want you to be alone with a man? Is that it? I wish to protect my sister's virtue, and for that you despise me?"

"You protect it for your own gain, Thomas. Not for me. But don't worry. Nothing happened, nor would it have. I may be desperate, but there are some things I'll not give up."

"If you weren't going to his bed, why did you leave with him? What was so important that you felt the need to lie to me and leave your family alone?"

"I went to find our father!" Anna shouted. "I wanted to know the truth." The wounds from that meeting resurfaced, and tears blurred her vision. But the time for lies was long past. "Lord Leedon is not our father."

"Didn't I tell you no gentleman will be willing to claim us? Yet, like with everything else, you don't listen."

Anna wiped at her eyes. "He admitted to knowing Mother. He said that she… that her work was… well, that she was a prostitute."

Thomas's lip curled. "Don't you remember the times she went to London? You even went with her at least twice. Didn't you find it odd that when she returned, there always seemed to be money?"

"I understand that now," she said, her heart aching as the tears fell freely. "I would never have thought—"

"We're bastards, Anna. Do you finally understand that? We're bastards! And you know something? You taking off with that man reminded me of her." He grabbed her arm, and she stifled a cry. "Now you know why I hated her so much! Because of what she did. For bringing us into the world as she did! Don't make me hate you, too."

Anna shook her head. "You can't mean that. Mother loved all of us. You don't truly hate her, do you?"

The laugh that erupted from Thomas was cruel. "Oh, but I do. I hate her more than you can ever know. But what does it matter anymore? She's just dust, and we're left here fending for ourselves." He released her arm and drew in a deep breath. "I'll write to Mr. Harrison tomorrow and inform him that you wish to return to work."

"But you told me I had until September," Anna said. "That means I still have two months! Besides, Colin is working on a plan so we can be together." As soon as the words left her lips, she knew she should have kept silent.

Thomas roared with laughter. "Christian, did you hear that?" he asked of their brother, who had joined them. "The duke's scheming to find a way for him and your sister to be together. I imagine he's speaking to the King at this very moment. Perhaps the invitations to their wedding have already been sent. You'd best go and press your best trousers."

Humiliation washed over Anna, and she clenched her fists in her skirts. "You don't know what you're saying. Colin is as good as his word."

"I believe her," Christian, who had been watching the argument with great interest, said. "Anna has no reason to lie, and she's always been a good judge of character. If she says it's so, I don't doubt her."

"Then you're just as foolish as she is for believing such nonsense!"

"Her story's no more delusional than yours," Christian said. "At least she's spent time with someone of worth. All you do is prance about wasting our money. The furthest you've gotten is speaking with a stable hand of an earl."

Thomas turned and pointed an accusatory finger in Christian's face. "You've no dignity for yourself or for Anna, another trait you inherited from our mother. Will you say the same when Anna is with child and brings another bastard into this world?"

Anna lifted her arm, intent on slapping Thomas, but he pushed her away, and she landed with a painful *thud* on her bottom.

With a roar, Christian pounced, and soon he and Thomas were rolling around in the mud, their fists pummeling as they cursed one another.

"Stop this!" Anna shouted. "Please, both of you, stop!"

Thomas threw Christian onto his back and landed a harsh fist to his nose. "Both of you sicken me!" he grunted as he pushed himself away and stood, panting. He pointed a finger at Anna. "You best pray that the duke proposes soon, for tomorrow, I'm sending word to Mr. Harrison that not only will you be returning to work, but that he also has my permission to marry you."

With that, he stormed into the house, slamming the door behind him.

Anna turned to Christian. Blood trickled from his nose and dripped off his chin. "Are you all right?" she asked, tearing a portion of fabric from the cloth she had used to bundle her clothes. "You're bleeding."

Christian pushed her hand away. "It's nothing. I think we've been needing to do that for a while now." He accepted the cloth from her and dabbed at his nose. "I doubt it'll be the last time, either."

Anna sighed. "Likely not. But what's become of us? Thomas believes I'll simply give away my virtue to any man who calls me pretty, you two are fighting, and poor Henry must watch it all."

"You act like this is all new," Christian said with a snort. "It's always been this way. Whatever happens, I know one thing for sure. If you don't marry this duke, our troubles'll only get worse."

"What do you mean?" Anna asked with a frown.

Christian glanced toward the house. "Don't tell him I said anything, but I found out that Thomas took out a small loan in order to pay another, and he put up the house as collateral. You know as well as I do that he'll never be able to pay it off. No matter what we do, we'll likely be the last Silverstones to live here. And once this property's gone, we'll never afford another."

Anna looked at the cottage that had been her home all her life. She had gone to London in hopes of returning with good news. That all would be well and they no longer had anything to fear. Instead, she came back with a promise from Colin. But a promise would not fix the roof or pay off a loan before it was called in.

As she stood thinking of what Thomas had said concerning Mr. Harrison, Anna knew one thing. If Colin did not keep his word, Christian was right. Her troubles would only worsen.

***

With a sigh, Colin leaned back into the cushions on the bench of the carriage as it came to a stop in front of Redstone Estate. He had spent the entirety of his return journey considering the promise he had made to Anna. Would he be able to keep it? In one moment, he had readied himself to tell her that all was lost, that they had no future together. In the very next instant, he was promising her the world. He did so because he cared for her. Or perhaps he loved her.

The Duke Who Loved Me

What did it matter what he felt for her? His family would suffer from such an outlandish decision. What Evan had said was true. Colin was being selfish.

He would greet his cousins and then write to his mother to explain his delay once more. From there, he was uncertain what to do. Perhaps time alone would give him the answers he needed.

His thoughts returned to the night of the party. Witnessing Anna's distress had torn at his heart. All she had hoped for was to better her life and that of her brothers. Who could blame her for that? But it was in that moment, as he held her in his arms, that he knew what he wanted. To make her dreams come true. And his. For what he wanted was to be happy, and Anna made him just that.

As he alighted from the vehicle, the hope inside him faded at the sight of a carriage bearing the Greystoke crest etched in gold on its doors.

His mother was here? But why would she come to Wilkworth?

"See my bag taken to my room," Colin said as he hurried to the portico.

Davis opened the door, and Caroline greeted Colin in the foyer.

"I'm glad you're here," she whispered. "Your mother is in the drawing room, but she did not arrive alone. A Lady Katherine is here, as well, but she's gone upstairs to rest."

Colin frowned. "What's Lady Katherine doing here?"

"I don't know," Caroline replied with a glance over her shoulder. "They arrived yesterday afternoon. Your mother has said less than Evelyn."

"Thank you for warning me, Caroline. I suppose there's no putting off speaking to her, so I'll go now and see what she has to say. We'll talk soon."

A pounding in Colin's head told him that he would need to rest soon if he were not careful. This was the last thing he needed, to see his mother before he had found a solution to be with Anna.

"Hello, Mother," he said as he entered the drawing room. "I didn't expect to find you here." He walked up to where she stood at the window and gave her a kiss on the cheek. She wore a bright red

212

gown, one he recognized immediately. It was her battle gown, or so he had termed it. Along with the red jewels, she appeared a queen ready for war. And that was likely what she had in mind.

"Have I ever told you about when your father and I first met?" she asked. "Lord Athwart was hosting a party, and I had not wished to attend. At the time, I had an eye for adventure, but that event, I was certain, would be far too boring. After all, the viscount had very few friends, so I did not imagine that the party would be very lively."

Colin pinched the bridge of his nose. "Mother, what are you doing here?"

"Despite my misgivings, I attended anyway," his mother continued as if he had not spoken. "Oh, I knew who your father was, of course, and we had been introduced in passing, but that night was different. We spent the entire evening speaking together. Soon, we were courting, and the rest needs no explanation."

She turned to face Colin. "I had no expectations the night of that party, yet going was the best decision I ever made. If I had been obstinate, if I had continued to refuse my mother's wishes, your father and I may never have married."

"That's a wonderful story," Colin said, unable to hide his impatience. "And I am, of course, grateful that the two of you met. But that does not answer the question of why you're here."

She took his hand. "My son, you have a wonderful woman ready to become your bride, a lovely young lady who will make the perfect wife. Yet you're willing to lose it all by making an absurd decision?"

"And what would make you think that? I planned to write and explain. You see, Evan and I—"

"Are conducting business of some sort together?" his mother finished for him. "Yes, Evan explained everything to me. And I do mean everything."

Colin's jaw dropped. "He betrayed me?" he asked, pulling back his hand. "What I told him was in confidence!"

After the years of camaraderie, years of companionship, his cousin dared to cross him? Colin had believed that the close relationship they had would keep Evan from ever turning on him as he did with others in their family. What a fool Colin was for trusting him!

"No, my son. What Evan did was not betrayal. It was a noble deed. You may be unable to see it now, but one day you'll understand. He saved you from ruining your name. Did you truly believe that you could marry some common woman with ties to a workhouse?"

Colin rubbed his temples. He had no interest in battling her today. "Mother, I've come to find Anna quite compatible, more so than any other woman I've ever met. She's everything I've ever wished for in a bride."

"But you forget the one thing she does not have," his mother snapped. "She was conceived out of wedlock, Colin, a bastard you sent to the home of Lord Leedon! Can you imagine the embarrassment that man must have felt? For God's sake, he's a married man with three children. Do you not care about the scandal this will bring down on them?"

Colin shook his head. "His family was not present for that meeting. I admit it may not have been the best way to handle the situation, but she had to learn the truth." He leaned against a wall and closed his eyes. This was far worse than he could have expected.

"Well, what's done is done," his mother said. "I'll write to the earl to apologize for your behavior."

Colin gritted his teeth. "You'll do no such thing. My behavior, contrary to what some may believe, requires no apology."

His mother sighed in what appeared to be defeat. "Then, one question remains. What will you do now?"

"Concerning what?" he asked.

"Lady Katherine. She's been weeping all day, by the way, believing that she's unworthy of becoming your bride despite being trained for such a position since birth. Oh, how can you do this to her, Colin? Perhaps you also plan to find a cobbler to marry your dear cousin Caroline? Why not ask the housemaids if they would like to meet the men of title they suspect could be their fathers? Perhaps you can ruin a dozen names this week!"

Guilt washed over Colin. He did not wish to hurt Lady Katherine. Nor Caroline, for that matter.

"Think of your father," his mother said as she lifted the hand that bore his ducal ring. "He wore this with honor. Will you throw it all away for this woman?"

The memory of the day he received that ring came to mind. His father had been on his deathbed, dying from a horrible disease that claimed him far too early in life.

"My son, this ring was given to me by my father, as his father gave it to him. It represents the dukedom, yet is so much more. Whoever wears it represents not only Greystoke, but the family name of Remington, as well. Wear it with pride and honor, for that is what you must possess to lead everyone who depends on you."

"I promise, Father. I always will."

With one last look at his mother's furtive expression, Colin replied, "It was my hope that I would find a way to marry Anna. Give me just a few days to find a solution that is agreeable to us all."

His mother sighed. "I'm sure you think me cruel for interfering, but I only wish to protect you. Recovering from ridicule can be a battle, and some never recover. Regardless, I'll trust that you'll find the right solution. Just remember that you must think of the dukedom, for you have many who rely on you."

Looking down at the ring one last time, he replied, "You have my word."

Chapter Twenty-Seven

Colin was desperate. The entire night and most of the day had been spent conjuring and then discarding plan after plan. He needed a way for him and Anna to be together. Yet nothing came to mind. At least, nothing of substance. All he could do was be forthright with his mother.

He found her in the library with Caroline. His cousin seemed to sense his need for privacy, for she rose and exited the room, giving him a faint smile.

His mother, who sat on the couch, closed the book she was reading and set it on the table beside her. "You appear as if you have something to say. Have you finally seen reason and put an end to this nonsense?"

"I've come with a request," he said as he sat beside her. "I would like you to meet Anna."

His mother sniffed. "Surely you don't think I can allow someone like her to come into this home."

Annoyance rose in Colin. "I'll arrange to have her meet us elsewhere, away from prying eyes. You'll see that she's not the woman you believe her to be. She means much to me, Mother." He reached out and took her hand. "We both know I can marry whomever I wish. But we also know the disdain from my peers will be great if I marry someone like her. What I would like is your support in my decision."

His mother drew in a deep breath. "I've certainly found ways to make events play in our favor, but this woman's dubious bloodline hinders her. The fact she was born out of wedlock only complicates matters. I'm not sure what I can do about any of this, but you're my son and my allegiance is to you."

"Then you agree?"

"Do you think me so terrible?" she asked with a small smile. "I cannot say that your request does not make me uncomfortable, but how can I deny something as simple as a meeting? Perhaps your prediction is correct, and I'll see the woman as you do."

"Thank you, Mother," Colin said as he stood, feeling hope for the first time. "Trust me, you'll find her delightful." He kissed her cheek.

At the doorway, Colin paused. What his mother had agreed to gave him some semblance of hope. Yet would she truly give Anna a fair chance?

When he turned back and saw his mother's smile, however, he felt a bit better. If one could not trust his own mother, who could he trust?

***

The ornate mantel clock mocked Colin as he watched the hands crawl, snail-like, around its face. An hour should not be this long. That was how long it would be before he met with Anna, where he would explain that their chances of being together hung in the balance.

He rubbed his eyes. The agony of their future had kept him awake at night and racked his brain during the day. No other solution had come except to hope Anna could win over his mother.

A shadow fell over him, and he turned to find Lady Katherine standing in the doorway. Her green dress matched her eyes, and her hair had been carefully styled into a precise chignon. There was no doubt she was handsome, but she paled in comparison to Anna's striking beauty.

"My apologies, Your Grace, but may I have a word with you?"

"You're not a servant, Lady Katherine," he said as he stood, pushing down his annoyance. "Of course, you may speak freely."

She nodded and closed the door behind her. "I've thought a lot about what I wish to tell you, Your Grace. It will not be easy, but perhaps it would be best if I'm completely honest."

"I agree. Speaking truthfully is always best for all concerned. Let's sit." He led her to the couch.

"Thank you, Your... er, Colin." A blush crept into her cheeks.

Once they were seated, he said, "Now, what is it you wish to say?"

She shifted to look at him, her knee touching his. "You see, I have come to realize that you are a man with certain... needs. As a woman, as your wife, I'll be meant to fulfill those needs. I believed we would wait until our wedding night, but I see no reason to delay."

Before Colin could respond, she slid the dress off her shoulders. "I'm yours to use as you will, Colin."

Alarm bells rang in his head as the dress came dangerously close to exposing far more than appropriate, and he grasped hold of her arms. "What are you doing?" he demanded.

"Giving you what you want," she said. "I know how the other woman pleases you. I only wish to do the same."

"But that is not what I want from you."

"Then tell me," she cried as she pulled away and stood. "Tell me, for I'm being pushed away, and I have no idea why!"

Frustration tore through Colin at the tears that glistened in her eyes. He had not realized how harsh the current predicament had been on her. She had done nothing wrong yet had suffered for it.

He stood. "This has nothing to do with anything you've said or done."

"You're kind to say so, but I know the truth." She placed a delicate hand on his chest. "Do you not find me worthy of your bed? Do I disgust you? If not, use me as you wish. No harm can be done if we are to marry, anyway."

When he made no move to do as she asked, Lady Katherine took a step back and gave an angry tug on the neckline of her dress and pulled it back onto her shoulders.

"All my life, I've practiced all that is needed to marry a titled man. And still, you refuse me. Now, I'm to return home without my promise of marriage, without a fiancé. I have no future. My family, my friends, our peers, all will see my shame."

She placed a hand on his arm and gave him a fervent look. "I only wish you would have given me a chance. But now I can see that I'm worth nothing."

With a great sob, she lowered her head and hurried from the room.

Colin frowned after her. From the start, he had been clear that he had no interest in her. So, why had his mother brought her to Wilkworth?

Lady Katherine's distant sob made him sigh. What she said was true. When he did not officially propose, her parents would be angry. But plenty of eligible bachelors would find her more than suitable for their needs. If she was trained to marry a duke, she certainly could use those skills to marry a man of lesser title.

None of what just occurred changed his plans. He would still meet with Anna and set up the meeting between her and his mother. It would be difficult to convince her that this was the right path to take, but his mother would see reason. She had to.

Finishing off the rest of his brandy, he considered that perhaps he should have taken Evan's advice and ended whatever they had the night of Lord Dundwhich's party. He had no desire to hurt her, which was the reason he had made the promise he had.

The promise that sent his confidence plummeting every time he thought of it.

When the time finally came, Colin left the house and walked down the dark path, a lantern in his hand. The sky had a scattering of clouds, behind which the moon tried to hide. He had given himself enough time to traverse the woods, treading carefully lest he stumbled.

It was a relief when he arrived to find Anna waiting for him. She, too, carried a lantern, its soft glow reflecting off the pool. Wearing his coat over a simple burlap dress, she had never looked more exquisite.

"Did you know a duke gave me this coat?" she asked with a smile as she held out her arms to admire the sleeves. "It's at least two sizes too large, but it does its duty of keeping the chill air off me."

Her smile eased the worry in his heart, but it could not take it away completely. "Then you are fortunate to have received such a gift,"

Colin said as he joined her on the fallen log. "I'm sure the man who gave it to you did so because he cared."

Anna laughed, but when he did not, she tilted her head. "There's something wrong. I can see it in your face."

There was no point in lying to her. The truth needed to be said. "When I returned to Redstone Estate, my mother was waiting there for me. With Lady Katherine."

"The woman you're supposed to marry?"

"Indeed. I was surprised that mother brought her, but we should not be concerned about it. To say she disapproves of us is being far too kind." His grip tightened on the handle of the lantern. "Lady Katherine is angry, and I cannot say I blame her. I'd not intended to hurt her, but that was what happened."

"So, you came to tell me there's no hope," Anna said as she lowered her gaze. "That this Lady Katherine is to become your wife."

"No, of course not," Colin said, although the words sounded flat to his ears. "I've spoken to Mother, and she's agreed to speak with you on Thursday. We'll meet where the road forks." He took Anna's hands in his. "Be aware that Mother can be very blunt when she so chooses, but I know you can contend with her. It's what is needed for her eventual approval."

"Eventual approval?" Anna asked, taking a step back. "Don't you believe I can win her over on Thursday?"

How he wished to tell her that she could, but if he did, he would be lying. "Anna, the days and weeks ahead will be trying for both of us. We'll need patience more than ever. I've no choice but to ask that you remain strong, for my mother can be brutal when it comes to matters of the dukedom and what she believes to be right. It's difficult to explain, but I must have her approval. Not for my decision, but rather so we have her support in the weeks ahead."

Was it his imagination or were his words as forced as they sounded? Was he saying all this to convince himself as much as Anna? Or was he denying the truth? That his mother would never approve. That he was delaying the inevitable. That not only would the road ahead be trying but that it might just lead them to the edge of a cliff.

The river burbled, but this time it did not soothe him as it had in the past.

"I must tell you something," Anna said. "When I returned home, Thomas was waiting for me. He learned about us being in London together." She turned to face the river, looking lovelier than ever in the faint glow of the two lanterns. "Do you recall me mentioning my employer at the workhouse, Mr. Harrison?"

"The man who believes women are there to serve his carnal needs?" Colin asked. "Yes, I remember. What about him?"

"Thomas says that he wants to sell him my hand in marriage."

"Sell?" Anger welled in Colin. "You're not a horse to be bartered, Anna. Surely there must be a way to avoid such an arrangement."

"Only one thing can put a stop to it," she said, her voice filled with sadness. "The man with whom I've fallen in love must save me. Don't you see, Colin? I love you."

Without thought, he took her into his arms, wanting nothing more than to hold and protect her. To promise that every problem that life threw at them would fall to the side. To assure her that they had a future together. But most of all, he wished to express that he, too, loved her.

Yet the words would not come, and Colin could not say why. Instead, he held her face in his hands and said, "Don't worry. I'll find a way. As sure as the sun will rise in the morning, I'll save you."

Now, if only he could convince himself that his words were true.

Chapter Twenty-Eight

With careful hands, Anna pushed the needle through the fabric. Her blue dress, the best she owned, lay on the kitchen table. If she was to make a good impression, she had to resew the fraying hem and mend the places where the fabric had worn through. If only she could replace the entire dress!

She could barely contain her excitement— and her uneasiness. She was to meet the duchess in just a few short hours. It was one thing to tease a duke she had found asleep from consuming too much drink and quite another to be presented to his mother.

The truth was, the dress should have been discarded months ago, but with no money to purchase fabric for another, she had held on to it. It was certainly better than the dresses made of burlap, despite its holes.

"What're you doing?" Henry asked as he leaned his elbows on the table. "Did you break your dress?"

Anna laughed. "A dress cannot break. I'm mending it so I can look presentable to an important lady."

Henry did not seem to find her explanation satisfactory. "But why do you have to fix your dress for her? Doesn't she like it well enough?"

Anna reached over and tousled his brown hair. "Sometimes we must take extra effort to make a good impression, which means having our clothing as nice as possible."

He scratched his head and scrunched his face. "If you say so. I'm going outside to play."

Thomas, who stood beside the counter with a glass of water in his hand, watched her as she worked. He had hardly spoken two words to her since her return, and he had surprised her by not giving an opinion when she mentioned this meeting. She hoped he would not use it now to dampen her spirits.

"This meeting with the duchess is important to you, isn't it?"

Anna nodded. "It's the first step of many that I must take to earn her acceptance. If only I had a better dress, I think my chances would fare much better."

Thomas made no comment before leaving the room, and Anna resumed her mending, relieved her brother had not shouted at her.

Although Colin had expressed doubt at the river two nights earlier, Anna knew better. Duchess or not, his mother was a woman and would surely understand what they felt for one another. Of course, Anna would have to prove she was worthy. The bloodline she once believed was hers did not exist, but she loved Colin. And love was what mattered.

So lost in her thoughts was Anna that she nearly jumped from her chair when Thomas dropped a large box on top of her dress. Did he mean to sabotage her plans? The box had at least an inch of dust on its lid, which would dirty the fabric.

"What are you doing?" she demanded.

"Mother told me that one day you'd require a dress," he said. "I asked her how I'd know, but she assured me that I would just know. It was her favorite dress, and now it's yours."

Overcome with emotion, Anna lifted the lid of the box to reveal a lovely blue muslin dress. "It's my favorite color," she whispered as she trailed her fingers over the soft fabric. "I remember Mother once wearing this dress, but I had forgotten about it."

Joy filled her as she did something she had not done in a long time— she embraced her brother. "Thank you. There is hope, Thomas. One way or another, all our lives are going to improve."

"I hope what you say is true, for I've given up thinking that anything good will happen to us."

For the first time, Anna could see the weight Thomas carried on his shoulders. He did his best to never mention his despair. He had to have dreams, just as she did, and she prayed she could help him realize them.

"Anna!" Henry came rushing into the kitchen, his cheeks pink with excitement. "There're two ladies here asking for you. Christian's talking to them now, and one of them keeps giggling." He scowled at this.

"Just two ladies? There's no gentleman with them?"

Henry shook his head. "Just them two."

Anna frowned. "Who could it be?" she wondered as she followed Henry to the front of the house. There she found Miss Caroline in a yellow day dress with matching ribbons in her hair. Beside her stood a young woman in a maid's uniform clutching two bags.

"Oh, there she is!" Miss Caroline gushed as she hurried to Anna and hugged her. "You must forgive me for calling over without sending a request beforehand, but Christian has assured me that it's no trouble."

Christian's cheeks were redder than any rose Anna had ever seen— a perfect match to Miss Caroline's.

"You're welcome here anytime," Anna assured the young woman. From behind her, Thomas cleared his throat. "Oh, this is my eldest brother, Thomas. And this young lad is Henry. And, of course, you've met Christian."

"I have indeed met him," Miss Caroline said with a sigh as she stared far longer than necessary at Christian. Then she shook her head and added, "This is my lady's maid, Beatrice. She's here to help me."

"Help you do what?" Anna asked.

"Yesterday, I happened to overhear my cousin Colin speaking to his mother about meeting you. Well, a lady must be prepared to look her absolute best, so I decided to bring over a few items to help heighten your beauty."

Anna stared at her in disbelief. "You're willing to do this?"

"Of course," Miss Caroline said as if Anna had said the sky was blue. "We are friends, but, more importantly, we're women. Although it can be a burden, we must prepare ourselves for certain men. Some deserve it more than others."

She glanced at Christian, a mischievous glint in her eye. It was clear Miss Caroline had fallen for her brother's rugged good looks, just as so many others had, despite the fact that Christian never did anything to garner their attention. Now, he stood digging the toe of his shoe into the dirt in front of him.

"Well, we really should get started," Miss Caroline said. "We don't have much time, so let's go inside to get you ready."

Anna nodded, but when they reached the door, she stopped and turned to face Miss Caroline. "You're more than welcome in my home, but I should warn you that it's not up to your standards. I have no comfortable chairs to offer you."

Miss Caroline laughed. "I don't care about that. Friendship is not based on what we own." As they went to enter, Miss Caroline stopped and placed an arm across the door. "I'm sorry, but when a woman prepares for a special event, she doesn't need brothers milling around and gawking. Go entertain each other with stories of war or whatever other mundane topics men discuss."

Thomas went to speak, but Christian grabbed his arm and said, "Of course, miss. Come on. Let's leave the ladies to their business. I wanted to show you what I've done with the white stallion you brought me last week, anyway."

Shaking her head, Anna led the two women into the house. "My mother left me this dress," she said as she pulled it from the box. "I've never worn it and forgot it existed until just before you arrived, so I hope it fits."

"It's very beautiful," Miss Caroline said as she fingered the intricate lace that lined the neckline. "Once Colin sees you in it, and after what Beatrice and I do, he may decide to elope with you no matter what his mother says!"

Anna could not help but laugh.

Beatrice went over and set several logs into the fireplace.

"What are you doing?" Anna asked. "It's far too warm for a fire."

The maid blushed. "I must be able to heat the curling tongs," she said, glancing at Miss Caroline.

"Go on, Beatrice. Anna doesn't mind, do you?"

Anna could only gape. "No, I suppose not."

"Good. Now, there's no time for shyness, so get out of that dress. I've brought a chemise and a short corset. I assume you have none."

"No," Anna replied, staring in wonderment as Miss Caroline removed the items from one of the bags. The stays looked rather uncomfortable in her opinion.

"I've also brought a variety of petticoats and gloves." She pushed aside one of the bags. "You won't be needing this gown. Yours is far lovelier. Now, I believe this petticoat will be better for your dress, would you not agree, Beatrice?"

"Yes, miss," the maid replied. "The other'll be far too warm."

Miss Caroline nodded. "Now, let's get you dressed."

Donning the chemise, Anna welcomed the fabric, which was far softer than even her good blue dress. She grasped the counter as Miss Caroline and Beatrice pulled at the stays on the short corset, its bone structure digging into her flesh. It took some meandering, but they managed to get it into place, so it was not so uncomfortable.

"Before you don the dress," Miss Caroline said, "we'll have Beatrice curl your hair. She can do wonders, I assure you."

Anna gave the iron a skeptical look. She had never had her hair curled before, not with a hot iron. She had used strips of cloth to wrap her hair before but doing so typically was not worth the time spent. Not when she was only going to the workhouse.

"Don't worry, Miss Anna," Beatrice said when Anna winced well before the iron touched her hair. "I've never burned Miss Caroline."

"That's true," Miss Caroline replied. "And she's always done excellent work. I've never left the house with my hair looking horrid." She turned to the maid. "And how many times must I insist that I'm simply Caroline when we're alone?"

"But we're not alone, miss."

Miss Caroline waved a dismissive hand. "I'm sure Miss Anna will not mind, will you?"

Anna laughed. "Not at all." She found the pair very entertaining. They clearly had a close relationship despite their differences in station. Then again, Miss Caroline was different from many women of the *ton*. She treated people with respect despite their place in society.

226

"There," Beatrice said after more than half an hour. The smell of burnt hair filled the room, and Anna could not help but wonder if she had any more hair to curl! "What do you think, Miss Caroline?"

Miss Caroline walked a complete circle around Anna. "Yes, that will do nicely. Now, let's add a bit of color." She placed several jars on the table, lifting each one in turn. "She does not need much. Perhaps a bit of rouge and some color on her lips. She's already so beautiful." She handed one of the jars to Beatrice.

"I must admit that witnessing this budding romance between you and Colin has been far better than any novel I've read. Do you realize that we'll become family when you marry? Poor Davis will have a fit! But who cares? You'll always be welcome at my home no matter what."

Once Beatrice applied the makeup, Miss Caroline displayed a selection of gloves. "Do you prefer any in particular? Or perhaps you have your own to wear."

Anna shook her head. "I don't own any gloves. I believe I prefer the ones with the blue lace at the wrists. They match my dress."

Miss Caroline beamed. "Those were the ones I was going to suggest. All right, Beatrice, it's time to help her with the dress."

Stepping into her mother's dress, Beatrice pulled it up to her shoulders. With practiced ease, she soon had the tiny buttons in place. Finally, she helped slide the gloves over Anna's hands.

"There," Miss Caroline said as she took a step back. "Now, what are we missing? Oh, yes! Fragrance. Every lady needs perfume!"

After dabbing the scent of roses behind Anna's ears and in the hollow of her throat, Caroline took one last look. "I must say, my work today is pure brilliance." She turned and looked at Beatrice. "Do you not agree?"

The maid grinned. "I do indeed, miss," she said, giving Anna a wink.

Caroline glanced around. "Do you have a mirror?"

Anna shook her head, her cheeks heating. "Only a small one. But it's cracked and would do us no good."

"No worries," Caroline said as she pulled out a large hand mirror from the bag. "You'll not be able to see the full effect, but you must trust me that you are absolutely stunning!"

Worrying her bottom lip, Anna took the mirror from Miss Caroline and gasped. Staring back at her was a woman she hardly recognized. Her blonde hair hung down her back in long ringlets. Her lips were stained with just a touch of red, as were her cheeks. But the dress was more exquisite than she would have ever imagined.

"Mother would be so pleased," she said before turning back to Miss Caroline and Beatrice. "Thank you, both of you, for making me feel so beautiful."

Miss Caroline gave a dramatic sigh. "You were already beautiful. We only enhanced what you already had. And you're most welcome." She kissed each of Anna's cheeks. "May your romance continue to bloom. And write down everything that happens and send it to me so I can read about it like one of my novels!"

Promising she would, Anna bid them farewell. In just ten minutes, she would begin her walk to the fork in the road. Although all felt perfect, doubt crept into her heart.

Would her appearance impress the duchess? Could a simple dress bring about such a miracle?

But the question that had a firm grasp on her heart was, what would happen if the lady rejected her?

***

Another night of tossing and turning had kept Colin awake. This time, however, it was not due to worry but rather because of hope. Today, his mother would meet Anna and thus would begin the slow and tedious journey of acceptance. It would take time, of course, but his mother would come to see in Anna what he saw. And when that happened, she would have no choice but give them her blessing. And from there, find a way to make it work.

But first, they had to meet.

The Duke Who Loved Me

They were not due to leave for another hour, so he took his time dressing. He wanted to give his mother no opportunity to devise an excuse to cancel their outing, and knowing her, she might do just that.

Colin sighed and made his way to the library. His plan was to spend the next hour reading in an attempt to pass the time. If he was able to keep his mind on the book, that is.

He stopped at the doorway. Evelyn stood peering out the window, dressed once again in her mourning clothes. This time, she wore no gloves, and her right hand was pressed against the windowpane. Although she had dined with the family the last two evenings, she had said little.

"Good morning, Evelyn," he said, hoping not to startle her. "I don't mean to disturb you. I'm just here to choose a book and I'll leave you to your thoughts."

She turned to him and smiled. "No, please stay. I had hoped to ask you something."

Colin joined her at the window. A gardener squatted, hunchbacked, as he pulled the weeds in one of the flowerbeds.

"Caroline informed me that you intend to marry Miss Silverstone."

Colin nodded, although he had not mentioned it to Caroline. The girl must have been spying. "That is my wish. But I'm afraid mother's approval will take time. If it is even possible. I may be nearly fifty before that day arrives."

He forced a chuckle, but Evelyn did not even smile. Instead, she pressed the tip of a finger against the glass. "I once had happiness," she said. "Though the odd thing is that I didn't realize I had it until it was gone." She turned to face him. "So often in life, we come to find ourselves wanting more or better things without realizing that perhaps this is the best it will ever be."

Colin found that he had no reply to her strange riddle. "Why are you unhappy?"

Before Evelyn could reply, the door opened, and his mother stormed into the room.

"We must speak now. Alone."

Despite the fact the house was hers, Evelyn bowed her head in acknowledgment and left the room.

"What's wrong?" Colin asked, surprised by the rage in his mother's eyes and the curl of disgust on her lips.

She clutched a letter in her hand. "What I would like to know, my son, is how you could have forgotten to tell me that this woman I am to meet today is the daughter of a prostitute!" his mother said with a growl as she held out the letter to him.

"A prostitute?" Colin asked as anger rose in him. "I would watch your tongue, Mother. You have no right to levy such accusations against Anna! I'll not have it!"

His mother thrust the letter against his chest. "Read it for yourself. I warned you that the woman was no good, but I had no idea how right I was."

"What's this nonsense?" Colin demanded as he took the letter in hand. "Who is this from?"

"Lord Leedon," his mother spat. "The man was gracious enough to respond to my apology."

Colin's ire rose so quickly that he thought his face would catch fire. "You went behind my back after I told you to leave the man alone?" he demanded, his jaw clenched in rage. "How dare you go against my expressed wishes!"

To his bewilderment, his mother took a step toward him and tapped the letter with a finger. In the softest of voices, she said, "Read it and learn what he has to say about this woman you wish to bring into our family."

What had come over his mother as of late? Meddling in his personal life had never been something she had done in the past. Not to this degree. Whispered suggestions on who he should marry, certainly, but to go this far? No, it was unlike her. What the letter had to say had to be serious, indeed.

He unfolded the parchment.

Dear Duchess of Greystoke,

The Duke Who Loved Me

I appreciate your offer of apology on behalf of your son. I shall not argue that the imposition His Grace put on me might have caused me a great deal of discomfort. I'm only thankful that I had the foresight to make sure Cecilia and the children were not present to witness such an atrocity.

Although I had never met Miss Silverstone before the day she arrived at my London home, I was indeed acquainted with her mother. The various charities I have supported throughout the years included one which helps women who have been forced to lead a life that is far less respectable than most. We worked with such women, gave them proper training, and found them honest work to put them on a path to better lives.

Miss Silverstone's mother, Rebecca, was one such woman. The truth is, and please forgive me if I cause you distress with my forwardness, but she was a prostitute. Unfortunately, she filled her daughter's head with nonsense, including informing her that I am her father. Any such relationship is purely fiction, I assure you.

The fault, I suppose, lies with myself, for I was the one who chose to spend time with people who live such terrible lives, ignoring the advice given me that I should keep my distance. Now, many years later, my choices have returned to haunt me.

I humbly beg of you to see that His Grace puts these rumors to rest. If not for me, then for the sake of my daughters, who are but children. I would hate to see their impeccable name tarnished by lies.

Respectfully yours,
Leedon

Colin's stomach ached and all the air was gone from his lungs as if someone had struck him.

"Do you understand now what you've brought upon yourself?" his mother asked. "The shame you dare wish to bring upon this family with this dalliance?"

"I did not know," Colin mumbled. "I had no idea."

But was that the truth? He recalled the night in the park during the party at the home of Lord Dundwhich. Anna had said that if she were to explain the situation pertaining to her father, he would be disgusted. Now he understood why. The fact she was born out of wedlock had not mattered to him, for many children were brought into the world through a love that could not be.

This, however, was far different. Any man who had bedded her mother for money could be Anna's father. How could he allow such scandal into his family? The truth was, he could not, and that tore at his heart worse than anything could.

"You've shamed me," his mother said. "To say I'm embarrassed with the choices you have made as of late is far too lenient. Why would you do such a thing to me? Have I done something to bring on this act of rebellion? Is this the reason you came to the home of your cousins? To hurt me for some infraction I have done to you? You've never been a vindictive man, but I'm afraid that this...whatever you wish to call it has clouded your judgment."

Colin folded the letter and placed it in his pocket. His heart, mind, and body were numb. "I didn't mean to embarrass you, Mother. The purpose of this excursion to Wilkworth was to find myself."

His mother let out a mocking laugh. "Find yourself? Do you not see what silly notions do? They threatened absolute ruin." She shook her head and took hold of his hand. "My son, you are a duke. I don't deny that you may have enjoyed your time with this woman, but you must now make a decision. Either you sacrifice everything and ruin your name or leave with me today and return to where you belong. I'll see that our things are packed and placed in the carriage while I await your decision."

Colin stared at the ruby set in his ring. Why had Anna not told him all she had learned? He would not have cared for her less, but it would have helped so he could navigate the storm in which he found himself.

Clenching his fist, he swore under his breath. Who was he fooling? The ship he commanded was sinking fast. Unless he abandoned it, he, too, would go down with it. His mother was right. He was a duke and had a responsibility to his family. The games he had played these last weeks were that of a simpleton. Although he cared for Anna, any marginal chance they once had to be together was now gone.

Knowing this made him close his eyes. He had no choice but to say goodbye to her this very day. Her heart would be crushed, but it was for the best. For both of them.

How long he stood there in thought, he did not know, but then the striking of the clock drew his attention to the time. What had begun as a day filled with hope had quickly turned to one of dread.

What he needed was time to consider how he would break the news to Anna.

Colin walked to the foyer and found Davis standing at attention. "Davis, tell my mother that I'm off for a walk and will return shortly."

"Her Grace and Lady Katherine are not home, Your Grace," the butler said.

"Not home?" Colin asked, alarmed. "Where did they go?"

"Her Grace did not say, but I did hear her mention something about 'putting an end to this once and for all' or something of that sort."

Colin closed his eyes. His mother had gone to see Anna without him. What was worse, she had taken Lady Katherine with her!

Hurrying outside, he had hoped to see the carriage, but it was gone. "You!" he called out to a startled stable hand, "Fetch me my horse. Quickly!"

The man dipped his head and ran inside the stable.

Colin would have to make haste to stop his mother. To stop Lady Katherine. To save Anna.

And, as he had done so many times before, Colin turned his attention to his ducal ring. A ring that stood for everything.

The Duke Who Loved Me

One question sat in the forefront of his mind. Was he willing to sacrifice who he was for Anna?

Chapter Twenty-Nine

If one were to chronicle the plight of the Silverstones throughout generations, he or she would have seen a common pattern. One particular individual would savor a windfall that filled his coffers only to lose it all within his lifetime. Another would find her one true love only to learn he had never been hers. Whether it be monetary gain or love, all ended in ruin.

Well, that misfortune would end with Anna.

Wearing her mother's dress, the stylish gloves Miss Caroline had loaned her, and the addition of cosmetics to "add to your beauty" as Miss Caroline had put it, Anna felt like a true woman for the first time in her life. The world belonged to her, or rather to her and Colin.

At the fork in the road where she was to meet the duchess, Anna stopped to pluck a single blade of grass from the roadside.

How often had she performed this ritual of allowing the wind to carry her away to her dreams? She had been no more than six or seven the first time she had done it. And today would be the last.

She released the blade from her fingers. It floated to the ground at her feet. There was no breeze.

The *clip-clop* of hoofbeats made her turn. The Remington family carriage appeared, and Anna's heart pounded with excitement. The moment had arrived!

Straightening her posture, Anna adjusted her shawl for the tenth time. A first impression could make or break a deal, or so Thomas had often told her. Not that it had helped him much, but the advice was sound, nonetheless.

The vehicle stopped, and the driver jumped down, placed the steps on the ground, and opened the door.

A lady alighted, her beige dress flowing around her ankles. Well into her middle years, the duchess was still quite beautiful. Jewels sparkled on her fingers, around her neck and wrists, and in her hair. Dark blue eyes inspected Anna.

Please, let me meet her approval!

Then, to Anna's surprise, another woman stepped from the carriage. Her deep-green gown fit her slender form perfectly.

Her lady's maid, perhaps? Anna thought.

"Anna, is it?" the duchess asked. Nothing on her features expressed her thoughts.

Anna dropped into a curtsy. "Yes, Your Grace." She glanced up through her eyelashes. Where was Colin?

"Rise, child."

Anna did as the duchess bade.

"My son has spoken highly of you. I understand that the two of you were in London together. Is this true?"

"Yes, Your Grace. We were there a week."

The smile that appeared on the duchess's lips held no warmth. "Do you see the lady behind me?" Anna nodded. "Her name is Lady Katherine Haskett."

Anna realized at once who the red-haired beauty was— the very woman Colin was meant to marry. "She is very... pretty, Your Grace."

The duchess laughed. "Oh, my dear, she's more than pretty. She's flawless. Not a single blemish mars her skin. Nor her reputation. Her entire life, she has trained to become the wife of an important gentleman. One such as my son. Do you honestly believe you can replace her?"

Jutting her chin, Anna replied, "I do, Your Grace. I may not have received the training that Lady Katherine has, but I'm willing to learn. I don't know if he has told you, but Colin and I have come to admire one another greatly. Although he does respect Lady Katherine, his feelings for her don't go beyond that. He has told me as much."

"Let's take a short stroll," the duchess said. "Lady Katherine, I'd like you to remain here." Once they had walked a short distance, she continued. "I can see that you've given this much thought, Miss Silverstone. You're articulate and well-mannered and clearly have strong feelings for my son. I must admit, it comes as quite a surprise that you seem as educated as you are. What you've shared has made me realize the right course of action."

All doubt began to fade. She could see just how much Anna cared for her son! Was that not what every mother wanted? "Are you saying, then, that you approve of me, Your Grace?"

The duchess came to an abrupt stop and turned toward Anna. "Can you imagine your wedding day? All the honored guests? An orchestra playing? You wearing a lovely wedding gown of white satin covered in intricate lace?"

Anna could not help but smile. "Oh, yes, Your Grace. I've pictured it often."

"Then, one of the guests will raise a glass and make a toast." She lifted her hand as if it held a glass. "'To the daughter of a whore!'"

Anna's mouth went dry, and any response stuck in her throat. How did she know?

"Do you think me a fool, child? Did you honestly believe that I would allow my own flesh and blood to marry the daughter of a prostitute? You're no lady, Anna Silverstone, and certainly not worthy to marry my son. Not even my driver would see you as a viable prospect. People such as yourself are a scourge on society. If you don't feel disgust for your origins, you are far lower than I believed."

The shame nearly choked the life out of Anna. Her chest constricted, and she had to force the words past her lips. "I'm not a bad person."

"You may have your hair styled by the finest lady's maid and the finest rouge from Paris applied to your cheeks. Even the dress you wear gives the illusion that you're a woman of worth." The duchess leaned closer and added in a harsh whisper, "Yet none of it will hide who you truly are— the daughter of a woman willing to take a man to her bed for money. You'll keep your distance from Colin if you know what's good for you. You're unworthy to even set eyes upon my son let alone marry him!"

The duchess leered with accusing eyes, leaving Anna to swallow back bile. She was an impostor who had deceived no one but herself. Why had she believed herself worthy to wear such a beautiful dress? To present herself as someone other than who she truly was?

Her gaze fell on Lady Katherine. A woman without blemish. From her porcelain skin to the exact cut of her dress, she was indeed perfect. Unlike Anna, she was a true lady.

Just as she considered running away, Colin came riding up to her. Despair turned to elation. He had arrived to tell her all would be well!

He leapt from his horse and approached the duchess, his voice echoing through the valley. "What did you say to her?"

"The truth," the duchess replied. "That she will make an unsuitable bride for you. That she's lower—"

"You have overstepped for the last time," Colin snapped.

Hope rose in Anna once again. What his mother or anyone else thought did not matter. Only what Colin wanted did.

"Take Lady Katherine, collect your things from Redstone Estate, and go home. And pray that you are already gone by the time I return, for what I'm likely to say will pale in comparison to what you said to Anna."

The duchess marched to the carriage without so much as a word, ushing Lady Katherine before her.

When Colin turned back to Anna, his look of despondency told Anna everything. The last morsel of hope crumbled to join the dust at her feet.

"Anna, you must listen, please," he said. "Leedon wrote to my mother. Is what he said true? Was your mother a… a—"

"Yes." A tear escaped her eye and rolled down her cheek. "I wanted to tell you, but I could not. It made me sick, knowing the truth. I feared you would no longer want me. Please tell me that I'm wrong."

Colin closed his eyes. "I'm sorry, Anna. You must understand, but we cannot continue as we have."

It was as if the entire world had come to a stop. The ground beneath her feet threatened to give way, and it took everything in her not to collapse where she stood.

"Why must I pay for the sins of my mother?" she asked in a near whisper.

"But it's much more than that," he said. "We come from two very different worlds, you and I. Two extremes that can never meet. Our bloodlines separate us, and nothing can change that."

A sudden breeze arose, and Anna prayed it would carry her away. Away with the dreams in which she once believed. "You swore to me that nothing could keep us apart. Do you mean to go back on that promise?" His gaze dropped, and she knew his answer. "I love you, Colin. And I know you return that love despite the fact you've not spoken the words. You cannot tell me there is no way to remedy this problem. Love can fix this, can it not?"

She reached for him, but he took a step back. She could do nothing to stop a sob from escaping her lips. The carriage with the Remington crest trundled past them, leaving dust in its wake. Just like their future.

"I've known this day would come for some time now," he said. "But I refused to admit it. That was why I made that promise to you. As much as it pains me to say so, it's the truth. I'm a duke, and I cannot sacrifice who I am for any one person— even you. I'm sorry. I truly am. Goodbye, Anna."

Everything around her began to spin and her limbs became heavy, as if weights had been placed around her wrists and ankles. If she were to walk into the ocean this very moment, she would surely drown. Tears flowed like rivers unchecked as her heart broke into a thousand pieces, and she collapsed to the ground, her skirts billowing up around her.

"Above all, you're Colin," she called out after him. "Never forget that!"

He stopped beside his horse, and for a moment she thought he would return to her. Yet he did not. Instead, he mounted the steed and rode away.

The dust covered her dress and stained her wet cheeks. For how long she remained there on the ground, she did not know. Colin could have shot her in the heart with an arrow and the pain would not have been as excruciating as it was now.

Her dreams were now gone, and the reality of who she was had been made clear. The duchess was right. Anna would never be a lady. How could she have ever thought she could? Never had she been more disgusted.

Placing her palms in the dirt, she pushed herself up and wiped away the tears with calloused fingers. She kept her gaze downturned. Humiliation clung to her, adding a new layer of shame with each step she took on her return journey home.

The cottage came into view, and Anna felt the grief of one in mourning. There would always be broken windows and a leaky roof, teacups with chips, and dresses that should be used as rags. Her life was destined to never change, and it was about time she faced that fact.

The front door opened, and Thomas exited. His face gave no indication of what he thought, but he had never been one for consolation.

Bracing herself for the unkind words that she was certain would come, she was shocked when he gathered her into his arms and said, "I'm sorry, Anna. I truly am."

"I believed that, for once, there was a chance," she said, sobbing into his shoulder. "That we would escape our lives. How many times did you warn me that this would happen? But I refused to listen. Now I see that you were right."

She drew in a deep breath and pulled from his embrace. Everything had changed, and now it was time to face the truth. "I'll return to work next week. I'll speak to Mr. Harrison and agree to his offer of marriage."

"No," Thomas said. "I'll find another way. We all will. Somehow or another, we'll work things out."

Anna shook her head dully. "There is no other way, Thomas. I don't want another winter of Henry complaining he's hungry. Or being unable to buy fabric to sew new trousers for Christian. This is the only way. It's the way of the Silverstones. We always do what we must to save our family."

She walked past her brother and into the house, where she returned to her room. As the tears fell, she thought of Colin as she removed her mother's dress. With great care, she returned it to the box, along with the shawl and gloves Miss Caroline gave her, and slid the box beneath the bed.

The time of dreaming had come to an end. The era of being a Silverstone had come to pass. Her life was to consist of hard labor and a marriage she did not want. Yet if that was her fate, she would simply have to accept it.

Fate had been cruel, for yet another Silverstone had everything she ever wanted within her grasp— a man named Colin, whom she had come to love. And like all the Silverstones before her, it had ended in ruin.

***

A week had passed since Anna had returned to work. Each day, the pain receded, and numbness took its place. It was on days like today, when she did not work, that she found rising from bed difficult. On those days she rose, cooked or cleaned without changing out of her shift, and then returned to her sanctuary beneath the covers. To be alone with the emptiness that filled her.

Although Thomas had advised her to not think of Colin, she found she could not. He had entered her heart and removing him proved impossible. She lay there, staring up at the ceiling and imagining the formal announcement of the engagement between the Duke of Greystoke and Miss Katherine Haskett. They would celebrate with a subsequent party where their peers would congratulate him on his lovely choice of bride.

"How perfect she is for you, Your Grace," they would say. And how right they would be.

But did that lady feel any joy in the fact she was marrying Colin? Did she appreciate how special he was? Or was she simply pleased that she would become a duchess and ignore the man— not the duke— she was to wed?

Anna doubted that Lady Katherine could never love Colin as she, Anna, did. Yet what did it matter?

Her hand wiped away a water droplet from her eye, not a tear but rather water from a leak in the roof. The rain had stopped before sunset hours earlier, but it had seeped into the thatch to drip into the house. Much like the sadness that had seeped into her soul.

Unable to sleep, she kicked back the covers and rose, slipping on the coat Colin had given her. Her mind returned to that day when she had first encountered him. A handsome stranger sleeping off an overindulgence of honey wine beneath a tree. She recalled tracing his face with a finger. The thrill of being in her shift as he pinned her to the ground.

From then, every moment had been magical. Sharing in a picnic. Meeting at the river at midnight. Colin donning common clothes to dance at a tavern.

Unlike her dreams, however, there was no happy ending waiting for her.

She walked out the front door and was surprised to find Christian leaning against the front of the cottage.

"What are you doing awake at this late hour?" she asked. "Are you not to go into Wilkworth early tomorrow?"

He pointed in the direction of Redstone Estate. "I can't stop thinking of Miss Caroline. Since that day she called over, I can't seem to push her from my thoughts."

"I'm experiencing the same problem," Anna said. "No matter how hard I try, Colin always remains with me."

Christian turned toward her. "You loved him, didn't you?"

Anna nodded. "I did. I still do. But it no longer matters because he doesn't return my affections."

Frowning, Christian looked toward the woods again. "I don't know if what I feel for Miss Caroline is love, but I do find her very beautiful." He shrugged. "But what does it matter? That deuced river separates us and always will. How does that happen? How can a body of water create such a divide? No, it's more than that. It's because we're poor and our surname is Silverstone. Not Balfour or Parker or even Lambert. I think it's unfair if you ask me."

Anna placed a hand on his arm. Although Christian was only fifteen, he was wise beyond his years. "Life *is* unfair at times, Christian. But we must always make the best of what we have. The only other choice is to give up and die, and I'm not willing to do that. Are you?"

"Then why can't we rise above this?" Christian demanded as he waved his arm to encompass their surroundings. "Thomas tries time and again, but he keeps failing. Are we destined to live like this forever? Always cold and hungry? Always with clothes that no longer fit? Shoes that are too tight or are so full of holes we may as well go barefoot? I don't care for myself, but what about Henry? Is he destined to be poor?"

Anna could not bring herself to tell him the truth. "No. One day, when we least expect it, something will happen, something that will allow us to better our lives. Until then, we must keep going no matter how impossible it seems."

Moonlight washed over the ground, creating a perfect glow. What she would not give to meet Colin at the river one last time!

"Thomas told me you're going to marry Mr. Harrison," Christian said. "You can't do that, Anna. You deserve better than that old codger. Don't let Thomas dictate your future."

Anna smiled at her brother. "I swear to you that Thomas was not who made that decision. I did. We need the money."

"Why? So Thomas can spend it before Christmas? We'll just be back where we started, and you'll be gone and married."

This time, Anna did not argue, for she feared that what he said was true. Thomas had no knack for business, but her marriage to Mr. Harrison meant a new roof for the cottage. And plenty of food for Henry.

She had gone to her employer and accepted his proposal last Monday. He had licked his lips and raked his eyes over her, making bile rise in her throat. She had no idea what terms he and Thomas had come to, but it was not her concern. The truth was, there was no other choice. Either she married him, or Thomas would be forced to sell the cottage. And she could not allow the latter to happen.

Christian returned inside, but Anna remained to stare up at the sky. Pulling the coat tighter, she imagined it was Colin embracing her. They would soon marry others, but she could not help but wonder how close he came to loving her. For, no matter how hard she tried to rid herself of it, the love she had for him would always remain.

Chapter Thirty

Colin was dying. It was not the physical suffering all men eventually succumbed to at the end of their lives. Rather it was the slow death of his heart. Society had won, and it was at a great cost.

Two weeks had passed since he had returned to his estate of Hemingford Home. With each passing night, his eyes grew puffier from lack of sleep. He spent his days pouring over ledgers in an attempt to rid himself of the constant thoughts of Anna. Yet that proved to be impossible.

Leaving her there weeping on the ground had been one of the most difficult things he had ever done. The destruction he had brought down on her sickened him to no end. He had found the perfect woman, one with whom he could see himself spending the rest of his life. A woman who spoke her mind without reservation. Who brought out the very best in him.

Yet he repaid her with heartbreak. Allowed her to believe that somehow he would put to rights all her troubles. No, he had outright promised her, and now his words were worth less than the ink on a scrap of paper he had tossed into the fire.

To make such a vow and then rescind it spoke of the cowardliness within him. He was no better than one who swindled the unsuspecting on the streets of London!

"Not only can we purchase the land in which to place the hotel," Lord Leedon was saying, "but we can also build spaces that we can later lease to shop owners."

The earl had arrived an hour earlier to discuss a venture in a new hotel just outside of London. Although he had no interest in such a proposition, Colin had promised to at least hear out the earl in exchange for the meeting he agreed to with Anna.

Feigning interest in the plans rolled out before him, Colin asked, "Are you certain this is the best location? Will those journeying choose to stop outside of London? Surely there is any number of hotels available to them within the Town, so many that they'll simply choose to bypass this area."

The earl straightened from his hunched position, his brows knitted with concern. "Is something bothering you? If you'd rather discuss this at another time, I'll understand."

Colin reached for his glass of brandy and took a sip. "Forgive me, Leedon. I've been a bit preoccupied, what with my upcoming engagement party and eventual wedding."

The inevitable had occurred once Colin had returned to Hemingford Home, and Lady Katherine and his mother began immediate plans for the upcoming festivities. The invitations were already written and ready to send out on Monday, announcing the party that was to take place in three weeks. His mother had invited friends and family from all across England, promising them all the grandest ball they had ever seen.

But Colin found he cared nothing for any of it. He did not want to marry Lady Katherine, but now he had little choice.

"And the young woman, Miss Silverstone," Lord Leedon said, leaning his backside against the table. "Do you still keep company with her?"

Colin shook his head. He would not mention that she did keep company with him in his thoughts. It would only add fuel to any eventual gossip. "I admit that I was taken by her tale about you and her mother. Again, my apologies for putting you in such a position."

Lord Leedon clapped Colin on the back. "No need to apologize," he said with a chuckle. "Just promise me that you'll not frighten me like that again. It's not every day a bastard child arrives on one's doorstep. Let's pray it never happens to you."

Colin frowned. "What do you mean?"

The earl grinned and leaned in closer. "Her mother, Rebecca Silverstone? I actually knew the woman quite well."

"Yes, you've admitted as much. Through a charity in London if I recall correctly."

"That was merely a story to get the girl to leave. Rebecca was no prostitute. She was a maid at a friend's estate. Oh, but she was beautiful. I was shocked when I found her virtue still intact. But how marvelous for me, don't you think?" He winked. "It's not often a man gets to bed a virgin. And it was so simple! Unlike the ladies we court, all I had to do was whisper words of love and promises of marriage in her ear, and she opened up to me like a ripe fruit."

He barked a cruel laugh that sent shivers down Colin's back like the squeal of rusty hinges. "Can you believe the woman was asinine enough to believe it? That I— an earl— would ever take a woman of her low breeding as my wife? But there she was, waiting for me to marry her— even after having two of my children!"

He shook his head. "Eventually, she learned that Cecilia and I had married and ended it. Such a pity, really. I enjoyed my time with her. She had the nerve to call over to the house— twice, mind you!— to beg for money to feed her bastards. The last time she showed, I offered her a hundred pounds to warm my bed. After all, Cecilia was away. But she refused, the silly chit. I sent her away with only twenty, which was more than she deserved for her foolishness."

Anger filled Colin. Anna had mentioned accompanying her mother to London twice, and now he knew why. The poor woman had only wished to feed her family. Rather than take responsibility for his part in the existence of those children, Lord Leedon had tried to disgrace her further.

"Don't look so glum, Greystoke. Trust me. I care nothing for either Silverstone. To me, she's like an old pair of boots— long discarded in the rubbish, where her kind belong. Of course," he added, lowering his voice to a whisper, "if you're interested in pleasing yourself with the daughter, by all means, do. I'll even give you my permission."

Colin let out a roar, grasped Lord Leedon by the coat, and shoved him against the closest wall. "How dare you!" he growled. "You destroyed Anna by filling her head with terrible stories about her mother being a prostitute. How can you discard your own flesh and blood like that?"

"Flesh and blood?" the earl asked, clear confusion on his features. "She's nothing to me. Just one of many bastards I sired." He narrowed his eyes. "And don't think yourself better than me, *Your Grace.*" He used the title as a curse. "A blind man can see that you have feelings for the girl. Yet where is she? Certainly not here. And why is that? It's because you're no different from me. Any acknowledgment of the chit would ruin your name. That's why she is not here. And why you, Greystoke, are no better than I."

Lord Leedon could have thrust a fist into Colin's stomach and caused less hurt. What he said was true— Colin was no better. But he could begin making changes now.

With his eyes level with Leedon he said, "You and I shall embark on a journey together, beginning this day."

"Journey?" the earl asked with wide eyes. "What sort of journey?"

"To becoming honorable men. Don't look at me as if I've insulted you. You've done that all on your own. Here's my offer. Publicly recognize Miss Silverstone as your daughter or reap the consequences."

Lord Leedon's eyes nearly popped out of his face. "B-but my wife has no idea the girl exists!" he stammered. "I can't just—"

"You can, and you will," Colin said as he pressed the fist gripping the earl's coat harder into the man's chest. "You cannot truly believe that I don't have the power to see you brought to your knees if you choose to ignore this request. And trust me, I keep my promises. At least you'll appear honorable, even if the two of us are well aware of the truth."

He released his grip and pushed himself away. "And just think. Not only will you gain a daughter, but you'll also be associated with a duke and to the Remington name. It's not as if you'll lose out on this agreement. See what being honorable can do for you?"

The greed in Lord Leedon's eyes spoke his agreement long before his words. "Very well, then. I suppose this association is well worth the effort."

"Good," Colin said. "We'll talk soon. You're dismissed."

Adjusting his coat, the earl gathered his documents and maps and stalked out of the room. He was likely contemplating his confession to his wife. Yet Colin did not care. The man brought it on himself.

Once alone, Colin walked to the desk and placed his hands on the desktop. What Lord Leedon had said was true. How could Colin fault the man for pushing Anna away when Colin had done so for the very same reason?

Bloodlines.

Even if she were not the daughter of a prostitute, he had always known a relationship with her could never be. The blood that flowed through her veins was like the water that ran through the property. It separated them.

Yet, had he not been happy when he was with her? Did he truly care for what others thought of him? No. His concerns were for who he truly was. Colin.

A memory of a conversation with Evelyn came to mind. At the time, her advice had been a mystery, but now he understood clearly her meaning.

"I once had happiness. Though the odd thing is that I didn't realize I had it until it was gone."

He *had* been happy with Anna. He cherished every moment with her and only wished for more. But that had come to an abrupt end.

He glanced at the ring on his finger, and Anna's final words to him echoed in his mind.

"Above all, you're Colin. Never forget that!"

He had forgotten. In all he had sought, he had discarded the one thing that could have saved them both— being the man who loved her. That was who Colin was.

He closed his eyes and allowed his head to loll between his arms. "You fool!" he said in a deep growl.

"What's happened, Colin?" his mother asked as she entered the office. "Why did Lord Leedon leave in such a hurry?"

He removed the ring from his finger, ignoring her question. "When father gave me this, he spoke of the honor one must carry with it. The ring is a symbol of the dukedom, but so is the man who wears it."

Confusion covered his mother's features. "And you wear it proudly, my son. Not even your father could have matched the integrity of the duke you've become."

"Who I've become?" Colin repeated with a mocking laugh. "The duke I've become has no honor, for he denies what his heart desires. But Colin? Now, he *is* honorable. He's a man of whom I may be proud."

His mother frowned. "You're talking like a madman. You're a duke and therefore—"

He slammed a fist on the desktop. "No! I'm Colin Remington! That's who I am."

"Of course," his mother said in a tone she often used to placate him. "I'm quite aware of that already."

"No, you are not!" Colin bellowed. "Don't you see, Mother? You know me as the Duke of Greystoke, just as I know you as the Duchess of Greystoke. You may also hold the title as my mother but I've no idea who you— who *Mary Ann*— is!"

Silence fell between them as Colin turned the ring in his hand. "You asked me if I'm willing to sacrifice everything for Anna, and I thought I could not." He shook his head. "That was the duke speaking, not your son. Not Colin."

"I can see that you're tired, my son. Perhaps you should—"

Colin spoke over her. "Despite Father's advice, denying my love for Anna would bring me greater shame than anything else I could ever do in my life." He held the ring up, smiled, and returned it to his finger. "Well, I'm no longer willing to do that. I'm off to find Anna."

"Colin?" his mother cried as he walked past her. "Colin, don't be a fool! Think of what you're doing. You're a Remington! A Greystoke! This is not how a member of the aristocracy should act."

Pausing at the door, he turned back to face her. For the first time, he saw what putting the dukedom before his own heart had done to him, what it would do to him if he continued on as he had. He would become just like his mother. A slave to her title.

"I cannot argue that statement, Mother. After what I've witnessed from Leedon, a man I once respected, I certainly want to be nothing like my peers. No, I prefer the actions of your son. I do hope that, one day, you can meet him, for I believe you would like him. I know I do." He kissed her cheek and then added, "By the way, Leedon lied. Anna's mother was no prostitute. She will become my bride no matter what anyone thinks. Goodbye, Mother."

As he walked to the foyer, he called out to the butler. "Pendleton, have my horse saddled and brought around front at once."

"Yes, Your Grace."

Colin paced in front of the house as he waited for the horse to be delivered. Perhaps he should have saddled the beast himself! No, the stable hands would be far more efficient with such tasks.

It was not long before a stable hand arrived, leading the beast behind him.

"Will you be gone long, Your Grace?" Pendleton asked as he stood on the portico.

"Likely," Colin said. Then he removed his coat and tossed it to the butler. "I don't believe I'll be needing this."

Pendleton's eyes widened. "I don't understand, Your Grace."

"That's the funny thing, Pendleton. No one does. Except Anna." He dug his heels into the horse's flanks, and it sprang forward.

As the familiar landscape passed by him in a blur, Colin could think of only Anna. How he cared for her and how he was lost without her. He had made a reckless mistake, but he would never do so again.

It took him several hours to arrive at the cottage, and what he found was that only hope held the house together. Cracks glinted in the bubbled glass of the windows, and it could have used a good coat of paint. But he was not here for the cottage.

"Anna!" he shouted. "Anna!"

A young man with hair to his shoulders exited the stable. From Anna's description, Colin knew precisely who he was. "Christian, is it?" The boy nodded. "Where's Miss Anna. I must speak to her."

"She's at the workhouse."

"Then I'll go there. Give me the directions."

Christian explained the route Colin was to take, but before Colin could leave, the boy reached up and grasped the horse's harness. "If you mean to break her heart again, don't go. Because if that happens, I promise I'll hunt you down if it's the last thing I do."

He did not seem to care that he was threatening a duke. Perhaps honesty ran in the family. Colin appreciated that far more than anyone realized. Even himself.

"I swear to you that I will not," Colin replied.

For a moment, Colin thought the young man did not believe him, but then he gave a firm nod and released the horse. "See that you don't."

Turning the horse about, Colin set off toward the workhouse. With each strike of the horse's hooves, his heart beat louder as it ached more for Anna. What a dolt he had been to leave her! But he would right that mistake.

It was not long before he rode up to a building that could only be described as a monstrosity. Dirty and rundown, it had likely been a barn at one time, but it no longer held horses. Now it contained another type of beast of burden, and Anna was one of them.

He leapt off the horse before it came to a complete stop and ran to the large double doors. Placing his palms against each, he pushed forward. The doors creaked on their hinges and opened to the dim interior.

***

Anna's eyes stung from the mixture of the sweat on her brow and the dust that filled the air. With a mumbled curse, she pulled tight the missed thread— the tenth thus far. Most days she had none, but her mind had not been on her work since her return two weeks earlier.

Once the thread was where it was supposed to be, she returned to her place at the front of the loom.

"You're not thinkin' of that duke again, are ya?" Molly Gibbons asked with a scowl. "Ever since you've come back, you keep missin' your weaves."

"I'm just tired is all," Anna replied.

The truth was, she had been thinking of Colin, of the night they swam together beneath the light of the moon.

"Well, you'd best stop your dreamin'. We've got work to do, and I don't want Mr. Harrison yellin' at me for your mistakes."

"Leave her be," Betty said, wiping her hands on her dress. "The girl's got every right to dream, don't she?"

Molly snorted. "If she wants to waste her time, then go right ahead. But you're better off accepting the life given you. Fair or not, it's what it is."

"Ye've no right to take away a woman's dreams, Molly Gibbons!"

As much as she wanted to agree with Betty, Anna knew that Molly was in the right. The workhouse was her life. She had enjoyed a brief reprieve from it, but there was no permanent escape. That was the lesson she had learned during her journey to London.

Having heard enough of the two arguing women, Anna stepped between them. "Molly's right. We've work to do. There's nothing more to discuss."

Betty shook her head, and the three returned to their looms. As the minutes ticked by, Anna thought about how prophetic Molly's words had been. Dreams no longer had a place in her life. Not only were her constant thoughts of Colin getting in the way of her work, but they were also affecting her sleep. The lack of either would do her no good in the end.

Pressing the treadle beneath the loom to adjust the warp, Anna resumed her work only to start when a hand touched her back.

Turning, she stifled a groan. Mr. Harrison grinned down at her. "Tonight, Thomas and I are meeting to finalize our agreement."

"I'm aware of that," Anna replied in frosty tones. Why did he have to remind her?

"I say we go away tomorrow, a short excursion, you and I, so we can discuss what'll be expected of you once we're married." If his eyes had been teeth, he would have devoured her. "Especially those important wifely duties a husband gets to enjoy most."

"That sounds lovely," she managed to utter. "But I must return to my work. It's unfair to the other women if I'm standing here talking to you rather than completing what's required of me."

"We'll have to discuss that sharp tongue of yours, too," Mr. Harrison said with a smirk before leaving by way of a door at the back of the large room.

Betty leaned in closer. "I know ye've no choice but to marry him, and I don't wanna try and talk you out of it. Just promise me one thing, will ye?"

"What's that?"

"Don't ye ever stop dreamin'. I don't care what Molly says, ye can't give up. Yer destined for better things, Anna, I'm sure of it. If anyone can crawl outa this life, it's ye."

Anna gave Betty a sad smile. "Thank you for saying so."

She refrained from adding that her friend was wrong. None of them could leave this harsh life no matter how hard they scraped at the walls of poverty. All they would be left with were no nails and aching fingers.

Returning to her work, she pushed all thoughts of Colin from her mind— not an easy task, that— and focused on the loom before her.

At one point, she stopped to glance down at herself. The skin on her hands was dry and cracking. Callouses covered her fingertips. Her dress was made of burlap, not the satin or muslin of the upper classes. And like many of her companions at the workhouse, she was a bastard.

Yet, what did it matter? Whatever life meant to bring, it did so without fault. Everyone had his or her place in life, and it was up to her to accept her lot. No amount of caterwauling would change the fact that she would always be poor.

Yet if she had grown up a lady in a country manor, would she still be of the same opinion? Not likely.

The Duke Who Loved Me

The doors of the workhouse banged open, and sunlight filled the room, making Anna squint. At once, the looms stopped, and whispers filled the air. The silhouette of a male figure appeared in the doorway, and those closest to the entryway dropped into curtsies.

Anna could not help but gasp as her eyes adjusted to the light. Colin marched toward her, his steps firm and his stride sure.

"What are you—"

She had no chance to finish, for her words were cut short as he lifted her by the waist, pulled her tight against him, and kissed her. Gone were the other women, the looms, the dust. For that one long moment, only Colin existed— he and his lips and his firm body pressed against hers.

"Anna, I love you," he said as he lowered her to the stone floor. "There's no life without you in it."

Her heart trembled. "You mean... are we...?" The words refused to come.

He took her hand in his. "You told me that, one day, the wind would carry you to your dreams. I'm here to tell you it cannot." Her breath caught in her throat as he scooped her into his arms. "But I will."

She wrapped her arms around his neck, allowing him to hold her against him as he carried her past the looms, past the other women, past the dust to cheers and applause. But Betty's voice rose above the rest as she ran alongside them. "Go on, Anna! Get outta here! Go live yer dreams! Ye hear me? Live yer dreams and don't ye ever come back!"

Once outside, Colin set Anna onto the back of the white stallion before heaving himself behind her. She loved the feel of his arm wrapped around her as he heeled the horse's flanks.

"What's happened?" she asked as the horse trotted down the lane.

"I finally remembered who I am, Anna. All thanks to you."

She turned her head and grinned up at him. "Are you speaking of Colin, the man I spent time with in London?"

He nodded. "I am. He's also the same man who loves you. The man who's willing to sacrifice everything for the honor of becoming your husband. That's of whom I speak."

Anna sighed and settled back against his chest. "And he's the man I love."

Chapter Thirty-One

Aweek had passed since Colin had saved Anna from the workhouse— and from a life she did not want. Mr. Harrison arrived that same night, shouting and cursing until Christian threatened to strike him if he did not leave.

Not only did Colin's return make her happy, but so did the truth about her mother. After Colin had explained what he learned, he had held Anna as she wept. Her mother had not lied!

Although the dream of meeting her father had not yielded her what she had hoped, something good came out of it. The man had agreed to recognize Anna and Thomas as his children. No relationship would form between Anna and the earl, she was sure, but the pain was not as terrible as she had thought it would be. At least the bloodline had been established.

Now, she and Colin sat beneath the very tree which Anna had first found him. A blanket was spread beneath them, and they were sharing dried meats, cheeses, and a bottle of honey wine.

"Must I remind you what happened the last time you drank too much of that?" Anna asked as Colin poured himself yet another glass. "It was really quite embarrassing."

He set his glass beside him, frowning. "If I recall, you took advantage of my drunken state. I awoke to one less coat, you sitting on my lap scantily clad, and my family ring nearly stolen!"

Anna glanced down at Colin's hand. He now guided the ring rather than it him, another thing about Colin she would forever cherish.

"If I recall correctly, you overpowered me as if I were nothing more than a child and threw me to the ground," she said with a grin.

"Did you know that I wanted you to kiss me while you had me pinned?"

His eyebrows rose. "Oh? Well, I want to kiss you now."

Before she could respond, he pulled her to him. Their lips met, and her heart beat with love.

"I'll be honest," he said breathily, "I wanted to kiss you then, too. But I've a rule I refuse to break."

"And what rule would that be?"

"To never kiss a thief!" he said with a laugh.

"Oh, you'll pay for that!" she said, joining in his laughter as she made a fist and playfully hit him on the arm.

He raised his hands. "Mercy!" he cried. "I cannot take any more. If I had another coat, I would offer it to you just to put a stop to your cruelty."

"Well, see that you give me one later in recompense," she said with a mock sniff. "If not, I'll call you out for a duel."

They settled back to their wine, and Anna looked out at the river. Tomorrow, Colin was to return to Hemingford Home to settle several affairs of business before coming back to her so they could begin the search for a new home together.

After repacking what remained of their meal, they made their way back to Redstone Estate. They spoke of their upcoming wedding, which would be a glorious affair. Miss Caroline, of course, had been ecstatic to learn they were to wed and had offered Redstone Estate for the party.

"She would have attended no matter where we had our breakfast celebration," Colin said with a laugh. "I doubt Markus could stop her, even if he wanted to. She's far too persistent for her own good."

"I'm still surprised he hasn't come to put a stop to it," Anna said.

Colin snorted. "Caroline can keep a secret when she must."

As they exited the woods, Anna's laugh died at the sight of a carriage sitting in the drive in front of the house, bearing the familiar crest of two ravens flanking a crown. "Colin?"

"Trust me," he said, squeezing her hand. "Nothing Mother says will make me change my mind."

His smile was like a healing salve on her fear. She did trust him. And always would.

As they approached the portico, the door opened, and the duchess walked outside. Her dark-blue traveling dress with its black trim unsettled Anna, for it was as severe as her countenance.

They came to a stop at the bottom of the steps, the duchess staring down at them.

"If you've hidden Lady Katherine inside your carriage," Colin growled, "I swear on Father's grave that I'll never speak to you again."

The duchess sighed. "Lady Katherine is not here. Nor will she be again. I sent her home with the understanding that she would not become a Remington— or a duchess. At least not by marrying you. She was not pleased, nor were her parents."

"Then why have you come, Mother? If you're here to dissuade me from marrying Anna, you may as well leave now. I'll not change my mind."

His mother shook her head. "Since I was a child," she said, a sad edge to her tone, "all I knew was that I would marry into a noble family. Not a single thought was given to what I wanted in life. My mother snuffed out what little resistance I was able to muster. I was told that my worth lay in my beauty, and once that was gone, my value would be depleted."

She drew in a deep breath and slowly released it. "I see that day coming, and it frightens me. I've no idea what will become of me when it arrives. You said something to me not long ago that had me consider something very important. I've been a dutiful daughter, a deferent wife, a respected duchess, a guiding mother. Yet I've never simply been Mary Ann. Even if I wished to be her, I've no idea who she is, and that thought bothers me greatly."

The pain in the duchess's eyes made Anna's heart constrict.

"You were right, my son. I know you now only as the Duke of Greystoke and have forgotten who Colin is. Therefore, I'd like to make a request. I wish to know you as Colin."

"I would like that," Colin said, smiling. "For I believe he will make you proud."

Anna was so happy for Colin and his mother. It was good to see them repair what was broken.

His mother smiled and turned to Anna. "We're two very different women from two very differing backgrounds, but I believe we just may find we have more in common than we realize. I just hope you'll give me time to learn what that is."

"I would like that very much, Your Grace," Anna replied.

Colin took a step forward. "What are you doing, Mother? Are you saying that you wish to be a part of our lives?"

"Yes, if you will accept me. If Anna is to become my daughter-in-law, allow me to help her." She turned back to Anna. "I would like to train you. If you are to take my place, you'll need guidance. I'm willing to do that. This new world can be difficult to navigate. Even with my extensive training, I found my first years in the position daunting. Besides, it will give us the opportunity to learn more about one another."

Colin had confided in Anna the issues he had with his mother, and she saw this as a way for them to reconcile.

Seeing the hesitation in his eyes, Anna said, "I believe her offer is genuine, Colin. If she teaches me, not only will it help me be a duchess others will admire, but it will also give us the opportunity to become acquainted with one another. But the decision is yours."

"This is why I wish to be with you," he said. "You understand what matters." A wave of joy washed over Anna when he turned to his mother and replied, "We both accept your offer."

The duchess smiled and snaked her arm through that of Anna. "I believe a nice cup of tea is in order. Will you come inside and join me?"

"I would like that," Anna said. Then she grinned. "But I don't think Master Markus will approve of me being in his home if he were to learn of it."

The Duke Who Loved Me

The duchess laughed. "He's as stubborn as I have been. But none of that matters, for you will soon become my daughter. Anyone's disapproval of you— or my son— is disapproval of me."

With a happy heart, the trio went inside, Anna being the first Silverstone in many years to be invited into a home without a broken window as an equal.

Epilogue

The following months few by in a blur. So much had transpired that Anna found herself struggling to keep up. Yet with the help of her mother-in-law, she was able to circumvent her new position.

Colin purchased the workhouse from Mr. Harrison, which he hired Thomas to run. Thomas proved to be a surprisingly efficient and worthy taskmaster. Not only did the working conditions improve, but so did the wages for the workers. This, in turn, improved production.

Another improvement made was to the cottage. The broken windows were replaced, the roof no longer leaked, and Henry had no need to complain about hunger again.

Christian also was able to extend the stable, which allowed him to house more horses. He even considered hiring help.

Later, Anna stood with Colin outside the dressmaker's shop in London, just as she had many months before.

"You know," Colin said, "now that you're a duchess, they'll come rushing to your side to grovel at your feet."

Anna laughed. "Your mother reminds me of it often. Not a day goes by that she does not mention the benefits of my new title."

She and her mother-in-law had become friends of sorts. Most days were spent in training, and Anna found she enjoyed it. Although the dowager duchess expressed her opinion whether it was requested or not, she also raised no fuss if anyone disagreed with her.

They resumed their stroll, acknowledging the nods and smiles that came their way. Anna was becoming accustomed to the attention, and although she did not mind, it was the fact that a new duke now possessed the title and guided the Remington Family that made her proud. His name was Colin, and Anna adored him.

"We've come a long way since we were here last," Colin said. "I'm just glad my cheeks are not stained with dirt this time."

Anna laughed. "I'm thankful that I don't have to worry that a barmaid will snatch you away from me."

The doorman at the restaurant where they were to dine opened the door for them, but Colin stopped and turned to Anna. "I do love you, you know."

"I do know," she replied. "And I love you. Now, shall we eat?"

Once inside, a steward took their outer garments. The headwaiter led them into the dining room, and Anna could not help but smile upon seeing her brothers waiting for them, all in their new suits.

Anna stifled a laugh. Henry pulled at his collar, and Christian sat so rigid one would have thought him a statue. Thomas, however, sat with his head held high, just as he always did. Colin had sent for them so they could all enjoy time together in London before Anna and he left for their belated honeymoon.

They all bolted to their feet when Anna and Colin approached.

"This suit's itchy," Henry said. "But Thomas said I shouldn't complain, so I won't."

Anna did laugh this time as she embraced him. "Well, you certainly look handsome, even if it itches."

"There they are!"

Anna turned to find Miss Caroline navigating the many tables. She wore a red dress and a large hat with a red ribbon that hung down her back. "Colin. Anna." She kissed each on the cheek and then pulled at the fingers of her gloves as she added, "There are so many unsavory characters in London that I feared for my life on my way here. But I feel safer now." She turned and smiled at Christian. "Much safer."

Christian bowed to her. "Fear not, my lady. No harm will come to you when I'm around."

"Such a gentleman," Miss Caroline said, her cheeks turning pink.

"Perhaps we should sit," Colin said, ushering Miss Caroline to her chair. "I'm sure young Henry is hungry, are you not?"

"Very!" Henry replied, making everyone laugh.

As they shared in whatever stories came to mind, Anna studied her brothers. They had changed and yet remained the same in so many ways, and for that, she was glad.

When her gaze fell on Colin, her heartbeat quickened. She had so much love for him, the world could never contain it. Her dream had always been to escape the fate that had befallen every other Silverstone before her. Although one would believe it was the money Colin had that saw that happen, it was not.

Colin had shown Anna one could sacrifice everything for love. It was why she had agreed to marry Mr. Harrison— for the love she had for her brothers. And why Colin had been willing to jeopardize his relationship with his mother and defy the expectations of the aristocracy— for the sake of his love for her.

It was that same love that caused her heart to beat with a new rhythm, for above all else, her dreams had come true.

Brought about by Colin, the duke who loved her.

Thank you for reading *The Duke Who Loved Me*. Find out what happens between Evan, Lord Westlake and a woman he once scorned in the next book, *The Baron Time Forgot*.

Made in the USA
Monee, IL
24 July 2022